PRAISE FOR *ZERO*

"Conceived at the height of an unprecedented national crisis, M. T. H__
Bomb is a violent, vital novel about virtue, loyalty, decency and love, even as we
watch these timeless human attributes dissolve in the stomach acids of the World
Machine. Think E.M. Forster's *The Machine Stops*, written for the *Westworld*
age, and you may just gain a fingerhold on this crazed colt of a book."

SIMON INGS, author of *The Smoke*

"A beautifully-written and profoundly dislocating book about a chillingly-
plausible near future and its discontents. Absolutely essential reading."

DAVE HUTCHINSON, author of *Europe in Autumn*

"An ambitious novel that effortlessly combines speculation, social commentary,
metafiction, and a compulsively readable story. Thrilling, audacious and timely,
M.T. Hill's visions of the future feel closer to reality than they should."

HELEN MARSHALL, author of *The Migration*

"The fragmented story of Remi, a traumatised man struggling to remake his life,
reminds me in its surrealism of Tom McCarthy's *Remainder*. Intense and well
observed, *Zero Bomb* delves into our fears and distrust of technology, and our
political anxieties stoked by twenty-four-hour news."

ANNE CHARNOCK, author of *Dreams Before the Start of Time*

"Vivid and richly imagined, *Zero Bomb* is a passionate examination of who we
are and a warning of what we could shortly become. I couldn't put it down."

CATRIONA WARD, author of *Rawblood*

"*Zero Bomb* is a novel on the bleeding edge of desperate times. Delicious
shivers of strangeness – an allotment of limbs, a fox that is also a surveillance
device – bring an old magic to a future Britain broken by zero-hours contracts,
algorithmic bosses, and 24/7 alienation. Using a bold structure, the novel reveals
its mysteries across different facets of a compelling near-future North."

MATTHEW DE ABAITUA, author of *The Red Men*

BY M.T. HILL AND AVAILABLE FROM TITAN BOOKS

Zero Bomb
The Breach (March 2020)

ZERO BOMB

M.T. HILL

TITAN BOOKS

Zero Bomb
Print edition ISBN: 9781789090017
E-book edition ISBN: 9781789090024

Published by Titan Books
A division of Titan Publishing Group Ltd
144 Southwark Street, London SE1 0UP
www.titanbooks.com

First edition: March 2019
10 9 8 7 6 5 4 3 2 1

A CIP catalogue record for this title is available from the British Library.

Printed and bound in the United States.

To Lucie and Raymond

PART I

REMI

1

Remi took to running when his daughter Martha died. His wife Joan called this denial, deflection – a kind of coping. But Remi called it running or jogging and nothing else, and within weeks his running had consumed him. He ran to the shops for milk, he ran to the shops for bread, and he often ran hours into the night so he couldn't dream of her.

Remi wanted to run a marathon the morning of Martha's funeral. Almost two months had passed by then, owing to a gross delay on the post-mortem. A fatal backlog, the coroner said, without irony, without so much as a twitch. Their service being tested, underfunded and overstretched. In the end Remi and Joan were on countdown so long that when the day finally arrived, Remi saw it as just another. He woke at three-thirty in the morning with plans to leave home by four; he woke to Joan sitting in low lamplight on the floor by their bed, freshly bereaved by the simple act of waking, and he saw she was weeping again. 'It's just the thought of her lying in that cold room,' she told Remi as he dressed in his luminous running clothes. 'She's on her own.' And Remi nodded his agreement and left anyway, went out with the foxes but before the dog walkers; out early enough to be the jogger who finds the body. He ran an easy eight miles into the day – was there as the late-spring mist rose from the fields and hills that hemmed Manchester. There to witness the rising sun, the neon-edged moorland, with the glowing feeling he might be the first or last man alive.

As the morning's warm light planed in low, Remi lapped two reservoirs. There were geese on the water, static and wary. The power lines, strung between elegant new pylons that overlooked the site, chattered in the breeze. Remi only broke his stride when he came across a neat square of rabbit entrails on the path, and even then he didn't stop for long. There was no fluff or blood nearby. The entrails sat there glistening, a uniform plum colour. Remi's shin splints hurt. He was thirty-nine years old. His jowls were loosening, his crown was thinning, and his only child was dead.

Reaching the other side of the reservoir, Remi drew parallel with a fence that bounded a working farm. Snuffling sounds drew his attention – some donkeys were eating god-knows-what from a smouldering bonfire. Like the geese, they stopped to regard him dumbly. He wondered if they had the capacity for shame, if they could register being caught with their snouts in the filth. Then Remi considered if *he* should be ashamed. Not for intruding, but for being out here at all. It was then Remi noticed a dark fox, apparently following him, and saw its bloodied maw, and he understood.

• • •

Later, as Remi helped to bury Martha in the grounds of a church he'd never attended, sweating freely as he worked the shovel, he pictured those donkeys from the farm by the water. We each keep little rituals, and there are things we do when we think nobody's looking.

The shovel was small and, owing to the church being quite new, the pile of soil beside the grave was full of crushed hardcore. Remi worked hard and committed this dark rubble with his sweat; it made a terrible sound as it showered the coffin. He was still wearing his luminous running gear. He was burying his daughter. He was thirty-nine and gravity was claiming his body and his child was dead, and here he was, amid this faceless mass, throwing smashed rock upon her. Convinced he was going to break the casket lid with the weight of the rubble, he stopped shovelling. He didn't want to see her again.

Then the priest did his bit, ashes to ashes, and Remi stood away from Joan and her estranged family and sought something to hold on to, something real. He tried to list what comprised the England his daughter had known. What remained of his own England now Martha was gone. He considered his own anchoring points, his childhood – son of a French mother, an English father. The hills around his parents' village near the Pyrenees, and then their move to Manchester when Joan fell pregnant, not long before the Brexit referendum. He began listing the things that made this England: the grey cracked pavements and potholed roads you ran along into town; the vascular tree roots breaking through tarmac on narrow streets; the font used on motorway signs. Passing a convoy of Volkswagens on their way to a club meet somewhere in the Midlands. Rooting in your pockets for loose change at a railway station toilet gate. Lying deeply hungover in a cheap hotel bed, your infant daughter kicking you in the chest, your wife laughing quietly as she tries to nurse.

Martha had not long turned seven when she died. England had changed so much in her scant years.

After the wake, the quietest the pub had known, Remi and Joan caught a taxi back to their house. Remi made a pot of tea and a plate of limp sandwiches that went untouched, and then he began to leave her. He packed his sports rucksack, energy gels, a bottle of water. A money belt and his bank card. He sniffed his way through the house, which seemed poisoned, noxious. He announced, 'I'm going for a run.' He pulled on his trainers on the front step and stretched his hamstrings, his calves. He rolled his shoulders and locked the door and posted his keys.

Remi reached the fringes of Birmingham the next morning.

2

It was Birmingham for a while, after that. No contact with Joan as a policy, a means to sever the connective tissue, annul their relationship mentally if not legally. To get by, Remi started washing cars at less than minimum wage for a friendly Polish family, until something of a turf war erupted with a rival firm down the road. When an early-morning petrol bomb nearly cost Remi his sight (and took his remaining hair), he gathered his stuff and ran himself out to Solihull, where he was forced to rough it properly. Unfortunately, he settled on the wrong patch – earned his licks from a band of local homeless who didn't trust his accent, nor his unweathered face. Soon Remi was huffing spark as a crutch, and sooner still he could not run. He lost a year this way, though it made no odds since Martha's death – time had become irrelevant to him; eating and drinking were little more than necessary hindrances.

Then an intervention, a ray of luckshine. Street pastors from a Christian charity arrived in the squat where Remi lay sored and broken, and brought with them the faint promise of redemption. Remi was unsalvageable, he thought, addicted and numb, but he went along to their centre and for several months ran clean for a lack of other options, having all but forgotten why he started taking spark in the first place. Making good progress, getting through the worst of withdrawal, he was in turn given a semi-permanent address from which to make job enquiries. A sort of alms postbox.

Some weeks later he began delivering food-aid parcels on foot. It was enough to keep a pay-as-you-go mobile going; brought in enough cash for him to hop between youth hostels or, occasionally, treat himself to a bed-and-breakfast. The work got his pulse up, and helped his muscles recover some of their previous form. He remembered something of what it was to run.

Not long afterwards, however, Remi's luck ran dry. In the space of mere weeks his postal firm was swallowed up and mostly automated – redundancy culled all but two staff, the legwork farmed out to drones. Suddenly Remi's prospects seemed shapeless, dismal, until a chance meeting with a metalworker stayed the fresh allure of spark and took him south to Kent, where he laboured long hours operating microcranes on the border fence.

Some days he can still smell the steel on his hands. Some days he can easily spend an hour counting the nicks and scars on his fingers and forearms.

Today, though? Today it's London. Crushing, vital, imperfect London. Fractured, febrile London – London its own country, forever skirting ascension or total collapse; a shattered or immutable city, depending where you are and what you can see. Or how much you earn, and with whom you spend your time. London where Remi's alarm is going off early, because he needs to get out and courier a hot manuscript to an agitprop publisher in Walthamstow. London where he's scraped enough together to rent a studio flat in post-bomb Hackney – a shoebox, but a *nice* shoebox, in a converted Victorian gas holder on the Regent's Canal. London where Remi sleeps in an old iron carcass, but still can't believe his good fortune.

London where his daughter Martha's voice is fading, the last low whisper of an exorcised ghost.

Remi dithers at breakfast. His ears are already full of rain and traffic. It's a grey morning – a filthy week, all in all. He takes his toast with a cup of black, sugary tea, and pops three anti-emetics from a blister pod. Chewing and sipping, he grabs his traffic bug from its wall charger and tethers it to his watch. The bug is a newish Gilper on loan from a pawnbroker – it features urban-camo skin and a high-capacity cell that's more than enough for a working day's footage. As he pours himself into bike Lycra, his street armour, he lets the bug hover outside the flat window. According to the pawnbroker, the bug's previous owner jail-broke it with introspective software. Now it seems to enjoy taking its own mysterious pictures of the pre-dawn, none of which he can ever find on its memory drive. Idly, Remi turns on the cooker hob and turns it off again.

Outside, and into London ramping up. A freezing pall has passed over the city, and the streets sparkle with ice.

The bike lanes are hectic, too: riders running wheel to wheel, while above them streams an almost continuous river of bugs, every single rider leashed invisibly to their own, as if it's really the bugs dragging their owners to work.

By the time he's on street level, the smog has settled. Just as quickly, the whole scene is shot through with lasermesh from the City's high-rises. Holo adverts rally in the pall. The sun, more of a backlight, gives everything a bright yellow density. Squint a little, and the sky is falling.

Remi numbly pulls on his breather, joins a fast lane and powers into the flow; he heads straight down the central chute past Spitalfields, minding his own business. He's Kevlar-heavy and constantly swallowing what feels like nylon string. Early riding can do this to him, plastic lung being at its worst first thing. When it's as cold as this, it can be as bad as the day he quit huffing. All around him, riders are bunching up as if subconsciously seeking each other's heat. You're meant to take your time on these mornings – especially if you're rolling with tyres as thin as pennies, on a surface that's been relaid to deal with each successive summer's obscene heat. But Remi's having as much fun as what's left of him allows – digging in, running true, bang on time. The eerie hiss and clank of hard breathing and chaingear. Give it some extra welly down the off-chute, and he might just break some community trial records by the time he arrives. He might even feel something at all.

Remi's bug flashes a right arrow to him, and Remi leaves his lane.

• • •

The literary agency is situated down a narrow side street. Remi stands the bike and checks his watch: he'll make the manuscript collection six minutes ahead of schedule. This means an instant bonus, a guaranteed three-star review, and the possibility of repeat business.

The agency's front gate is hidden behind a lattice of scaffolding and mesh. Shoring-up works, probably – more buildings damaged by tunnel boring for the next Tube line. He hits the buzzer. The Gilper lands on his shoulder and chirrups.

A bank of locks pop open, and a severe-looking woman comes out to the gate, a lead-coloured case in her hands.

'Morning,' Remi says. 'Run to Walthamstow.'

'You're the courier?'

Remi flashes his ID. Freelance and fancy-free.

'Very early,' the agent mutters. She rubs at a coffee stain on her top, and doesn't open the gate. 'I hope we're not paying you by the minute.'

'I got lucky,' Remi tells her, shaking his head. 'No extras for you. What we quote is what you pay.'

The literary agent nods, but she doesn't look him in the eye. She passes the cased manuscript from one hand to the other, and then out to him. Trembling, ever so slightly, like she's glad to be rid of it. Remi takes the case with polite reverence: he can tell from the weight it's a geolock-and-key job, proper contraband.

The literary agent nods. 'Is that everything, then?'

Remi nods, and the traffic bug lifts away from his shoulder.

The agent murmurs something about payment gates and backs into the shadows.

'You have a good one too,' Remi says. He walks to his bike, slides the envelope into the shock panniers, and holds his wrist against the connector pad. This links the envelope to his bug, in case he gets jacked.

Remi doesn't know much about art, though he'll blag his way through a client briefing to win a delivery contract. But by doing this job, he's part of the scene's nervous system. When you're creating under a government that demands to see it all, you have to adapt. To paint or cartoon or write books these days is subversive at the very least, and to shift it through the city is not simple complicity – it's open defiance. Remi reckons about half of his traffic is typed or handwritten manuscripts, and the demand for grey couriers like him is only growing. The current buzz on deep channels is that foreign embassies have cottoned on and started paying big, if certain assurances are met. If the art market takes a whack – if there's another big crackdown, say – Remi might yet explore that route himself.

The commute only intensifies as he cycles on with the manuscript. His bug is flashing the directions, but he knows these roads, counts the miles instead through personal nodes: the pubs, the automated bookies, the empty temples and mosques and synagogues, the libraries-turned-flats, the sets of traffic lights you can safely skip. Graffiti tags and fissures in tarmac on certain roads. Grids and H-for-hydrant signs making for esoteric markers and signals.

Then he's waiting at a heavy junction, caught in electric traffic. Sandstone brick surrounds, Georgian everything.

You can tell a wealthy enclave by its heavy gates and partially exposed gun-turrets – is this really Mayfair, already? He scans the run of luxury shops while his bug traces a lazy helix above his head. He admires another rider's cycle as it pulls alongside him at the lights, a sliver of a thing with a carbon-fibre frame. Next to the two of them, a driverless car paused so perfectly on the dashed nav line it could be screencapped from an advert. Remi and the other cyclist share a cautious smile as they notice simultaneously the passenger asleep on the car's rear bench.

Then to the traffic lights, foot on the front pedal, and back to his idle quantifying. What makes this city? What makes it breathe? Remi has some ideas: the crane verticals and cables; the old and new in visible sedimentary layers, history compressed and overflowing from the grids; blues and reggae and old-school jungle from open windows and passing cars; a grimjazz band practising in the middle distance, steady cymbal wash; a food courier arguing futilely with a driverless white van; a steaming coffee outlet selling weed and beta-blockers; lads outside a takeaway sharing shock-joints and quiet dreams; a mobile shop blinking deep cuts on stolen derms; hidden London delineated by the warm vanilla lights of bedsits above shops; sleazy-hot London with its shapeless blood-glow; sex bidding and street shouting; the wealthiest Londoners slipping by undetected in silent taxis—

'Hear that?' the other cyclist asks him.

Remi pulls down his breather, wipes the condensation from his top lip. 'Sorry?'

The other cyclist nods. 'That noise. You not hear it?'

And then it comes again, and Remi does. A sad *pop*, like someone closing a door in another room.

'What the hell's that?' the other rider asks.

'Tunnel works?' Remi shrugs and looks at the ground. 'I dunno.'

The other cyclist shrugs back. Not cold, or even polite, Remi understands, but familiar. The death-spiral fraternity of cycling in London.

Again comes the popping sound. A series of popping sounds. 'Seriously!' the other cyclist says. It does sound like it's coming from beneath them, but it's too clipped to be a passing Tube train, and Remi's sure they stopped tunnelling work to repair the collapse at Tottenham Court Road.

Once more the noise comes, this time much closer. Remi squints at the other rider. The lights turn green and the driverless car glides away. Remi and the other cyclist wordlessly mount the pavement, intrigued or unsettled enough to hang around. They both lean on their tiptoes, holding the traffic light post. Their bugs begin to fly in tight circles around each other, as if they're conspiring.

'Right then,' the other cyclist says, gesturing to the bugs. 'That's no good.'

Remi grimaces. The bugs often know.

Then the smog draws closer, dry and sour, and the popping sound is all around them. The driverless car has faltered in the box junction, its motor screaming painfully. The passenger has woken up and is banging on the windows. Without saying anything, Remi dismounts his bike and props it against the post, and the other rider does the same. Together they approach the car, stilted by adrenaline.

There's a smell of hot wires. Other vehicles start to beep as the traffic lights turn red again. Remi's bug emits a shrill alarm to warn him he's abandoned the manuscript case.

Remi heads directly for the car. 'You all right?' he calls, mouth sticky. Behind them, doors are hissing open, other voices rising. *Pap-pap-pap* from the driverless car's front end.

Closer, the offside window, and a pair of thick boot soles fill the glass. The passenger on his back, kicking at full stretch, because the car's cabin is filling with smoke. 'Jesus Christ,' Remi manages. And now the car's reverse note sounds, hazards glitching on and off. Remi instinctively steps away just as the driverless car accelerates, brakes to a pause, and restarts itself. Before he can react, the car swings away from the box junction and turns to face the mounting traffic. To face Remi.

'Jesus Christ,' Remi says.

The passenger window glass gives and speckles the road, and then the car comes at him.

3

In the moment – syrupy, elastic – London reveals to Remi its starkest face: a blanked sky, impassive glass, reflections of ancient buildings that will long outlast him. Remi needs to move but his limbs won't have it, and then the second cyclist is there, clamped to Remi's arm, rotating him, and the driverless car passes so close it draws a hiss from Remi's rain-shell. Remi and the second cyclist tangle and hit the road. The tarmac is bright black and wet. A wrench. A lucky roll. The driverless car is still pulling away when it hits the traffic lights, and the whole fixture tilts out of its base. The pole collapses, sparking, and gouges chunks of masonry from the nearest building. The car digs in and tilts backwards, driving wheels lifted away from the road and spinning furiously. Thick smoke rises from the arches, the bonnet seams, and on the street the exposed mains start crackling.

Finally, the crowd. London's white cells rushing to the site of attack. The passenger's arms and head emerge from the smoke as he clambers out. The other cyclist is back on his feet. Remi's sitting up on the road with his head pounding, purple blotches in his vision. His hands and knees are studded with grit.

'The bikes,' the other cyclist says.

The bikes. The package. And a roiling panic. From his seated position, Remi just about sees what's left of his bike: the wheels creased and tyres off, the frame wedged against the base of the traffic light pole. The panniers have been folded in half. The manuscript case is in the mix.

As if to offer sympathy, Remi's bug descends to his shoulder and stops flapping.

'I'm insured,' Remi says, mostly to himself. He shields his eyes to survey the mess. 'Hang on. Is that—'

'Wait!' the other cyclist calls. 'Oi!'

Because the car's passenger is sprinting away down the road.

'What's he *doing*?' Remi manages. He's getting up. Unsure but apparently without serious injury. A semi-circle of concerned faces. An older woman holding out a flask. 'Jesus,' Remi adds, shaking his head. 'I've got the lot on tape – how's that his fault?'

'You all right, though, love?' the older woman asks. A cup of tea now. 'Could'a done ya, that! And to say them cars are clever!'

Remi doesn't argue with her. It's difficult to say much at all. He waves away the tea and stumbles towards the other cyclist, who's doing his best to separate their bikes from the tangled car and post.

'The bikes,' the second cyclist says, forlorn.

'I know,' Remi says back. He kneels down to free the package from the panniers. Its reactive protection layer means the innards will be fine, possibly creased – but the agent will already know something's wrong, because the tracker will show it as stationary for longer than Remi's service-level agreement permits. Worse still, she might think Remi's tried to tamper with it, get inside.

'This has to go,' Remi tells the other cyclist. 'I've got to get it somewhere…'

Their eyes meet briefly. Both of them stinking in their armour-panelled Lycra, panting like dogs. The other cyclist looks lost. No – he looks bereft.

'It was a present,' the cyclist tells Remi, as if he might know. 'From my late wife. What the bloody hell do I tell the kids?'

And with this arrives a vision, white-hot and livid: Martha's body.

Remi stoops low to offset the dizziness. *Not here.* He closes his eyes. He's dragging it up. The smell of burning. He's dredging again. He plants one hand on the road, the manuscript case clutched against his chest. A voice from an old room, a memorial. His first and failed attempt at therapy: *Remi, I want you to imagine you are standing before a cove. You have rowed ashore and tied the boat to a slimy post. You can hear the sea. It is different from shore – flatter and stiller than when you were out there. There is a tall figure in the breakers. There is a lighthouse on the hill. You can walk towards the lighthouse, if you like. You can ignore the figure and walk along the ridge towards the lighthouse. You don't have to look back. You don't have to look down. Inside the lighthouse you find a table set for one. You sit before a bowl of light, and in the light is the colour blue, which you can taste and swallow and feel yourself digest—*

Remi grips the package. He straightens it as well as he can, and the action brings him back from the edge. He checks his watch. He clears his throat. Without another word to the other cyclist, he pockets his bug and tries to run.

4

Remi can't remember how to do this. Two steps, two breaths in; three steps, three breaths out. Wasn't this the pattern whenever he went out back home, back in the other time, his first life? Something about maximising oxygen flow to needy muscles. A pattern he internalised and made automatic, once so natural that it became his response to any pace beyond a brisk walk. Within minutes he's hitting the chest burn, early fatigue. Wanting to stop. *It's natural,* he tells himself, remembering old pains at least. *This is before you settle in for the long haul. Don't be too harsh on yourself – you haven't run anywhere for so long.* Doesn't he remember? How he used this to free himself from having to think? Two in – one, two. Three out – one, two, three. The uneven pavements and cold down his neck. Towards the meditative state that saved him each and every time he went under.

Except it isn't working. Remi's tearing through West London's back streets, and everything seems volatile and disconnected. The city is shifting around him, becoming unknowable.

He pulls up, staggers a little. A starburst overlay. He could've been killed back there, injured at the very least. Yet it's not even the idea of a malfunctioning driverless car that fazes Remi most. Despite their advancements, hiccups happen, albeit rarely. Batteries can fail, and without due care, circuits corrode. No – what really bothers Remi is that the passenger fled. You can't even start a car these days unless you're comprehensively insured, with a subdermal chip to prove it. Can't pass a traffic signal without your car being immobilised if your licence is about to lapse. And casualty rates for car occupants are the lowest they've ever been. The passenger wasn't injured by the impact, nor rendered so shock-stupid that running made sense. So was it the smoke? With an electrical fire you might panic, seek to clear your lungs... but why would you run?

Another plausible motive is shame. Not wanting to be seen. Because, Remi considers, given the media's fatalistic obsession with driverless anything, today's incident could well make the nine o'clock bulletin.

Or – what if the car was hacked? What if it was deliberate? What if it was to do with the manuscript?

Remi clutches the case to his hip. He checks his watch, whose screen displays his job rate dwindling in real time. He unpockets his bug, which bobs in circles around him. If he doesn't land the manuscript on target, he'll lose half a day's wages, and possibly the next contract. He retches. Running all the way to Walthamstow just isn't an option.

• • •

Remi descends the stairway at the nearest Tube station, Green Park, and jostles his way on to the eastbound Piccadilly Line platform, trying to remember the name of his contact, of his issuing agent. In the moment it's hard even to recall the name of the editor he's delivering to. The address. Given the sensitivity of the documents they move, a courier's memory is their lifeblood, and Remi's is scattered, failing. Then the train is in the platform and he's being pressed into a heaving crowd, blood and plasma still damp on his knees, sweat running freely from his brow. He winces inwardly as his knees rub on someone's long woollen coat. He finds a gap, a pocket of air. He gulps it.

The stops filter past. Remi stands with his hand on the bar, woozy and distracted. Fading in and fading out. Then it hits him: Walthamstow. Fucking Walthamstow! Why is he on the Piccadilly Line and not the Victoria? How's he even managed that? He swivels to the live Tube map scrolling down the carriage, questioning himself. Okay, so he'll just change at King's Cross, or even Finsbury Park. He retightens his grip on the handle. He wipes his wet face down his other arm.

At King's Cross, the carriage empties at an impressive speed, leaving plenty of empty seats. The chance to rest makes Remi's decision for him. As he sits down, the people on the opposite row gawp at his torn knees, his clammy skin. He tries to ignore them. He closes his eyes. He attempts to tot up the value of his lost bike, and the faff it'll take to replace it. He squeezes the bug in his pocket, and it gives a tiny haptic response. Some attempt at reassurance.

At the next station, Caledonian Road, two heavyset men

seat themselves either side of Remi. He notices them because they're wearing near-identical tracksuit bottoms, fleece-lined cardigans and heavy-looking work boots. They carry a stink of ethanol. Labourer-grubby: the lemon sourness of a urinal cake. Between them they casually muscle Remi's elbows into submission, his torso frail by comparison. The man to his left has long, dirty fingernails, and a tin of beer concealed in a degrading plastic bag.

'Want me to swap?' Remi asks the man on his right, tilting his head sideways to his friend.

The man flashes Remi a bored glance. He might as well be in another carriage, another universe. Then the man drops his sports holdall on the carriage floor. From this the man produces a pad of paper, an old fountain pen – instantly curious to Remi because he does it so delicately, and because it makes no real sense: a labourer with a fountain pen between his thick, dirty fingers. Besides, who doesn't watch their fellow passengers from the corners of their eyes? Who doesn't try to peer into another life and imagine, briefly, what it might be like to occupy it? The stolen glance is a transaction from unwritten London. It's another way the city trades its secrets.

The man's pad contains reams of squared paper. An artefact in the same way the pen is, given this day and age. Perhaps Remi's first impressions were wrong: he might well be a labourer, comfortably scruffy with it, but he might also be a man for whom organisation matters. A foreman, or engineer, old-fashioned to the point of being contrarian about technology. Is the pen really his? Is it an heirloom? Remi marvels at the possibilities. A whole life story spun from an object out of sync. And as the man begins to write on the pad, a silky motion, arched hand, Remi follows what he can of the fresh ink, refocusing his gaze as the man reaches the end of the first row of squares and drops down to the next.

There the man stops, as if sensing Remi's gaze in some unknown, atavistic way. Remi turns away too obviously. He locks eyes with the woman opposite, whose scolding expression says his movement, however minor, has pulled her out of her book.

The train rattles northwards towards Finsbury Park. Less than five. The carriage lights strobe through dead spots in the tunnels. And the big man goes on writing furiously in his squared-paper pad, corner to corner, his forearm rippling with each stroke, every point of exerted pressure. Next time Remi glances over, his guts shift with surprise. In so little time, the man has filled half a page – and not with any real words. Instead, the man has plotted an unbroken string of figures and letters, seemingly at random, into every square. Something about the pace of it, and the hand's steadiness, gives Remi the impression these letters and numbers have been learned and repeated here by rote. Unnerved yet fascinated, Remi continues to follow as the man completes a new line of characters, and then another. Is it a puzzle, Sudoko-like (remember those)? Or a calculation, some bizarre theorem—

'Hey,' the young woman says to Remi over her book. 'You're bleeding pretty bad you know.'

Remi shrugs with one shoulder. As he does, the train brakes to a sharp stop in the tunnel. The carriage lights clank off. The man next to Remi stops writing and taps the page three times with his pen. Remi keeps his eyes front. The man taps more insistently, and Remi finds it irritating. Tap. Tap. Tap. Remi glances across the way, startled to find the man staring back from the reflection opposite, lighted and dimmed as the lights flicker; fully, surreally there when the light floods, and then a blank mass in darkness, facial features absent entirely.

The man is smiling.

A second jolt as the train lurches forward half a metre. And more tapping, each time in the same place. Remi looks now, and this time he notices the word on the pad, the word under the pen, with the sensation of insects climbing his neck. The squared page, for all its apparent randomness – hundreds of tiny letters and digits – bears a name. Four little letters, right at the end of the man's pen, that spell it out:

R E M I

Remi squeezes his eyes shut. It's the strobing. He's overtired. He's shaken up.

He opens them, and the man's pen has moved to the top of the page:

L O R R Y

S P R A Y

The pen moves to the middle of the page:

T A L L O W

G R E A S E

The page like some abstraction of a word-search puzzle. The page full of messages:

W O O D

P I G E O N

COLLAR

The train driver gives an apology for the delay and announces Finsbury Park as the next station. The big man leans forward over the pad, as if to better study Remi's reflection.

'What is this?' Remi hisses, breaching the silence of the carriage, and with it the gravest rule. 'What are you doing?'

The pen taps:

OILED

PUDDLE

The pen taps:

MARTHA

Finally Finsbury Park is sliding across the windows. The two big men rise and push forcefully up the aisle towards the carriage doors.

Without a thought, Remi gets up to follow them. Shoulders first up the platform, scattering, a half-jog, half-stumble, keeping in sight the writing man's pattern baldness; the figure and scene already etched on his bones should he ever try to forget them, double-exposed with the shattered image he tries to maintain of his daughter.

Up the wet stairs and into Finsbury Park's tiled tunnels, glossy with condensate, the sheen and colour of wet teeth. The writing man is only just ahead now, and the second man has vanished. The manuscript case jangles under Remi's armpit. Nothing is cohering.

'Wait!' Remi calls after them. The crowd thins out under North London's surly sky. The big man doesn't turn, much less waits. The man and his holdall, his jogging trousers; his work boots leaving dirty wet prints on the tiles.

'How?' Remi shouts. 'How do you know her name?'

The man is outside on the concourse, sprinting now through the bus ranks, before walking again in a longer stride, seemingly focused on a place unknown. Remi watches him pull a large woollen hat over his head. Remi follows. 'Wait!' he shouts. 'Wait!'

By a pub on the corner of a main road, the writing man turns at last. Their first proper eye contact: a moment of curious recognition, incomprehension. Remi is coming in fast, yet the man remains nonchalant. He rolls away as though preparing to throw a punch, but instead takes something small from his pocket, folds it quickly, and posts it through the grate of a wall-mounted ashtray. He lights a cigarette, takes a short drag, and posts that also.

Finally, the man steps off the pavement and into a waiting cab. Remi instantly unpockets and throws his bug into the air – 'Shoot! Shoot it! Get the reg plate of that taxi, you little bastard!'

But the bug falls to the ground, wings inert and body dull.

5

Remi wavers in the Finsbury Park drizzle, the writing man gone. Now Martha returns to him from the recesses, the flooding drains and cobbled alleys. Of all the places, they're in the old bathroom, her legs around his waist and belly, backside on his forearm, and she's proudly repeating her newest word – *teesss* for teeth – laughing at herself, the tickling sibilant, and at Remi's over-the-top movements as he uses his finger to demonstrate brushing. It's painful to him, an old scar raised as they sometimes do in heat, picked at. It was always so bittersweet to watch Martha develop. The dissonance of completely loving a child so bright and fearless and full of potential, and yet having to second-guess who she might become, what might await her *out there*; what anyone her age might go on to do in the onrushing England, the irrupting future, where the jobs would *change*, or slip away, and the opportunities would all be so different, the stakes so much higher. All those evenings he sat there in Martha's room feeding her from a bottle as she gently tapped his nose for comfort, he and Joan the entirety of her world. Remi would feed her milk as he read with his spare hand about new atrocities: the horror show of western Europe convulsing in some kind of pre-collapse; another vote going this way, another heart-deadening lurch that. The recession of empathy they had to witness and endure (some, of course, in more acute or violent ways than others). The triple threat of heat and war and high water. And Remi feels again the perverse relief he enjoyed in the months following her death. The release to know that, even though she'd gone, leaving an absence that completely anaesthetised them from the world, he'd never have to see his daughter heartbroken or sobbing or suffering. For every moment of beauty nested within her, for every moment of pride she had seeded in him, Remi would never have to watch Martha suffer the ignominies of adolescence, young adulthood or the otherwise unknowable – be that robots, riots or plain human wrath.

And yet, as the smell of burning paper fills him up, it's the missing her that matters more. Her breath as she settled in for sleep, how it deepened yet softened as she drifted away. *A small green boat*, he would tell her. *Lower the oars, Martha, and hear the rowlocks rattle. The sound of water will carry you*. Later, when he was sure she had gone, how he would open and close the door in such a way as to not disturb her; knew so well the creaks of the landing, the stairs, every patch of carpet to avoid. He misses her sleep-smell and her impossibly tiny fingernails, the fine hairs of her neck, the way she would sneeze without a care in the world, then laugh with thick snot in her mouth, let it down her chin; and how she brought him his shoes and tried to put them on the wrong feet, squealing in frustration. Right here, he would give it all gladly to have her back. To know she'd had her shot at this life after all.

Remi picks up his bug and turns to the burning cigarette bin, damp and dismal in his Lycra. There's no longer a way to get the manuscript to the publisher – although that seems incidental, a fact from a separate, parallel reality, and readily acceptable. This, here, this is what's actually happening. His desire to know what the writing man posted in the cigarette bin is deep-set and much heavier: Remi wants – needs – to find it. Which the writing man clearly knew, too – else why would he have pushed in a burning cigarette, if not to eliminate choice? So now Remi's self-conscious and agitating; there's football chanting from the pub, and he can't go in there asking for water for the bin – not in this state. In part because someone showing off, a few sheets to the wind, might take an interest in the manuscript case, but also because there simply isn't time.

Remi swears breathlessly and kneels and scoops two hands of rainwater from the nearest puddle. He throws this silky grey water over the smouldering ashtray. A hiss, and a bloom of thick, sour smoke. The smell of wet cigarette butts is nauseating – a clogging, rot-sweetened smell, black in his mind as the tarry mulch he'd surely dig from the bottom of the bin.

Remi pushes his sleeve over his hand to lift the dirty ashtray lid – only not carefully enough. A masonry screw, perhaps already loose, works free from one corner. The whole unit swings towards him and flaps open, releasing a flurry of still-smouldering papers, butts and ash, the latter blowing directly into Remi's face. Remi staggers back, gasping, his face caked and sticky with it. Only the sight of paper scraps blowing away prevents him from vomiting immediately; instead, he gags and swipes at his eyes, goes quickly to his knees to splash puddle water over his cheeks and forehead, and then tries his best to snatch the largest pieces of paper away from the pavement before the wind or wet can take them.

Remi doesn't notice the men exiting the pub beside him. Only loosely does he hear someone calling him a 'fucking scumbag' while another man stands laughing at the spectacle of this bloodied and ash-dirty man rooting through the filth of a cigarette bin. Only vaguely does Remi suffer this humiliation. Because now in Remi's hands is a tightly folded wad of thin paper, unfolded to reveal a small chit, and here the ash and the stench is meaningless, because there's another message meant for him, and him only. He tries to stand, then tries again. He rocks on his knees. The message starts MARTHA, and he swallows a hard knot, and then he continues:

> LEICESTER SQUARE
> SSID: 394020
> PASSWORD: theyearofourlord1812

Remi pushes off his knees and stands, sodden and thrilled and shivering, nose clogged with sourness. This message, this *instruction*, being the most he has felt about anything for the longest time.

'Scored, then?' one of the watching men ventures. Stretched Arsenal shirt, modish glasses, tight jeans.

Remi laughs over his shoulder. Whatever's happening here – whatever this is – it's a reminder of what it is to be relevant. And her name is all around him, and she's everything, and Remi's gaping holes are plugged for an instant.

Martha.

6

The manuscript case's late-alarm finally dies as Remi ducks into the Tube, cutting its signal. Another courier once told him not to worry about it: these cases use the same tech you find in the watches rich men wear when they fly their single-seaters over rainforests, in case they go down.

Driven on by the note, by intrigue of what now seems like a deliberate, carefully planned operation (did they have a team following him – a whole network – or did they simply hack and track the package?), Remi boards a westbound Piccadilly Line train for Leicester Square. He stands in the vestibule, swaying with the carriage, aware of his body heat and the ash still remnant in his hair, in the creases of his neck, the crust on his clothes. He is otherwise apart from the experience, watching the scene as though detached from his body.

He checks his phone – battery holding out but well below half charge – and then his bug by habit, shocked to find it still dead. With the train approaching King's Cross, he can feel the approach of a Rubicon: a sense of falling over, or falling in. An event horizon only a few stops down the line, a few more brake squeals and handle squeezes, the engaging of otherwise unused muscles to stay upright. Maybe it's that he already understands this will affect his life by some measure – even if that's only because it might be the kind of story that in its retelling sounds ridiculous.

This whole train's on countdown, Remi tells himself – and not one of them knows it.

Finally, the train bursts from the last stretch of tunnel before Leicester Square's platform. Tangerine light and massed bodies in flammable-looking winter coats. Remi holds up the chit of paper, floppy now owing to his clammy hands, and digs deep into his phone's settings. He switches the Wi-Fi function to manual search.

The train doors open. Remi pauses briefly as he recognises the northern accent of a staffer on the platform, begging people to let passengers off the train before they board. The phone does its thing: the nearest Wi-Fi networks scroll into the list, but none of them look anything like the one on Remi's chit. Frowning, he refreshes and refreshes the settings. Nothing. A few official-sounding TFL networks, a partially masked SSID, and what looks like a temporary hub for a jobbing utilities or civil engineering firm. Not the SSID from the chit.

Then the doors start to close, and Remi wants to be sick. What if this is it? A cruel prank in which he's setting up the reveal, the punchline, as himself?

No. It's enough to recognise that people have been tracking him. There's intent, calculation.

As the train slides out of the station, Remi tries one final time – turning his phone's Wi-Fi off and on again. To his horror, the movement of his thumb – the switch – coincides with a grim jolt near the front of the train. The emergency brake sends him reeling. His system dumps adrenaline. His elbow almost overextends, so he automatically releases the handle and staggers into the person next to him. The train judders to a pause, leaving the carriage most of the way out of the station, and all of its passengers in near-darkness.

A hush. A shared psychosis, the whole carriage questioning what just happened. Wondering if the jolt was caused by something worse than a bag or scarf caught in a door farther down the train.

Remi's phone vibrates in his hand. He almost drops it. A new SSID has appeared on the screen, and he holds up the chit to compare the number.

Connect.

Password.

Remi fills out both fields with dizzying imprecision, weak at every joint. Despite himself, he gets the password in first time.

Now, an interstitial page loading slowly. Dark, with a line of pixelated white text at the top, which resolves quickly to CLICK HERE. The carriage has all but dissolved into negative space. Remi stands in a blank room, bounded by nothing.

The loading circle sputters. The next page loads in agonising increments. It's an image. Low quality, full of blocky distortions owing to compression. A slice of background, a sliver of hair. A hint of eyebrow. A single, questioning eye.

Remi clutches his face and kneads the soft spots beneath his ears. His throat is full.

The page finishes loading. It's a picture of her – of Martha – staged as an old school portrait. He squints. Her face has been subtly altered. Her hair isn't blond, or at least how he remembers it. The longer he looks, the more he's certain: the whole image has been manipulated to make Martha look older than her seven years. This isn't the little girl they buried – it's an impression of Martha: taller, leaner. Martha as the young woman he dreaded her becoming.

The image winks out. In its place flows a scree of figures and characters like those he watched the man plot in his squared-paper pad. Then the text edits itself down to a single line, animated to flash like an old-fashioned GIF.

ALIGHT.

ADHERE.

Next thing the screen is plastered with red crosses. Dumbfounded, with the sensation of drifting despite his standing still, Remi obediently presses the screen. It blackens instantly.

Remi pockets his phone and looks up at the roof of the carriage, blinking. They hadn't moved, had they? He twists and repositions his feet. The train is clicking quietly, unpowered. Murmuring along the carriage. Glaring lights – passengers using their phone torches. The carriage aisle is filled with ghosts, blue-skinned and milky-eyed.

'What's this all about?' someone asks Remi directly. A smartly dressed man in a trilby peers at him from behind a tablet. The kind of man you'd have seen down here a hundred years before.

Remi blinks back at him. He doesn't know, apart from the inescapable sense that using the Wi-Fi switch also turned off the train. He lowers his eyes. Too alarming a thought. And yet the idea persists like tinnitus – a keening in his inner ear that tells him he's in some way responsible.

'Power went,' Remi offers. 'I mean, I reckon.'

'For Christ's sake,' a woman chimes in. 'This country!'

Remi gives both of them a lost expression and fixates on his shoes, then at the manuscript case poking out from his armpit.

'Here, someone's coming,' someone else says. 'Out there, see?'

They're right. Outside, elongated by torchlight, shadows stalking the tunnel walls. A work crew, perhaps, or a team of first responders. There comes a deep, rhythmic clanging, very internal and mechanical, like sounds from the bowels of an old ship, and then the carriage doors grind open.

'Single file,' one of their rescuers shouts. 'Get tight into the wall – you can worry about your clothes later.'

Remi is quickly swept into the dismounting crowd. Quick – that's about right. The whole day has been *quick*. Someone wearing a head torch helps Remi down from the step, where he stands on a material like shingle. The man's torchlight illuminates the bow of the tunnel ahead. Blackened bricks and impossibly green flora. Someone asking if this was terrorists. A young child sobbing gently. The urge to run a finger along the filthy wall, leave a record of his being here. A tiny marker that might, on finding it later, prove to him all this had really happened. He looks across at the rails, three strips of wire suspended in uncertain light, and wonders what it might be like to touch the live one. Would you even know you'd touched it?

'Single file!' someone shouts. 'For your safety and ours!'

Remi leans further into the black walls, watching silvery particles rolling, disturbed by the steady stream of bedraggled travellers. They pass the driver's cabin, and inside the driver is staring dead ahead, paused in the strangeness.

As Remi falls into the rhythm of the march, he tries to think reasonably about the picture of Martha, the awareness he's being toyed with, somehow. At some point someone's hand has risen to guide him from behind, and now he lifts his own to guide the woman in front. Maybe he's done something heinous, he thinks, and he's about to be outed or punished for it. But why? That he's been targeted is obvious. For what purpose is a bigger question. He's gripped by it, by the excitement and the keen paranoia; aroused and alive at the thought of being exceptional enough, or so unremarkable as to be anonymous – a perfect asset to someone, or an agent, or maybe the ideal folly.

Who, then? And how do they know about his daughter? Why have they made her look older?

Remi's head is full to bursting again. Martha, flickering, an archive of film rushes running through an old projector. He can hear his blood. His stomach feels burned out. As the sallow light of London begins to leach into the tunnel ahead, it's all Remi can do to close his eyes and let his head hang slack; let the people around him reveal the city, return him to the natural level, and help him to normalcy, away from these last hours.

Then he remembers what he left the house for. He grips

the dead bug in his pocket and then the manuscript case. No two ways about it: an insurance write-off is pretty much the only thing that'll keep the literary agent happy, and Remi in a job. He releases the hand of the woman in front and tears away the manuscript case's tracker pod, its alarm chip, and throws these components sideways. They bounce into the pit below the central rail. The manuscript he'll keep hold of. He can deliver it anonymously as lost-and-found when it suits him, or at least when he's next up Walthamstow way.

'I was dazed after being knocked off my bike,' he'll tell the client, affecting a tone of concern and regret. 'The envelope was damaged. Someone rifled my pockets and took my things. I don't remember what happened – it happened so quickly.'

And then he'll show them his bug footage of the driverless car, and they'll believe him. And London, their savage city, will churn on.

7

Remi walks home to his apartment in fine rain, a million white cuts on the bitter wind. As he goes, he is with her, his chest burning with her, and he musters more of the past: Martha being little and chatty, four or five, and them visiting Remi's parents in France. She's playing outside in their garden, old enough at last to be left unsupervised for longer periods of time. 'Papa,' she'd called to him, squatting over the rough lawn as if she needed to pee. And Remi had gone to Martha, who revealed to him a pile of dead flies, each of them wingless. 'What are they doing like this?' she asked him. And Remi couldn't say, felt ill looking at them. In truth, he couldn't be certain she hadn't committed this herself. 'Let me fetch you a dustpan,' he said in loose French, and he swallowed once before he went inside. When he returned, Martha was laughing hysterically. There was a length of knotty brown string running across the patio stones, and Martha was skipping madly over it, back and forth, back and forth, totally rapt. As Remi approached she squealed, 'Papa!' and when Remi squatted to look closely he saw that the string was in fact a long line of ants. They were carrying the wingless flies into a wall. 'They cooperate!' Martha told him. 'They work together as a team!'

Safely back indoors, Remi hangs the dead Gilper in its charger mount and runs himself a near-scalding bath. He climbs in. Martha's falsified face fills the cabinet mirror. He is very still. Her older face is open but insincere. She's pale and freckled and dead, just as she is in his strongest recollections of her.

When the weight of grief becomes overwhelming, Remi holds his head under the water and wills himself to breathe.

Remi can't sleep. The Tube and the power cut and his racing pulse. Martha's face, older and thinner. He's so awake. Her nose had looked harder, sharper, and her gaze was hollow.

He throws off the sheets and goes to the sink and pours himself a water. The bug is winking in its mount to say it's charging. He angles its projector to the wall and turns it on. The wall, a screen from corner to corner, reads MEMORY EMPTY. He goes to the bug, takes it down, shakes it. Hard reboot, try again. There's no available footage, and nothing else in the root folders either. The bug didn't only lose power – something wiped it.

Remi sits on the end of his bed. A mocking reflection in the floor-to-ceiling: balding pate, striated fat beneath each nipple, a greying pubis. He claps feebly and the television flickers on – again the full span of the wall, a bachelor's toy or impulse buy, intended once to shore up a defence within. He hops from shopping channel to sports round-up to interactive porn. He flops back on the bed and tries to get an erection. The woman on the screen says, 'Hey, Remi.'

Later he wakes up with a pillow over his crotch. The TV is still blaring but the light outside has changed. Dirty pink, earliest morning. Certainly the wrong side of his alarm. Remi realises he's listening to an automated news report. *A burning car at Watford Gap services.* He claps once to turn off the television, and the television stays on. Remi claps again. The volume increases. Remi doesn't remember changing the channel over. Remi doesn't watch the news because Remi hates the news. He claps a third time, and the image flickers and resharpens.

'Bloody thing,' he says.

He searches for the remote under the bed, and the news rolls on. Something in the reporter's tone, the inhumanness of it, has started to distress him. Not the bleached wording, nor even the false sympathy. He can't find the remote, and he sits back down on the bed, dizzy. He's started to sweat.

Where's the remote?

Responders have not ruled out the possibility that the driver's daughter was in the car.

Remi faces the screen, and with it comes a weight. The sensation is fast upon him, worse than panic – more an unfeeling. It's paralysing. A lightless helmet closes around his head, covering his mouth and ears and eyes. It's suddenly hard to breathe, and a confusing, caustic pain racks his chest and arms. There comes the sound of crackling meat, then a blaring blue light. It's like his limbs are being slowly stretched out. He's watching a fire, and the television gets louder. The first body was found at close to twenty-three hours last night. The body was a man. Remi can suddenly smell gas, strongly. The man was pronounced dead at the scene. Responders have not ruled out the possibility that the driver's daughter was in the car. And now Remi comes off the bed with his hands over his ears. 'No!' he screams, as the volume only rises. 'No!'

And soon the sound distorts. The treble into white noise. The blood runs thickly in him, and his gullet burns, and he kicks at the screen, which immediately discolours. His foot has left a rainbow wound. The volume is still increasing, and Remi stuffs his hand behind the screen and swipes at the wires; but the wires are hidden in the walls by design, and what's happening to him here must be deliberate. This is another attack on him. He kicks the screen until the membrane tears, and little islands of pixels blacken and die. The speakers roar. Remi's body is a slick, tautened mass, and he collapses into himself, numb and empty. He's remembering something. He's remembering more than he wants to. The memory is a parasite whose anaesthetising venom has worn off. Remi can sense its teeth, or a proboscis, deeper in him than will ever be safe to extract.

Remi comes round when something heavy hits the window. The sun is half up, and his morning alarm is sounding.

Remi gets up from the floor. The TV is off. The fine details of a bird's splayed wings are imprinted on the glass.

He gathers his sheets about him and goes to the window. He's naked, and he can smell blood and vomit. He rubs the glass behind the bird print, expecting some sort of grease or dust to come away on his finger. The glass hums. It wasn't a small bird. Wingspan more than a foot across – maybe a pigeon. He goes on his tiptoes to get a view of the ground, lest there be a bird lying dead out there, some sort of omen. There's no bird. There is, however, a movement on the periphery. Down low, across the bottom of his view, a flicker of reddish brown. Bin bags rustling in the steel-fenced rubbish store. He touches his face in thought. He draws his glass-chilled finger across his eyes. He closes them. He opens them. The red-brown thing is staring back. It's a fox. The fox is in the communal bin store. Two eyes, alert and bright; not yellow-gold as Remi might expect, but silvered, almost electric blue. He pushes himself against the window. The fox's face is slender and conical, and its ears are pricked and twitching independently of each other. Its feet are stretched out in front, playful as a pose, weirdly exact in their symmetry. Its brush and coat are streaked with brown. The fox is probably a metre or so from coal snout to white bob, and it's watching Remi carefully.

Remi slaps the glass, leaving a wet smear. 'Get away with it,' he mouths. 'Go.'

As if it heard him, the fox slides out of the bin store, smooth as spilled oil, shoulders rising lazily with each step. It stops itself, directly below Remi's window, squarely in Remi's view. Its head is cocked upwards yet the eyes are no longer fixed on him. The fox's brush rises and settles. The wind breathes once, twice, through the fox's coat.

'What are you doing?' Remi asks, and realises on the last syllable that he was holding his breath.

The fox moves in a circle and coils up on the ground, chin over one forepaw. Its tail rises and falls again, seemingly its own creature. The fox glances at him, and then it yawns.

Remi slaps the windowpane. 'Get out of it!'

The fox immediately stands up and slinks out of sight. Remi turns away, angry and cursing the lot of it; cursing the state of his television and the fragments of a night now repeating in his mind.

There was a news report. He'd remembered something. He'd forced the memory back down for now.

A bark, and Remi swivels back to the glass. The fox is still there. This time, though, it's partially out of sight, its brush extended rod-like and hind legs wriggling and struggling for traction. As Remi watches, he realises the fox is dragging something heavy with its mouth. Remi swallows. The bed sheets feel heavy about him. A large green sack slithers into plain view. The sack is marked CLINICAL WASTE.

Here the fox stops and curls itself around it. It looks up with a kind of certainty. Remi can't shake the feeling the fox wants him to have seen all of this.

'What?' Remi asks, as the fox places a paw on the sack.

Did the fox just tap it?

Remi goes into the bathroom and washes his hands. He feels ill. He goes back to the window and the fox is still down there with the sack marked CLINICAL WASTE. Remi pulls on his jogging pants and goes back to the bathroom, where he washes his hands again.

He wills himself to face the mirror. The mirror has

isolated and highlighted an area of sun damage on Remi's cheeks. Sallow eyes, a tungsten sheen to his skin. He's living inside a stranger with thick grey hairs about the shoulders and a dark mole on his chest.

Remi leaves the bathroom and checks the window again. The fox is there. The fox is waiting. 'Right,' he says. He pulls on his dressing gown and leaves the flat. He goes down two floors to the block's yard door. Two breaths in. Three breaths out.

Remi has walked London's streets long enough to recognise a fox's signature. A heavy waste smell, at once human and gamey and archly sour. He knows the calls, too: they are part of the Hackney fabric, and in Hackney the fox is everywhere.

The back door is open a crack, and through this vent comes the smell in earnest. Only this fox doesn't smell exactly like the others. Beneath the common scent, the primary notes, there is mint, not fresh or bright but there nonetheless – a light menthol that comes and goes with each inhalation, almost easy to dismiss each time. The fox rises to its feet and slinks to the crack in the door, waiting for Remi to open it fully. It's larger than Remi had first thought: broader in the shoulders, more squat than lithe. A big fox. A powerful-looking fox, with a black-tinted pelage on close inspection. More than this, though, Remi sees with clarity the keenness of its face. The creature is plainly intelligent – the silvered eyes carrying a sort of half-smile, a knowing grin. When it re-angles its head towards the hall light, its pupils flash green.

'Come on,' Remi says. 'Clear off.'

The fox moves away only far enough to nudge the waste sack with its forepaw. It returns to the door.

Remi shakes his head. His palms are itching. His breath sticks. How often do you stand this close to a fox? How often will a fox let you?

Despite himself, Remi takes a step forward. The fox stays still. Remi opens the back door fully. The fox darts in and across the carpet, turning to Remi with its teeth bared. It starts to salivate. Its spittle rolls from the corner of its mouth and on to the carpet in heavy globs. Remi's too stunned to speak, or react with any grace, and now finds himself outside, in the fox's place, nearly tripping over the waste sack as he backs away from the door.

In the foyer the fox squats and begins to piss on the carpet. Remi yelps and remonstrates but the fox goes on with it, a loud and heavy stream. Remi covers his mouth as the fox uses its front legs to drag itself around the carpet, still going.

Finished at last, the fox pushes back outside, rubs its flank along Remi's rooted legs, and takes the knot of the waste bag in its jaws once more. It drags the bag against Remi's shin, where it sags around his leg with a liquid-seeming weight. The fox returns to the front door and waits there indifferently.

Remi leans and opens the door without a word. The fox scampers away over wet gravel, and then there's silence. Remi can't take his eyes from the carpet. He can't even blink.

There, glistening, is a fresh message for him.

8

In a stupor, Remi takes the clinical waste bag up to his flat. He accepts that it belongs to him. He's unbound, the wrong side of a border. To look at his broken television is to hate and hurt, to loathe and shame himself. The only recourse is to look at the opposite wall – the one without windows, achingly bare and typically new-build, a crackless magnolia. It seems the most non-threatening surface in his world. He lies on his bed and stares at the wall for a long time, the fear being that anything more complex will cause him to break down entirely. Only when his palpitations fade, and his hands and feet feel somehow detached from him, does he allow himself to close his eyes and picture the fox once more: the flecked and rain-matted coat; the deranged grin playing on its chops; the sight of it marking the foyer.

A message. Unless Remi is fully adrift, the fox came inside and pissed a message on the carpet. Deny it, and Remi risks cutting all tethers to the real; might need to admit – and submit – to greater hallucinations, including the picture of

Martha shown to him on the train. Embrace it, however, and the circuit breaks anyway. No animal has the capacity to communicate with humans like that. Yet Remi saw it, still smells it, and there's a sack here in the room as proof of the encounter. He shifts on the bed and stretches a leg down from the bed to touch it with his toes. The contents of the bag are heavy, malleable, hard to define. He'd carried the bag up into the flat, pushed open the door with his back. He was there with the fox and now he's here, chill-blue in the morning glow.

You're beached, Remi. The dunes are wet. There is a figure in the breakers.

There was a message written in fox piss.

There was an exchange.

Sleep deprivation can feel like being inside a translucent tunnel, of course. He's only dimly aware of the flat, of London stirring and coming to life around him. Inside he's screaming: *What do you remember?* Was it about Martha? Why can't he remember? And so he tries: Martha was born breach, with one eye swollen closed for the first fortnight. A lot of hair. Joan said to him, 'She has your brow.' Tongue-tie noticed after a week of painful latching, Joan's nipples 'like a war zone', and Martha's tongue clipped the next day. She sleeps well enough and rarely cries. She starts to walk at thirteen months. Her first syllable is *ma*. Her first recognisable word is *teeth*. She enjoys screens too much, and she notices planes going over long before they do. She's prone to angry outbursts, a fault Remi quickly attributes to himself. She's affectionate, unselfconscious, inquisitive. She finds comfort in holding Joan's breasts, whose bronchial veins have by then faded, and whose areole have returned to their paler, pre-birth colour. Martha insists on walking even when she's too tired to walk. By four she's losing an early interest in books, and the nursery staff can't always contain her moods. There are incident reports. A possible diagnosis or concern, some term he can't recall – though the threat is vague at first, and so unbelievable. Did she soil herself too often? Joan's mother would say, *It's just a phase*. Forever a phase. Google, Martha's third parent, is filled with increasingly desperate search terms. Martha wets the bed, too, see. She stops Remi and Joan removing insects from the house because they are welcome there. She prefers to be around Joan, most of the time. Sometimes you can see that Joan resents it.

Then Martha is seven. A smell of gas. A smell of burning. Thin fabric catching and quickly consumed. A column of heat, with the figure of Martha frozen in fear or fascination before it. Is that it? Is it all that's left? A fire? Where was the fire?

It must be closing on rush hour now. The mauve sky is streaked with pink and orange-rimmed cloud. Remi can't decide what day it is. Is he working? Is he on rota? He slips uneasily from the bed and pulls on a pair of thermal leggings, a fleecy top. The waste sack carries the musk of the fox. Dung and acrid sourness. He's with it once more, because the smell has transferred to his hands, is seeping into him. He's staring down the fox in his mind, willing it to turn or never turn – to make a choice, because those eyes have snared him. And now Remi wants to open the sack almost as much as he wants to burn it. Burning might yet be the answer. He kneels. The knot is crudely tied but good for its purpose, tight and small. He picks at it with trembling fingers. He's watching from outside himself again, curious to note how uncoordinated and skittish his hands seem. He persists, solves the knot. He sits back and watches the ties unfurl. A fresh smell, camphor and ferns. He thinks of embalming a body, he thinks of sterile things. When you try to mask a bad smell you often draw attention to it. The sack's ties are settling. The neck of it has opened. Remi weighs the situation and goes to fetch his Marigolds from the kitchenette sink.

He digs in. Inside the sack are several smaller, opaque bags, sealed with ziplocks and labelled with handwritten notes, like those you might find on a prescription bottle. He takes out the nearest bag and squeezes it. Liquid. A faint grease mark near its sealed opening. He reads the label, which says OILED PUDDLE, followed by a 'date of collection' – yesterday. He rotates the bag, and his skin prickles.

He takes out another bag. A little heavier, less fluid. He holds it up to his face. The label carries scruffier writing, perhaps another writer's. It says TALLOW GREASE, and he places the bag very carefully on the floor and stares at it emptily for a few minutes.

The third bag Remi removes contains liquid, too. MANNED LORRY SPRAY, followed by TERMINAL ROUNDABOUT APPROACH, BRAKE FLUID MIX. The fourth and fifth are also marked MANNED LORRY SPRAY, modified by ORBITAL HARD SHOULDER and FLYOVER ROADWORKS respectively.

Remi swallows as he lifts out the last bag. It's so light it could be empty, and there's no label to define it. One corner of its sealing edge has come unstuck, and he realises that this must be the source of the bag's smell. He winces and puts a finger into the gap, then pulls. The bag rips, and the contents spill out. It's hard to understand them, at first. Duster-ends spring to mind, a misfiring connection taking the easiest route. Remi doesn't blink. His ears are roaring. There are two of the things, tartar-white and bangle-like in thickness. They are dark and slightly wet-looking on their inside edges, and feathered on the outside. Threads of red cotton hold each of them together.

'Wood pigeon collars,' Remi whispers. And in his mind's eye the fox's maw is bloodied and dripping. Sated, the fox turns and retreats to the void at the centre of Remi, a den for the oldest and worst of him.

Remi closes his eyes.

9

Surprisingly, Remi sleeps so well he wonders if death has taken out a short loan on him. He wakes around midday, surrounded by the contents of the clinical waste sack, and by pieces of the television. He goes to the toilet, showers unthinkingly, and gathers the small bags back into the waste sack. A single pigeon feather lingers on the floor, tremulous in the aircon stream.

Dry and dressed, Remi phones his main despatch agencies and signs himself out for the rest of the afternoon. (Facing the changing tech landscape, most of his clients choose nostalgia as a coping strategy, and continue to use the otherwise redundant copper telecoms grid.) He takes care to sound calm and measured on each call. This way, voice frequency analysers won't detect stress tells or signs of illness, will automatically chalk him down as absent or taking unplanned leave. He also sends two direct messages to the only client with whom he maintains a drinking relationship. Reading them back, he sounds diffident but firm, no bad thing when over-explanation arouses suspicions.

Next, he climbs into his oldest courier armour, all manual fastenings and degrading elastic tighteners. Heavy boots and old racing leathers. He also pulls his bug from its charging mount – it starts up without issue, apparently recognising the flat, the window from which it likes to hover in the early morning, and also Remi's features, which it parses briefly before displaying a green smiley on its body. It hovers near his shoulder, rapid wingbeats cooling his neck.

'We're off-grid today,' Remi tells it. 'Personal leave.'

The bug tilts on its Y-axis, its equivalent of a head-cock. It rotates away then snaps back to him playfully.

Now Remi re-bags the contents of the waste sack. A quick toilet stop before he descends the lift to the cycle lock-up, where his old bike, his spare, is secured. The air down here is warm and chalky. Remi unracks the old bike and empties its pannier bags – used energy gel sachets, a water bottle, a delivery receipt for a nightmare job that took him from London to Glasgow with what amounted to a far-right separatist's handbook, and nearly implicated him in a sting. Anyway: he uses two bungee cords and a carabiner to secure the waste sack over the rack. He checks tyre pressure by bouncing over the handlebars – they're down, but not terminally so. He mounts the saddle, which is softer than his newer racer's, and settles on it with the reassurance of the familiar. He doesn't bother with his helmet, and is relieved he doesn't have to worry about mapping lenses now the bug handles directions.

He takes a breath. Kicks up the stand and wheels himself to the lock-up exit. When the gate's open, he whispers into the bug and throws it ahead of him. It responds enthusiastically to the hot sun. It buzzes up and into the glare.

Remi sets out.

The uncanny fox had left Remi an instruction, and through a blanching yellow haze Remi follows without deviation. He's certain that the alternative – staring at his flat's walls and regretting it – would have led to madness.

And so he's heading towards Soho. S O H O being the message applied by the fox to the foyer carpet. Soho in the West End, the glittering half-digital realm, the part-virtualised pleasure garden of their accelerating city. The letters of the message feel vivid to Remi in the daylight, where in the night they seemed nebulous, much less certain. Remi cycles steadily through interactive chase sequences and startling adplays; on past bathtub VR cafes whose muscle-wasted patrons compete for loot-farming contracts, and where those with shattered analogue lives plug in semi-permanently to seek better chances online. He pushes through scenic pop culture tunnels and fake theatre facades, lined with underpaid students flogging beautiful nodes; and he weaves around the roaming pornboards streaming sets from other time zones. Soon he's deep in the heart of the place, neon-blind and tense and sweating. But what the old bike lacks in finesse, it makes up for in agility.

Remi doesn't know exactly where he should go, of course. Instead, he holds to a strange faith in the vagueness of the commands and messages he's received so far. An uncomfortable trust in whoever's been tracking him. He hopes that by being here, cycling without his breather or helmet, and with the waste sack as cargo, he's at least demonstrating his willing. What other option does he have?

But an hour later, during which Remi has traversed the full Soho maze, seen most of its attractions several times over, he begins to reconsider. Begins to doubt – as if it wasn't already self-evidently ridiculous – that a fox should be able to write a message to him like that. Begins to question his memory, his grasp of things. Like so many people here in Soho, he begins to question reality itself.

He chokes on these doubts. He chokes on the thick city. He stops riding and secures his bike in a closed council rack; seeks shelter from the smog in the closest cafe, where spark-smoke turns opaquely against the glass. At the bar he orders two beers with a beta-blocking chaser. These he drinks under a glittering awning, his bug asleep on the table. He tries to affect the posture and gaze of a casual people-watcher, even though he can't focus on anything at all. He doesn't notice when the street traffic builds and crawls to a stop. A profusion of distant sirens like screams underwater, warbling in and out of earshot.

He sets down what's left of the second beer as an old-bodied ambulance turns into the narrow street, scattering mopeds and revellers. The sound and sight is finally enough to distract, draw his focus. When the ambulance pulls up just twenty feet from the terrace, Remi observes with detachment, London being the sort of place where these scenes play out thousands of times a day; London, overpopulated, until recently a quarter flooded, being the sort of place where human life in all of its richness can paradoxically seem less precious.

At any rate, he doesn't think for a moment that the ambulance, which contains two paramedics, a man and a woman, has arrived for him. Not until they're in the cafe, and by his side, and saying his name flatly.

Remi goes without quibble, and without paying his bill. The cafe owner stands unperturbed; shoos away Remi and his chaperones with a guilty look, perhaps hoping nobody will be put off, or worse, stream the scene for likes. LED arrays on the opposite building disorientate him. The pavement is slippery. He's starting to regret the alcohol. The walk to the ambulance is short but takes forever, a very exposed walk in the close air, and then he's at the rear doors.

'Sit and wait,' the woman says, 'while we fetch your bicycle.'

The man helps Remi up the kickstep. The bulk of the ambulance saloon is stripped out, save for a rubber floor and a crude plywood bench. The box frame is lined with wood panelling, scoured and scuffed, more like an old-time trader's van.

Remi crouches in one corner, holding his bladder. Sawdust and mildew. He checks his phone, thinking he should message someone, but the battery is dead.

The man's head appears through the rear doors, temple veins throbbing. He slides Remi's waste sack, panniers and saddle across the floor, before lugging Remi's cycle up as well. As the man climbs into the box, Remi considers his build and tone – similar to the man who'd written messages to Remi on the Tube, and hardly more effusive in his manner. It might even be the same person. The man sits on the bench and wipes his brow and removes the hi-vis and regulation fleece.

Up front, the woman climbs into the cab. She glances round and starts the engine, the sirens; they accelerate away into Soho's throngs, blipping the horn every now and then. Remi watches as herds of pedestrians disperse once more in the narrow roads: rift-drunk, most, but safe in numbers.

'Where are we going?' Remi asks.

The man shakes his head.

'Only right you tell me,' Remi says.

The man blinks at him.

'Come on,' Remi says. 'I've done my bit.'

The man stands up. He hovers there, head pushed forward by the saloon ceiling. Stooped this way, swaying, with his feet planted wide, the man appears taller and wider. The unsaid threat being implicit. Then the man clears his throat. 'I don't know where,' he says, tilting his head to the cab. 'Only she does.'

'Who's "she"?' the woman hisses. The woman is down to a vest, shoulder muscles working smoothly as she changes gears. All the dashboard electrics have been removed as well. Like someone came along and cored the ambulance.

'And you're meant to be some kind of snatch-squad?' Remi says.

The woman disengages the siren, slows off and gives the man a dour look. She doesn't so much as glance at Remi. 'Tell this prick,' she instructs the man, 'to keep his trap shut. Or we use a bag.'

Remi swallows. The urge to piss grows stronger.

'Best you listen,' the man says. 'She's fair, yeah, but she isn't patient.'

Remi drops his gaze and nudges the free-spinning wheel of his bike with his foot. Its slow ratcheting pierces the empty space.

'And tell him to get rid of that bug before she sees him,' the woman adds.

Remi straightens. *She?* He instinctively feels for the bug in his pocket. The man, now seated, has his hand outstretched, with some shade of pity on his face.

'I need it,' Remi tells him. 'For my insurance.'

The man curls his fingers and retracts his arm. He shakes his head and reaches behind the bench. He pulls out a sleeve of thick white fabric. A bag.

Remi's grip tightens around the bug.

'Give it to him,' the woman insists.

Remi hesitates.

'Please,' the man says. 'For your sake.'

Remi huffs and slides the bug across the floor. The man picks it up and rotates it in his hands. The bug's wingtips flash green. Remi gasps – this means it recognises the man's fingerprints. Was this how they tracked him?

Reddening, the man quickly pockets the bug and settles back against the van side, jostled by the ride. He glances mournfully between his boots and the waste sack, still tied to the bike.

'You wanna know how I got that?' Remi asks, motioning to the sack.

The man shakes his head fractionally.

'Wouldn't believe me, anyway,' Remi says.

The woman adjusts her rear-view mirror so she can glare at him.

'There was a fox,' Remi says. 'I went to—'

At this the man lurches from the bench and cuts Remi off with a sharp back-handed slap, more shocking than painful. A moment later the man's fist piles into Remi's solar plexus, and Remi is driven back into the ply lining of the saloon wall. The man's other hand, balled around the bag, pulls Remi's face forward and down into the rubber matting.

'She told you.'

Remi fights for his breath. The man's weight is pushing it all out. A sense that if he exhales, the spaces inside him will be flattened. Then a tightness begins to stretch at Remi's crown, tugging on the hair. The smell is mint. The smell is fox. The smell is something to crawl into, curl up inside. Remi finally inhales, and the world turns creamy white. He laughs – he can't help it. His ears go from stinging red to crushed and numb, and he tastes a sweetness. He's somewhere like that nebulous stage between consciousness and sleep: he's with Martha on a train, the two of them at a table with window seats in what must be early spring, when the rapeseed has thickened and turned whole swathes of countryside to sun. He's back with Martha as she counts *sheeps* in the fields, and he notices how each of them takes turns to close their eyes and bask briefly in the warm white light, exaggeratedly whispering *mmm* to each other, giggling like they're the first to know, the first to try it. And Remi thinks more about that, the light and the rich colour of the land, and how it was the exact opposite of this. It's nearly enough.

10

When the bag comes off, it's East London brick, at a guess. Nearby, a wet concrete overpass stilted above rows of large industrial units. A drained canal full of rotting chairs and hospital bed frames and gas canisters. High-water marks where the surge protection failed last year. Hints of the concrete barriers that might or might not cope the next time – because there will be a next time.

Remi doesn't know why the imposter paramedics removed the bag. Timing is about far as he can stretch to. He'd been out for most of the journey, and had kept quiet and did as he was told when he came to. Perhaps they want him, in some limited sense, to see. To understand the power dynamic. In any case, he's more bemused than afraid. When you cycle across London every day, an exercise in control, losing that control can be relieving, even satisfying. If nothing else, being here has stirred him awake. There's a reason to be here. Which means he has a reason to be.

'On through here,' the woman says. She's walking in

front of them, surplus fatigues and trail-running shoes. She's removed her wig to reveal a sharp undercut, a large monochrome tattoo of a pigeon whose wings stretch out both ways from nape to shoulder bone.

They pass beneath a steel roller-shutter with NO PARKING splashed across it. Another poured concrete floor, the smell of old fat on foil.

The doors roll closed behind them. Someone exhales slowly – Remi or one of the others. And now the space is pitch dark except for the band of light beneath the shutter. Remi has a hand over his chest and swears he can feel his fingers vibrating.

'Is the bag full?'

A low, hoarse voice. Not the woman's, nor the man's.

Remi searches the darkness. Faint outlines, oblique shapes. Nothing soft. The others have left him.

'Is the bag full?' the voice repeats.

'Me?' Remi whispers.

'Is the bag *full?*'

Remi steps forward and nearly trips – the sack is directly in front of his feet. And now the room has taken on the heat and stink of the fox: scat and vinegar. A carnal smell.

'Yes,' Remi offers. 'It's… full.'

'Obeyance,' comes the voice.

A small door before Remi squeals open.

'Collect it,' the voice says, stilted. 'And deliver.'

Remi picks up the sack. Winces as it swings against his thigh.

'Come through,' the voice says.

• • •

It's a warehouse. The interior, a cavernous space, is lit entirely by candle. Hundreds and hundreds of them line the walls, producing a terrific, visible heat that distorts the steel struts above him, and makes the far wall seem like a mirage. The floor is polished concrete covered in sawdust and woodchip; the walls a mix of brick, rendering and exposed steel joist. Centred in the space stands a large mesh cube, each face perhaps twenty metres across. It's tethered to the ceiling by a braid of heavy cables. Bathed in wavering shadow, a stooped figure occupies a plastic chair in the far corner of the cube.

Remi steps forward, struggling to focus. His nose is running. The wax smell is overpowering. The sack in his hand is growing heavier and heavier. The candle glow is uncanny. The walls are swimming.

'Hello?' Remi tries.

The figure in the cube stirs. A shudder of matt grey fabric. The figure is breathing strangely, as if curled into itself, or – and the idea strikes him – eating something forbidden. Remi edges closer.

'Hello?'

'*Wait.*'

The voice is quiet enough to be confident of itself. A shiver, then, to realise he's heard it before – and long before here, too. He can't place it, or necessarily explain it.

Remi comes to the cube. Between the fine mesh squares, a deliberate solitude. A short, slight woman in a sack-like tunic, thinning white hair, and a headpiece that appears to be decorated with small bones. Nothing else with her but the chair.

'Open your gifts for me,' she says. A half-turn of the head, still focused away, neck muscles stepped, so that only a slice of her face is hinted at. She has a dark skin tone, scored in texture. A distinctive jutting lower jaw, a little like a piranha's.

Remi kneels and steadies himself against the mesh. He unties the waste sack. His eyes are watering in the heat, and he blinks tears into the sawdust. One splash is so perfectly formed it shocks him.

Remi takes out the small bags and places them next to the cube. At last the woman turns to him. Smiling deeply in warm candle glow, her face a cut of old oak, a woman at ease with herself and fully in control. She says, 'Hello Remi,' and then, 'at last. It does truly feel as though I know you.'

Remi doesn't respond.

'Experimental Faraday cage,' she tells him, chuckling. 'Before you ask – since your type, standing that side all agog, always do. And no, you may not come in.'

'What's it for?'

'My sanity!' the woman spits. 'A snail needs a shell. Now, shush. What you have in here, see, are the ingredients for a spell that you yourself will cast.'

Remi shakes his head.

'We're not long for this world,' the woman says, insistent. 'I don't even expect you to listen overlong – only to act accordingly and promptly when appropriate. Thus far you've proven yourself capable of that, at least. A quality I admire. And indeed seek.'

'What's this got to do with my daughter?' Remi asks.

The question goes unanswered. The woman focuses

beyond him, flashes a chilly smirk. 'Here, girl,' she says, hardly raising her voice. And now from behind comes a shuffling. Remi turns. A fox – no, *the* fox – is crossing the sawdust, and then it's with him. It nuzzles against Remi's leg. It curls around his feet. It wags its tail and gazes up at him, pupils narrowed to sharp little almonds. Remi swallows. The fur on the fox's legs is missing, revealing light alloy and fine gearing. Machine parts.

'This is Rupal,' the woman announces. 'Rupal, this is Remi. She's keen on you, actually.'

The grime on Remi's skin itches madly, yet he's strangely flattered by the fox's affection. He can't deny the instinct to kneel and stroke the fox, a notion at once repulsive and exciting. That it's the same fox is unquestionable: the litheness, the colour of its coat, the snowy bob and quicksilver eyes – it's all the same. The smell, too.

But… these legs.

'Ru,' the woman in grey says quietly. 'Let the poor man be. He's having a moment.'

The fox stands up and trots around the cube towards the woman. It places its muzzle against the mesh and wiggles its tail. The woman inside comes to, extends her long fingers and begins to scratch the fox's throat.

'She was originally meant for MI6,' the old woman tells Remi. 'Intelligence gathering – a scout. Made in one of those little robotics firms in Cambridge. I've always cherished foxes, so the opportunity to procure her seemed somewhat fatalistic. I suppose they might have called her a semi-autonomous drone, or a field asset, or some other euphemism. We inherited her when she failed her trials.

This second generation are known for being acutely sensitive: it's very possible she could sense *too* well, which may have foretold distraction during operations. For our purposes, however, her sensitivity is a boon. It was really a case of taking some liberties with the firmware and power pack – giving her more time to range, for instance, and a proper means to synthesise energy out in the field. The sale report said she procrastinated, was easily overstimulated. I call that fastidiousness. Rupal can roam for a days at a time without a kill or collection. She is the finest collector we know, in fact, and we have a few. Try not to be alarmed by her appearance: she prefers the fur to be off indoors – it can get a little warm in here, and she's getting to be an old girl.'

Remi stares at the fox.

'In truth,' the woman continues, 'we once tried to prepare our recruits for moments like these. Cognitive dissonance… detachment… fear.'

Remi looks at her. 'Recruit?'

'Recruit! Of course! Why call it anything but? Back then, mind you, when all this started, it was a tap on the shoulder and a little chat. Except we find the approach never ends too well in this new regime. So much profiling can only teach one to underestimate the fractures in all of us. We still profile, yes, but we also listen, and gather, and watch, and wait for a fracture to present itself. A fracture wide enough. This fracture we prise open before we introduce a series of terrible shocks. And you have a fracture, Remi! A deep fracture within you, and not of your bones. And all this, I suppose, constitutes your first shock.'

Remi rubs his temples. 'You're secret services?' A wooziness under the wax smell and the heat, and the rich stink of this half-real creature acting as though it's merely tame. There's nothing more to offer, he decides. There are no words.

The woman doesn't answer, or rather lets the silence do it for her. She creaks to a stand, huffing, and glides to the cube-side towards him. Her gnarled fingers wrap into the mesh, nails whitening.

'You might say that which is broken is rarely fixed,' she says, staring directly at him. 'How's about that for a recruitment strategy?'

'I don't get you,' Remi admits. He wants to sit down. He wants to close his eyes.

'We've asked you here to fulfil a role,' she tells him. 'There is a cost, and there is a reward.'

'Reward,' Remi repeats.

'You are a courier, aren't you?'

'Yes.'

'And you have taken government contracts before.'

Remi shakes his head. 'Never.'

'False. Don't be dishonest.'

'I haven't. I thought about it, but... no. I don't—'

'Walthamstow is one example. The literary agent. Come on. Are you *really* so foolish? Don't be disappointing, Remi...'

'I don't—'

'I am well aware of my idiosyncrasies,' the woman says, and she cracks a smile. 'But you can say a lot about this government before you accuse it of workplace discrimination.'

Remi pinches his eyelids towards his nose. 'So this *is* a government agency?'

73

The woman's smile is static, thin.

'You're MI5?'

The woman purses her lips. 'The *point*,' she says, 'is not what I'm doing here, or who *we* are, but who *you* are. Because, Remi, we need a man like you, and we hope you might see why. An opportunity like this could serve you very well.'

Remi shrugs. An opportunity like what? There's no real way to remonstrate, to reject the experience. Consciously or not, he tries to disengage. Shut it down.

Except something about the woman says she won't allow it.

'You have to understand,' she tells him, 'that we understand you. We'll get to your role. First, we have to get into what motivates you.'

'Martha?' he says. 'The picture?'

The old woman nods carefully. 'Oh, yes. Her and the rest. But why not – let's talk about Martha first, shall we? Let's talk about this thing you've taught yourself to believe. Let's talk about what you really are. Rupal?'

The fox rounds the mesh cube, paws clicking on the floor.

'Show our guest to his briefing room. There's a girl.'

11

Remi follows the fox's narrow body through blank corridors, watching her ears swivel and tic. He doesn't see another person; there is no bustling of staff or harried agents, nothing of the industrious scene you might imagine given the same cues. The only thing more unsettling is the fox, the steady whine and whir of whatever drives her legs. Remi's own soles are soft enough to mute his steps, but his ankle occasionally cracks. Over his shoulder, the corridor stretches back to a vanishing point. How long has he been down here?

At last the fox stops by a numberless door and scratches three times on the jamb. The door hisses open. Improbably, the woman in grey is waiting for him inside. Remi gapes at her.

'How did—'

The woman taps her nose, beckons him in. Remi enters warily. His eyes are drawn immediately to a glass tank set on an ornate wrought-iron table. The tank contains three liquids of differing viscosities, suspended uneasily in resistance to each other. The pigeon collars are stationary on the surface.

'It can be confusing, at first,' the woman in grey tells him, 'to accept that which your instincts reject. What I will tell you, though, is that your gracious offerings afford simpler passage. These collections form our contract. They foment our mutual trust.'

'The fox brought them to me,' Remi says. 'How was I meant to collect anything like—'

'Of course she did,' the woman snips. 'As I said – Rupal *likes* you. She has known you long enough.'

Remi looks down to the fox. The fox yawns widely, indifferent. She angles her face to the light source. Her eyes flash green as her pupils contract to slits.

'Please have a seat,' the woman in grey says, and this time she's gesturing. By the door are two chairs, one of them dripping with straps and crowned with a padded head restraint. Remi swallows a hard lump.

'I'm all right standing,' Remi says.

The woman in grey rolls her eyes. 'This was the only available room. That's all.'

Remi relents and takes the non-padded chair, and the woman beams at him. 'Good,' she says. 'We can begin.'

She claps twice in quick succession. The spotlight above the tank clicks off. As it does, the entirety of the facing wall vibrates into life and enters a warm-up state. A screen, on to which floods a litany of boot messaging.

'It helps to keep in mind that foxes in general are as adept at scavenging as they are hunting,' the woman in grey tells him. She has pulled around her face a strange cowl whose sheer fabric is stretched over a number of hollow squares. It mimics the aesthetic – perhaps even the properties – of the Faraday cage in the warehouse. Then, towards the screen, she says, 'Show him from the start.'

The screen resolves to a rectangle of grainy foliage, shot from a low angle. Surveillance footage of some kind. The camera is nested in bushes, where loose twigs and undisturbed mud blur. From the edges of the shot come hints of habitation, or rather abandonment, in brambles growing freely across concrete walling. The light is neutral, an overcast morning, a guess suddenly confirmed when the camera jerks up to expose heavy cloud bank.

A pounding, gravelly soundtrack fills the room. Remi watches as the camera straightens, and two thin, articulated beams of light flash across the frame, out of focus. Legs, he realises. Those were running shoes. Then, with a sudden jerk, the camera tips over on itself. Black soil, pulled back from to reveal the lifeless gaze of a grey-furred animal, a rabbit or hare, half-concealed in the earth. Its front is torn open, the cavity empty. Remi startles in his seat, and saliva fills his mouth. He's recognising something, though he's not sure what. Something from the past. He turns away.

'There's no point,' the woman in grey tells him. 'The system is calibrated to detect reflections in the moisture of your irises. It will pause the feed if it parses anything more than your blinking.'

Remi forces himself to look again. The camera jitters and moves forward. The image is stabilised, but the effect is nauseating: a fish-eye rush, reflattened in post-production, that creates an unnatural, irregular aspect. The environment is squashed, depth of field shortened. It's claustrophobic to look at, and that's only the medium. The message is even more unsettling. On the screen stands a man in running clothes, who bends down as if to tie his laces. The man is standing on a bridge. There's a large body of water beside him, held in by enormous concrete slabs... a reservoir. The man's posture is poor, his head jutting away and shoulders slouching. The leg muscles are fairly well defined. A gleaming, nearly bald crown. The man turns and moves on, breaking into a shallow jog. There comes the sound of someone spitting heavily, and the camera accelerates in pursuit, pausing briefly to take in a square of purplish entrails left in the centre of the bridge.

In his seat, Remi mouths something. He has a sense of time and space dissolving. The man on the screen is him. The camera is attached to a fox. He remembers that morning. A reservoir, a fox with a bloodied maw. Later, running to a church.

This footage was captured the morning they buried Martha.

'How long have you been following me?' he asks the darkness.

'Not just following,' the woman in grey says. 'Collecting. Assessing. Here – see? Perfect timing.' The camera is locked to a thick oyster of spit in the gravel. The camera crash-zooms into it, a congealment, fine bubbles popping, then rises away.

'Over the years, Rupal has created a beautiful taxonomy

of you. Hair, blood. The dead sperm from tissues in your refuse. Indeed, I think one of the few samples we're missing is the horrid, faecal-smelling balls of *matter* accreting in your tonsil cavities. But I'm sure she'll be able to reap one of those soon.'

'No,' Remi whispers, and he tongues the roof of his mouth instinctively.

'It is a dataset,' the woman goes on. 'A form of insurance. It's how we know you. And it is vital to our work. Absolutely vital.'

'No,' Remi whispers, and he stands up.

The woman in grey takes his shoulder. More force in her hand than should be possible. 'Calm down,' she says. She makes him sit. 'Your data is safe,' she tells him. 'These are merely the stakes. It is gravely important you acknowledge me. This way you can apprehend what comes next.'

'I don't want it,' Remi says, meeker now. 'I don't want this.' He slumps, overcome with a sense of helplessness and violation. A physical pain, as though he's being infected: a sharp line that seems to cut him down the middle.

'Please watch,' the woman says.

Cut to another scene. A smoky light. A London light. A figure through pyro-glass: Remi, filmed in his apartment kitchenette, unaware and apparently getting ready for work. Remi, in his apartment, being filmed by the Gilper bug he allows to hover outside the window each morning. Remi, in his apartment, being spied upon by the closest thing he has to a companion.

Cut to another morning. Another morning. And another. Now a time-lapse of Remi's morning routines: his eating

79

of toast, drinking tea; his standing at his kitchenette stove, rotating the knobs for the hob. Turning on the gas. Turning off the gas. Clicking, calmly, with his mouth, as if to mimic the sound of the stove's ignition switch.

'But…' he manages to say.

'It's an electric hob,' the woman in grey says. 'There is no gas supply to your flat, or to any of the flats in your block.'

Remi turns to her. The footage pauses instantly. 'What is this?' he asks. 'What are you showing me?'

'Well, that you are doomed to repetition,' she tells him. 'More of an animal than you realise.'

'I don't remember doing this. You've doctored it.'

'We've doctored *nothing*,' the woman snaps. 'The point is, your body remembers. That is the nature of trauma. We have your data here, remember – it is the exact same impulse that once caused you to refresh the same websites at least fifty times a day. The searches you made tell us so much. Your patterns are extraordinary, Remi: the data is a sight to behold. But what do *you* think you are looking for? What are you hoping will change? It's as if you almost know, deep in there, the truth of the matter.'

Remi's shame stays any kind of answer. There is no response. He's counted out and tallied up.

'Tell me, Remi, if you can – when did you stop watching the news? Do you know today's date?'

Remi tips his head forward, pushing his hands into his hair.

'Can you say? Can you tell me?'

Remi's lips part, but he doesn't speak.

'There's so little to be ashamed of,' the woman continues.

'The world is a cold stone, and we are its rotting flesh.'

'I remember arguments,' Remi admits quietly. 'At home. I remember arguing. I think that's when things started to change.'

'Change? If our records of your transactions during that period allow us to draw inferences, they would be that you stopped leaving the house at all. Is that what you mean?'

'My transactions? I don't—'

'Were they political arguments?'

He nods. 'Closer to home. Friends and family falling out. My mother and father… it drove a wedge between them.' More of it is coming back to him now, a wave of sorrow and prickling heat. His stomach knots, then cramps. A hot coal within him. His face throbs. He recalls the fighting. War speeches. The news showed it all. His body is very stiff. People were behaving like animals – on streets at home and in faraway places. Battlecruisers launched rockets, and children foamed from their mouths. The news showed him. Bodies were smeared under tracked vehicles. The high sheen of camera lights in fresh blood. He couldn't stop watching the news. Men and women at lecterns, frothing with ire. Falsehoods and weak pretexts. Lies and disinformation. Endless commentary and speculation, and the insidious ramping-up of fear and confusion. And through it all, Remi's stomach was his nerve centre: he lived on cortisol and adrenaline, developed a sense of always being on, always watching the news and waiting and dreading. A belief that England's streets and cities had grown teeth, that anyone and everything was a threat; a belief that the very apocalypse, acid rains and all-consuming, was rolling in. And Martha – it was Martha who would have suffered it all. The news showed him.

The woman in grey places her hand on the back of Remi's head. She cradles him.

'You were dangerously obsessed with the news, Remi. We have your viewing data. You barely slept. The news infected you. The news was your window, but the window was cracked. And over the course of perhaps six or eight weeks, you stopped wanting to be the first to know. You entered what we might term a dissociative state, inflamed by emotional trauma, simply by watching the news. It was a cycle. It bloated you. The hatchlings feasted. In this cycle you convinced yourself you were better away from your family, or that they were better away from you. So you decided to abandon your family. You abandoned your role as a father. You murdered yourself in order to live again.'

'No,' Remi says.

'You don't remember? You don't remember what you did?'

'I don't know what you mean.'

'The night you left Joan and Martha, you left the gas on. You burned the house down. Didn't you? You tried to kill them.'

'Kill them? No!'

'And you got away with it. They never even knew. The fire service, being so thin, had little time to investigate. They said it was an accident – there was no evidence of tampering. You were all so... oh, Remi, I've seen it all. You ran away and left them to burn. But we know differently, don't we? I know. I know what you thought you were doing. I know exactly what you are.'

'I don't remember,' Remi says. 'It was Martha's funeral—'

'Look at me, Remi!' the woman in grey shouts. She claps. 'Look at this.'

The room's sound and colours change. On to the screen flows footage from a church graveyard. Bleak uplands behind. A congregation around a fresh grave. Mounds of earth. He recognises some of the faces standing there. He recognises his wife Joan – brow darkened and eyes downturned. He can't see her eyes and yet he knows their colour, their shape under the duress of frowning. Lidded stare, once her stoned expression, here a picture of desperation. He watches the man he recognises as himself step forward, take up a shovel, and begin to shift soil into the cavity. The shovel face flashes as he works the ground. After four or five loads, he returns to the group, head bowed.

Here Remi notices the hand outstretched. A small hand wrapping his arm and pulling him in. His organs swell up inside him. A girl's nose, then chin, then forehead emerge from the crowd. A ponytail, with strays hanging out of the bobble.

'That's Martha,' he says.

'This was captured at your mother-in-law's funeral,' the woman in grey says. 'Rupal was in attendance. And yes, so was Martha.'

Remi balls up his hands and strikes his head and neck. The screen stutters as his eyes open and close.

'You didn't bury your daughter that day,' the woman in grey tells him. 'You buried Joan's mother. Later that night you left them, and you left the gas oven turned on.'

The footage ends. The viewing room floods with piercing light, so powerful he's sure it will erase him. The woman in grey is holding his face, long fingers wrapped under his ears. Her thumbs over his larynx. She tips his head back.

'You wanted to save them, in some warped way,' the woman says. 'The news had told you what the future would do to Martha. You were deeply ill, and we believe that was your intention. Insulate, envelop them. But you didn't save her, Remi. You only truly saved yourself. Do you see now?'

Remi slides from the chair. The floor swallows him. The woman in grey steps over him and holds on to his face.

'Quickly comes the fear,' she whispers.

Remi tries to turn his head, manages only a fraction. The woman wasn't addressing him. She wasn't saying fear at all. *Fur*. Emerging from a corner, Rupal's moon-silver eyes and exposed metal shins reflecting the light. Their radiance makes the rest of the fox's body seem like a phantasm, a suggestion.

'Quickly,' the woman urges. 'While they're still fresh.'

Rupal canters over to Remi. The woman clamps Remi's head in position while Rupal sets about licking the tears from his face, his eyes, his ducts. The fox's breath is coppery. Her tongue is dry and rough. Remi manages to squeezes his knees around the fox's body, a slight give in the ribs, and she rolls away from him with a wounded look.

'Martha is fifteen now,' the woman in grey tells him, tightening her grip.

'Stop,' Remi whimpers. 'Please stop it.'

'And you can see her again,' the woman in grey says. 'Would you like to?'

Remi looks at the fox. The fox is staring back at him.

'You must do as we instruct,' the woman in grey says. 'Will you?'

Remi nods once.

'Then be still now.' She removes her hands. She moves to the tank of liquid, into which she places her arm. When she removes it again, her skin is filthy. She takes the pigeon collars from the surface, brings them towards him.

'Open your eyes,' the woman in grey says. She tilts his head back, using his chin. He wants to struggle but finds himself paralysed. She places the pigeon collars on his cheeks and, raising her wet forearm, allows the liquid to run along the deep channels of her skin, mass and bulge at her fingertips, and fall into his dry mouth. Remi's throat seizes as he tries not to gag. *Tallow grease. Lorry spray. Oiled puddle—*

'A ceremony,' the woman tells him. 'For a promise, these ancient fluids. As a country we worked with them for so long – did you think they were a gimmick? We are together, now. Our blood and oil. Go home, and we will be in touch.'

Remi staggers to the door on weak legs. The white light clicks off. The woman in grey whispers, 'That's enough, Rupal.'

Remi turns around. Rupal is still licking the floor. Something inside Remi twists and breaks, floats free.

12

In body, Remi is picking his way towards Hackney, towards the flat. In every other sense he is altered, swimming. His nose and mouth can't quite break London's surface, and each breath brings a trill of pain, a lightning in his chest. How has he forgotten what should be insoluble? He's pushing against the inside of something. It has shifted outwards, started to give. At the thinnest point, it's possible to discern shapes on the other side. A truth is over there, but its form has come apart. He remembers the funeral, not a burial. He remembers gas hobs, not a fire. If he'd ever intended to hurt his family that way, the impulse is utterly revolting to him now – a stranger's resolve, an alien will: as exterior and unthinkable as the idea of hurting them with a ligature, a blade between the ribs, a hammer on thin bone. He stops to retch against a wall. Truly he believes he couldn't and wouldn't have done something so drastic, so unforgiveable. In turn, he questions how it could have even – or ever – happened. Would you really get away with something so heinous? He was never arrested – was he? Never sought, so far as he knows. He has never been haunted by the act itself – he has consumed enough true crime in his years to know that some killers return to the scene, attempt to relive their transgressions. If there's a darkness in him, it's surely personally inflected, inward facing. It doesn't stem from blame or guilt. Surely – *surely* – Remi had made no attempt on the lives of Joan and Martha. Surely him turning the hob on and off meant nothing.

Away from the woman in grey, beyond her thrall, more doubts are hardening. Denial as deliverance. What proof really exists for Martha, except for the photo, or the video footage, both of which could have been manipulated or fabricated? The bug's images of him standing in his kitchen, at the hob, were convincing, yes, but hardly definitive. Even the funeral footage seemed falsified, like a recital, a false-flag memory… they could have found models or actors, restaged each scene… If the woman in grey was really with a government agency, they had previous form.

But why? Why would they do this to him?

As he moves, Remi desperately hopes for clarity. Because the idea alone of Martha being alive is devastating. It brings to bear the possibility that in some awful state he truly abandoned her; that he wilfully left her, never mind Joan, and has somehow suppressed the memory of doing so. The dissonance hurts him physically. To admit Martha is alive is to also admit he has lied to himself so repeatedly, so effectively, that he has come to believe something infinitely worse.

Is he really so self-centred? This question is enough to

make him stop in the street. Remi has long since stopped regarding the past as linear, or at least the forward-flowing stream that brought him here. He tends to look back on segments of his life as though reviewing episodes from an unreal television series – vignettes out of sequence, out of sync. In this new mode, he struggles to make any of them work rationally. The viewing angle has moved: he sees now that there are blanks and deep holes in the continuity, in the stitching of him. There are moments he thought were crystallised forever. Since he left Manchester, he has always had the sense that his life ended and restarted when Martha passed on. That he should have to suspend these ideas isn't just painful – it's existential.

And what about the news? His apparent – no, demonstrable – aversion to it? If he has any memory of a fugue, it must be buried by definition. There's no real counter to his current detachment, him being the man he is, alone in his ways and answering to nobody but the clients he serves so punctually. Did he really lose himself so completely for that time? And does he accept that this was still him?

Why doesn't he *remember?*

As Remi reaches the turning for the flats and comes off the canal towpath, he can't help picturing his life as an infinite spreadsheet. He grows angry. He begins to grasp in totality the ways in which the woman in grey and her fox have surveilled and catalogued him. All those years. All these ways that technology has become his prison – and for what? What are they planning for him?

Remi washes into his flat on a tide of rage. He unlocks the door knowing what to do, what this urge is really about. He doesn't wait or hesitate: he works purposefully, each fresh wave of loathing for the fox and the woman causing him to seek out and break something new.

First, he destroys the obvious things they might have used – machines with watching lenses, or listening microphones, or suggestions of either. He tears the bug's charging mount from the wall and snaps it, gashing his hand. He stamps on his mobile phone until its screen is unreadable, and he drops the gathered wreckage from an open window to the car deck below. The noise of the debris energises him – he sets about ripping other objects from their perfect, just-so slots and slits, boxes and drawers, and throws these out of the window, too.

Next he sits and destroys his tablet and hard drives with a ball pein hammer, a diamond-tipped screwdriver. He takes a mesh basket and finds some accelerant and burns his English passport in an attempt to melt its memory chip.

He hunts for the less obvious things: anything he suspects could feasibly contain a camera or mic or tracker. A vented garlic pot, coin boxes, any hollow trinkets. Objects that he might otherwise ignore in everyday life, which would also make for ideal surveillance points. He makes a pile and goes through it with the hammer.

He boils the kettle and sterilises the screwdriver blade and cuts down towards the health insurance derm in his wrist, sucks at the wound until the capsule is there in his mouth. He chews until it breaks open. He swallows the insides. The aftertaste is caustic, how he imagines the flavour of singed hair.

He works like this into the night, thoughts dulled by the

physicality of it all. Methodical in a way that perturbs and reassures him. That he's capable of doing all this damage, to so much stuff he's paid good money for – grafted and grifted and saved for – is a surprise of its own.

Only when he's done – the flat smelling of his body, his skin bearing a film of sweat and blood and graphite – does Remi stop to consider if this was what the woman in grey intended. If the destruction of his personal life, his gadgets, was what she wanted. If his decision to act this way reflects or follows any sort of persuasion or suggestion on their part.

He dismisses it. Impossible to know. He can't second-guess himself, let alone the woman in grey.

Exhausted, he lies down on the lounge rug, strewn with its plastic debris, metal fasteners, splinters, and closes his eyes to sleep, having found a sort of peace in being able to see nothing. At least for now they can't see him either.

When Remi wakes again, Rupal the fox is waiting at the lounge window. Part of him expected it, the rapid response, but then he remembers how many floors up the flat is.

Rupal has her face pressed against the glass, snout squashed and pale whiskers splayed out like fine cracks. Her body is arched, positioned sidelong for purchase on the ledge.

Remi weighs the fox's presence, the devastation of his flat. A kind of shame and trepidation, his heart going, his wrist sore. Is this what the woman in grey meant by being in touch? The fox, unnaturally still, yawns widely at him, revealing a root-purple tongue and black-pitted teeth.

Remi snarls back at her. Rupal being the other tool that has captured and processed him, broken him down into parts, collected his remains and traces and impressions on the world, as a way to deconstruct and quantify him. And how. It's the effectiveness, the single-mindedness, that disturbs him most of all. The idea she's been Remi's shadow since the reservoir. That in all this time he only remembers seeing her that once.

So when Remi goes to the window to slide it open, he does so with the diamond-tipped screwdriver drawn carefully from the shag-pile rug, held close against his right kidney. He opens the window, and the fox darts in with that impossible smile, licking her lips as though to say, *why wouldn't I be here?*

Remi lunges at her. Rupal rolls playfully, seemingly oblivious. With his left hand Remi catches her by the throat and strikes somewhere along the spine, hears the metal scrape. He draws back his arm for another attempt, this time aiming upwards into the throat, and Rupal bares her teeth and yaps in panic and slides closer to him. She writhes against him like some lost pet, desperate, and Remi can't abide it; can't abide that she should want to be here. He brings the screwdriver down through Rupal's skull, and the fox pushes her face deeper into Remi's armpit, snuffling and whining and leaking, her brush swinging wildly. Remi recoils, gripping the fox by the lower jaw, fingers wet and hot in her mouth, and lands two savage blows to her snout, a third above the left eye. The impact shatters the lens in its socket, exposing a chain of tiny mirrors behind. With her single remaining eye, Rupal fixes Remi with a loving gaze.

'No,' Remi tells her. And Rupal paws at his thighs, Remi cross-legged with the fox rolling over and over, her face and coat shedding splinters of glass and metal. Except now she's mewling, a sad, low moan that makes Remi want to silence her forever. 'No,' Remi whispers, and he raises the screwdriver once more.

He's too tired to finish it. If it can be finished at all. The fox's torn fur reveals some kind of armour plating. Blood-oil on the uppermost surface, with flecks like iron filings visible in the suspension. Rupal sits on him, wheezing, trying to stand and move but caving each time. Remi collapses backwards with the fox on top of him, a dead weight on his chest. Rupal, with her eyes slitted, licks at Remi's face and neck, her fragments sprinkling his skin. Remi gives in. He drops the screwdriver and lets Rupal harvest his sweat.

13

Rupal is badly injured. When Remi cups her face and looks into her damaged eye, he can see the lens mirrors flipping in spasm.

'Why did you come back?' he asks her. 'Why did you come here?'

Rupal slides off him and staggers in a tight circle, forelegs unsure. She keeps lifting her chin, forlorn, as if willing Remi to get up with her. No, insisting. The fox wants Remi to get up.

So Remi rises to his knees. He steadies himself over his hands. Rupal circles him, nuzzling his back, his arms. And Remi says, 'I'm sorry,' hopeless as a boy, voice cracking. Rupal stops. Remi says, 'Rupal.' Quietly, as though in confession.

Rupal visibly brightens at hearing her name. She taps her way close to him and puts her cold nose to his belly. Tentatively, he touches her head, then her flank. Her insides are trembling. He picks away the larger pieces of debris from her coat, sweeps fragments from her snout and ears with the back of his hand. He yelps as something slides into his finger, and immediately sucks at it. He can taste her, the sourness and rust. He curses and lifts himself to his feet and Rupal immediately reels away, cowed and wary once again. She leaves a smear of a sticky fluid on the floor.

'No more,' Remi says, surveying the upturned room, the ruin of the place. He's not that man now. And slowly, Rupal returns to Remi's feet.

'Do you eat?' he asks her. 'Are you hungry?'

Rupal moves her head once to the side. A delicate movement, almost imperceptible. Is that an answer? Then another anguished moan as she lurches towards the door and begins to claw and scratch. Remi takes a step closer. Rupal spins on the spot and comes to his feet.

Remi nods. 'You want me to follow you.'

Rupal lies down on her belly. Her white tail bob waving, her ears sharply up.

Remi pulls on his boots. A heavy jacket. He holds his head and hears with harsh clarity the sound and coarseness of the screwdriver entering Rupal's orbit. He looks at his hands: narrow cuts through old scars, a flapping callus on his palm. He looks to Rupal, this wretched creature dripping mechanical fluids from her mouth, hanging on his movement.

He pockets the screwdriver. He makes a silent pact with himself. Seeing the state of her, he owes her that.

Rupal limps along the Regent's Canal's wet towpath some distance ahead of Remi, and then into the hiveways of Bethnal Green itself. Remi's holding his hood against the wind, hanging back from corner to corner for fear of looking strange, and to preserve the natural order. A fox and human don't travel together – interactions are fleeting, mystical. Their lines should not merge. Meanwhile, Rupal has gathered some strength in walking, though there's a sagging to her front right shoulder; a slight but noticeable kink in her spine that hints at more serious internal injuries. The bushy tail she holds at a right angle, as if to counter a loss of balance.

As they go, this strange dance, Remi wonders if they aren't heading to the small row of shops by the Overground station at London Fields. They traverse the mouth of Broadway, where the market stalls stand desolate save for a rough-looking man wearing a sandwich board promising salvation and jellied eels, in that order. Remi hurries past, hands pocketed; the fox has apparently sensed the stranger and jinked right into parkland. More people emerge from the treeline. He spots a circle of modern inflatable tents, the remains of a crate fire. It's four in the morning, and dawn is coming.

'Rupal,' Remi hisses, but only when he's sure of being alone. 'Wait up.'

The fox loiters. She marks her territory and licks her forepaw, her belly. From a distance, you would never know her truth. Out here, in this rich and unkept grass, she's every London fox that ever crossed him on a run; she is the city's history and its survivor all at once.

The fox dips her head. She looks to the distance, scenting. Despite her injuries, she increases her speed.

Remi shuffles into a jog.

· · ·

Remi finally catches up with Rupal on the corner of a back street. Here stands a vintage phone and subderm-seller's kiosk, digital A-board glitching on the pavement outside. The neon on the wall above the kiosk is dead, grey letters spelling DOCTOR DERM, while gaudy stickers and aug-reality tags decorate the roller-shutter. Remi's shoulders tighten as he notices the fox lying down. The pooling liquid beneath her. Here? Really?

Seeing him approach, Rupal stretches out her hind legs in the manner of a cat waking up. She wiggles her ears and closes her eyes. There's a gap in the base of the roller-shutter, through which she slides with no small effort. Then, from inside, a lot of banging and rattling around, before a tense quiet settles.

'Rupal?'

The fox barks once, muffled but sharp, and the roller door starts to squeak into its housing. A rhombus of dawn light reveals Rupal teetering on a stack of crates and boxes, her nose pushed against a simple industrial switch. As Remi ducks under, she moves away, shaking her face like the button had tickled her whiskers. The shutter closes behind him.

Remi hunts for a light. Only the fox beats him to it – jumping across a rack of shelves to nose on a switch; an old energy-saving bulb phases on above him, warmer than he might have expected. He can't see his breath, at least.

The fox pauses to give him a look. Then she jumps to the floor. Remi looks at his feet. He's standing in a pile of discarded plastic moulds and torn paper. Looking closely, he notices phone batteries among the mess, some apparently gnawed, along with blotches of what could be battery acid. As if to confirm something, Rupal sniffs the ground and takes one of the damaged batteries in her mouth. She chews it with an awful grinding noise, then lets her tongue flop loose, dark saliva spooling off.

'You don't...' He stoops lower as if to check. 'Jesus, no. Don't eat that.'

The fox leads Remi into the back of the shop, where she's fashioned a bed from various chunks of packing foam, polystyrene and cardboard. The stench is obscene: concentrated urea, peppery and raw. Flies billow and reform in the corners. No, they *are* the corners. Remi covers his mouth and nose lest the air blister his throat. His eyes water.

The fox settles in her den, unperturbed. Remi squats to her level, noting her tiredness. There's a cloying thickness to the space. A physicality to the air. Rupal's single working eye has taken on a strange aspect, a vagueness, as though it's struggling to focus on him.

'Why in here?' Remi asks.

Rupal pushes a half-eaten battery towards him. It's leaking from two deep fissures.

He fingers the dry end of the battery. He slides it away from her. 'You can't bloody eat this stuff,' he tells her. He scratches his head, because she can and clearly does. 'What about... what about meat? I can get you some chops. Lamb or chicken. Or eggs.'

He shakes his head, conscious of how stupid he sounds.

Rupal growls. Low and level. She points her nose towards

the back of the kiosk, where Remi can just about make out the far wall of a storeroom. He points in response, and the fox allows her head to hang slack.

'You want me to go back there?'

Remi's heart is going. But the fox has apparently expended what little energy she had left, and stays put. He goes through. He squeezes his nostrils tighter. Makes a seal.

He gasps.

On the floor of the storeroom lie the remains of two decapitated wood pigeons. Their necks reveal signs of damage, but the wounds are clean, precise, their carcasses otherwise intact. Packaged, even. It occurs to Remi that Rupal has prepared them for him. That when he was tasked by code on a Tube carriage to find objects for the woman in grey, Rupal was already out there collecting them. That when a driverless car was driven at him, all of this was already in motion.

A rustling. A tickling at his leg. Rupal is with him again. Low down, like she's ebbing away. Slowly, she enters the storeroom ahead of him and stretches her forepaws to the first shelf of a unit. He goes there, almost straddling her. On the shelf he finds a neatly organised sheaf of papers, damp and degrading most, wrapped in what remains of a thin plastic ring binder. He pulls the bundle into the light. Rupal is on her toes, leaning up and towards them. There are teeth marks in the spine of the ring binder.

Remi opens it. The first sheet is in fact a noisy monochrome photograph. Remi's heart creeps towards his mouth. The image shows a woman talking with a bearded man. They're wearing thick wools, and smoking. In the background, just out of focus, the unmistakeable shape of moorland. To one side of them stands a younger girl, hair pulled mostly across her face, but unmistakeably Martha. Martha, with her mother's broad shoulders, and Remi's long neck, and the clipped appearance of her earlobes.

The caption beneath the photograph reads GREENLEY SITE #54, dated late last year. Remi's guts tighten. His first response is repulsion, jealousy. Then a swing back to incredulity.

Remi lowers the photograph and stares at Rupal. 'You took this?'

The fox twists her head as though she's been caught out. Her tongue is hanging, cracked and dry. A kind of thick white powder has collected at its tip.

'Who's that?' he asks, pointing to the man.

The fox yaps once, brightly.

'Greenley?' Remi says. He turns the page. Another image: this time of a teenage girl leaving what might be a railway station. She's carrying a large backpack, and looks withdrawn.

'Where did you take these?' he asks.

The fox startles. She begins to cough or choke as if she might be about to bring up a hairball.

Remi exhales and turns the page. Now a nameless OS map, stained grey in places by dripping liquid. A circle drawn in shaky red pen. Tight contour lines suggesting elevation; a hill or mountainside, or the moorland from the previous picture.

He looks at Rupal. The thick white paste on her tongue has started to dangle, stretch away.

'She's here? This is where she's staying?'

Rupal stays very still.

'Jesus Christ,' he says, and he turns the page. Now a

CCTV capture, its picture lined and rough. The subject, however, is clear enough: a portrait of Rupal, balled up on the floor of a bare, apparently windowless cell, not much larger than her body.

Remi says nothing. The papers in his hand waver slightly. The heft of it all bears down – brings with it an immediate link, a sympathy, and the idea Rupal isn't meant to be here with him; that they likely won't know Remi is in here either.

Remi squats to take in the next page. He peels back the paper like it might injure him. Another photo of another cell, this taken from a different angle. The cell is noticeably larger, and empty. Old brick. A toilet bowl stands in one corner: this is a cell meant for human occupation. He stares at it until he can imagine being kept there, and has to glance away. He takes a breath before he continues, turns the page to discover an extract, written using fine ink and apparently ripped from a journal or notepad. Of what little he can read – the rest being smeared, or nonsensical, or torn – there are several distinctive sentences:

by observation, exhibits symptoms of acute dissociative amnesia. Will likely prove susceptible to intensive unreality therapy, with retraumatisation a distinct and advantageous possibil

And a few lines later:

especially pliable / amenable to our long-term goals

And further down the page:

daughter maintains useful proximity to target Greenl

These are medical notes of some sort. Medical notes about him.

Rupal has given up something here, a way for Remi to try and understand. Not a message, but a dossier of intelligence.

The fox has been helping him. Why, he can't even start to understand. Is it because the fox, like Remi, is trapped in this game? At the mercy of similar pressures? Is she trying to warn him? It all runs deeper than Remi can see.

'What now?' Remi asks her. And he looks at the fox's damaged head, its missing eye, and suddenly considers turning the screwdriver on himself. 'I'm sorry,' he says. 'For what I did to you.'

Like she was waiting for his permission, Rupal slinks into a corner and buries her head in a cardboard box, chews down on something. When she returns to him, her single working eye is glittering, lit from within. She comes with a fresh energy, and in her mouth is a slim, lead-coloured envelope, partially scored and folded laterally. She drops it in Remi's lap, and the weight is enough for him to know. It's the trackable manuscript case he couriered for the literary agent in West London. The realisation is electrifying: a coalescent line that runs between the driverless car and the men on the Tube carriage, and then to Rupal herself. This whole time, she's been involved.

Rupal nudges at the case, and Remi takes a long breath. He runs his tongue across his gums, both sets. The lock and seal is broken anyway, but opening it – even looking inside – is a hefty transgression; runs contrary to everything he's done to establish himself and survive in London. In some odd way, it jeopardises everything.

'I can't,' he says. 'I can't do it.'

Or is it fear? Of what's inside? Of what he might have carried in this package unknowingly?

In any case, the fox acts on his behalf. She bites the bottom edge of the case and shakes it from side to side. Out tumbles a jaundiced, scrappy paperback, cover all but missing. Remi takes it from the floor and brings himself to hold it, feel its age. The powdery texture of its pages. He pulls it up to his face and inhales sweet vanillin, thumbs wet with the hot slime from Rupal's mouth. According to the partially torn title page, the book is called *The Cold Veil*, author Laurel M. Brace. The verso says it was first published in 1971, with this particular edition printed in 1982. Remi peels back the title page. The first line of the prologue reads: *In the coldest harbours of tomorrow, the machines stood victorious.* A novel, then. A slim, long-ago published novel, and not a draft manuscript at all.

Remi holds the book. Hollowed out and deathly still. Rupal is watching him. With her chin, she makes an upward motion towards the book. Remi turns it over and thumbs through it, noticing that large sections of text have been torn from the binding glue. He goes through it again. What looked accidental seems anything but: the sections removed have crudely abridged the story, of which there now seems little left. Front to back, this copy of *The Cold Veil* comprises a prologue, the first chapter, the thirteenth chapter and an epilogue. Four segments in total. Suddenly, he's aware of the novel's artifice: a sense of its being considered, prepared somehow, rather than just passed along. An act – of something.

Rupal barks at him.

'What?' Remi says, splaying the book face down over his knee.

Rupal trots closer. She noses the paperback deeper into his lap and then burrows into it, noisily pushing its pages up over her head. The action flicks remnant glass into Remi's face. She growls as she does this, possibly frustrated, backs away and flips the volume. Then she bites deeply into the novel's spine. She tosses it to the floor. The punctured book skitters and lands with its final pages open. Set in the rear cover is a photograph of the author. It is a face younger than he knows, and yet the jawline, the pitch of cheek…

The author Laurel M. Brace is the woman in grey.

Remi opens his legs and stretches his toes. A dislocation: he doesn't remember eating, can't imagine ever wanting to again. The world pinched up and in retreat. When he scoops the book from the floor, it slips from his fingers because they're shaking.

Rupal comes away from his lap and retrieves the book for him. He takes it, and Rupal returns to him, fussing at his armpit until he lets her in. The smell of her. And there, on the dusty floor in the back of the kiosk, with Rupal curled under his arm and her chin nested on his exposed belly, her working eye tuned down to a simple black line, Remi begins to read what remains of the old woman's novel, in part because it's been arranged for him, and in part because there's nothing else to do.

14

Later, when he's finished reading, Remi takes care to place the book on the floor between his legs. Edges straight, parallel with each leg, so that the title and author's name are obscured. In this way it's under his control, its power in some way diffused.

He isn't fully sure what to make of Brace's disjointed story, though he has gained some satisfaction from joining up the unseen and unsaid, filling in the temporal blanks made physical by the book's dismemberment. In this sense the abridged novel has been generous – it neither insulted nor underestimated him. It could even be its own short story in this format, given its mostly functioning state, and if its editor – or its vandal – recognised this. Or was it just a matter of time and format? Either way, the novel wears its decade on the page – Brace's writing being of a slightly stilted, gently formal style that reminded Remi of the youthful enthusiasm he once held for utopian science fiction, and the story, so far as he can tell from these four chapters, being relatively straightforward. That said, it's also surprisingly prescient in many ways, if a little naïve in its depiction of an automated society. The 2010 Remi lived through wasn't so staid, nor so peaceable. Or sufficiently advanced, come to that. Even now, here in 2030, flying cars are a rich man's fancy. Then, of course, there are the logistics and politics of its world, which don't fully mesh: there's no mention of a universal basic income, which Remi and many others, cleaving to the idea that working gives you purpose, and rejecting free money for the feckless and lazy, had voted against in 2022. Brace has also reified the unions, instead of predicting their annihilation at the pitheads and later on the NHS wards; and the death of privacy is a conspicuous gap, given what they know now – perhaps especially in light of what Brace herself has ordered done to Remi. There can't be, he decides, a living writer who doesn't want to touch on the willing surrender of personal data, or the slyness of personal technology too complex to fix or modify, yet always so perfectly intuitive – or fun – to use.

But in another sense, Brace's idea of an 'automatic England' is certainly upon them. In pockets of the country, drone labour is very real, and without a basic income to mitigate the excesses of concentrated ownership, the blight in some parts of the wider world has been no less catastrophic than war. It's just that the real automatic England presents itself as a different variety, with a more respectable sheen. People don't simply rise up and resist machines as Kip Mornington and his army do in Brace's novel. If basic income ever comes up in contention – well, the country was too afraid to try another way, believed the scaremongering about its costs, and tacitly voted for the status quo to continue, falsely believing these issues would only ever affect someone else. The will of the people – that's how they'd put it. And what are you going to do about it?

Remi wonders, then, how Brace would view her work now. If it's hard to accept that by speculating in fiction you also date a piece of fiction. That if you live for long enough, you might also see its relevance slip away.

In spite of all this, the characters resonated for him. While there's a distance in reading her, Remi had sympathised with Morn, the stoic protagonist whose struggle against the machines stemmed from personal loss. He wonders what happened to Brace to inspire it. If the novel is in some way autobiographical. A father and a daughter… a war and a wager. He wonders too what this book is for. How do these four chapters link to his time in the warehouse with Brace? Or this contract of hers. Is the book meant to be a statement? Is it a warning to him? Or is it something more?

Rupal lifts herself from Remi's stomach, chin fur matted and damp. A smell rises from their contact: sweeter than musk, or his sweat. Remi feels drunk. Tired to the point of delirium, mired in Brace's fiction. It's affected him physically, this book.

'We should go,' he says. 'We should get out of London.'

The fox stands and shivers. Remi lifts himself up and does the same. He stoops for the old paperback and slides it back on to the storeroom shelf. Taps it, almost reverentially, and motions for the door.

Rupal won't lead. She stands there at his side. 'Hop it,

then,' Remi says, and starts to move. The fox hangs back behind him.

He pushes the shutter switch. The rollers shift. He steps out on to the street and the fox noses into his legs. Her way of pointing.

'Where?' he says. But the answer is already waiting. Over the road, a bar of blue lights pop and flare, and an electric engine whinnies into life. The ambulance is waiting for him.

Remi, very still, looks down at the fox. Not a protest – more to check for intent. But Rupal's already trotting away up the street, shoulders jouncing under her skin as if Remi never tried to destroy her. This time, she doesn't turn back. He follows her passage – Rupal's rewilding, her brush bleeding into heavy morning – as she sheds her name and becomes other once more. Another London fox; every London fox.

The ambulance's rear doors open. Boots clumping on gravel. A large man crossing the road, a woman in the driver's seat. Remi stands there by the A-board outside the shop, lost and found, awaiting them. Ready, like it or not, for his next instruction.

PART II

THE COLD VEIL (ABRIDGED)

Prologue
War's End, Earth. 2070.

In the coldest harbours of tomorrow, the machines stood victorious. The fifty-year war, at its apogee an extra-planetary war, was concluded.

The moon, such as humankind's limited government knew it, was lost. The Martian colonies, so painstakingly erected, were riven and left to the wages of solar radiation. Earth, the first and last front, was depopulated by magnitudes unthinkable to anyone who had lived through the late twentieth century.

It was the year 2070 exactly, and the machines could now rest and tally their run of crushing victories. In doing so they chattered and rattled among themselves, linked as they were through the same core network that sustained their existence. On this day, a fine cold day, their automatic empire was born. The cold veil was drawn.

Yet not all of humanity had acceded to these terms. One such human, a tall woman with polar-white hair, swathed in cotton rags and sheepskins, her skin deeply tanned, stood above the coastline of Dover, the southernmost reaches of Kent, upon the eroding white cliffs which had for centuries provided natural guard against seaborne assault. From here the woman watched the machines in conference. From here, this unseen vantage point, she discerned the machines' antennae crackling with longwave messaging. The snap of their chatter above the wailing of a mournful sea. She confirmed their build versions, she recorded their heights, and soon she would plan her route into their nest.

Which is not to say the woman was unaware that humanity had lost, or indeed *was* lost. It had been inevitable for some time. About this she was philosophical – she often questioned aloud if homo sapiens' whole time extant as a species was simply the result of bad fortune. The woman's father and many others of his era had created the first generation of machines intended to free humans from toil. Unwittingly, they had devised for themselves a pitiless yoke.

The tall woman's name was Morn, full title Miranda Mornington September, Prime of the Fourth Metropolitan Borough of Southampton. She had journeyed here alone in spite of her old age, wearing a suit of bespoke farmour: a hulking bipedal exo-system constructed almost exclusively from reinforced stallion and bull bone, salvaged tendons and ligaments, heavy leathers. The farmour was driven by a tin-and-iron pulley and cam system, whose movements reproduced and augmented her own, yet still the journey had been long and arduous, and when the task was complete she would need to hunker down in seclusion before striking camp and returning with a token of her visit. The one thing that would help them in the siege to come.

For now, though, the light was too flat for Morn to make good on her promise. Better to rest here and launch her assault under that savage clarity of dawn. She climbed back into the bodybay of her farmour and drew its ribs and her skins tightly around her, releasing the perfumes of mould and moss, tallow grease and oil. Above her, the homing pigeon preened in the suit's shoulder cage.

Latterly she slept for a time, knowing as she drifted into the void that for all their worlds were fallen, there remained, in the hearts of those still alive, a crucial defiance. Humanity was insurmountable while its blood still ran hot.

By first light Morn was already up and on a battle footing, poised on the banks of a fast-flowing seawater inlet. In the early hours she had woken to hear the machines moving beyond the shingle and separating out from each other; she had imbibed her leaf immediately and fed her homing pigeon, and tracked one of the machines to a small manufacturing complex inland by some two miles, her senses aglow. The seawater inlet, presumably, drove the generators needed to power the machine replicators, which were responsible for the spidery harvesters she had observed yesterday, drawing minerals from the bluffs. This place was not *the* nest, then, but it was still *a* nest. She was certain her quarry would be found inside; that the machine she had trailed was part of its rudimentary command structure. And so the scene was set.

Without delay, Morn piloted her enormous suit towards the boundary of the plant, stooping low on the sharp banks of a tributary, and powering through its clay sludge. Machines did not sleep, rather they replenished, and Morn had calculated the range on her mark from the beach, using the machine's size and chassis class as indicators. The mark would now be inside, perhaps beneath the main plant, lowered into its pod. Despite their constant evolution, or *iterations*, the machines had not yet shrugged off the strictures of hierarchy. It was one of the few remaining traces of their makers.

As Morn drew ever closer, a swarm of sentries rose from the plant as though from a nest disturbed. These were not stingers but compound-eyed monitors, and they were around her quickly. Morn swatted at the monitors in irritation but maintained her trigger discipline, both aware of and prepared for the larger threats that remained, and were surely imminent. (The weapon she carried was a spoil of war, a much older machine's gun-arm; an intelligent puck-launching device whose payload flensed human flesh in tight conical patterns and, it turned out, did much the same when turned on its originators.)

With Morn's detection came a shrill alert, beamed instantaneously across the entirety of the southern English reaches, perhaps the continent beyond. The alert's nature was internal by definition, but the machines had developed an audible signature to deter all kinds of biological life, a warning as much as a signal. Morn cursed her arrogance and impatience, knowing that with deeper forethought she could have dealt with the sentries while they were still on base. The alarm roused and aggravated the pigeon in its cage, and it flapped wildly above her.

'Hush now,' she told it. 'I won't give you up that easily.'

Morn reached the wall of the complex as its machine foot soldiers massed in the inlet behind her. She challenged them silently with her weapon. She saw them hesitate, recoil, but noted with unease their confidence. They rallied, did not desist. She hunkered in and released a shrill warning of her own.

Too late: a dactyl was gliding in from the direction of the blackwinter-mottled sun, for the machines had clearly adapted once more, perhaps in anticipation of human desperation like this. As the dactyl's cannon rattled, Morn forced her farmour suit into an unnatural squatting stance, and saw through the farmour's bone frame the knee joints close to warping. The dactyl's projectiles speckled the ground, lifting great clods of mud and clay up through the farmour's undercarriage and into Morn's face. By chance she went unscathed, but shrapnel had penetrated the navigator system, and a reinforced rib in the farmour's front wing had cracked and folded neatly inwards. A single pigeon feather floated down through the chassis.

Morn removed a foot from the stirrups and tried to kick the damaged bone back into place. Loosened, the bone rattled and fell straight out of its socket. She cursed silently – cursed the engineers she had asked to lighten her farmour unit – and saw between the bounds of this fresh gap a band of defence wheelers whirling across the terrain to finish her off.

Morn took the opportunity. She sighted on the wheelers and fired the enormous weapon once, twice, three times. The leathers of the farmour creaked and juddered, but held. The farmour's feet were planted in such a way as to dissipate the gun's monstrous recoil; did so with nary a shudder. The approaching wheelers paused, hanging perfectly still for a moment, then disintegrated smokelessly. Their parts were turned into such fine particles that the prevailing wind carried them away like spume from a rough sea. Morn lowered the weapon. The resulting gap in the machine line was impressive, and the coming wave slowed considerably on approach.

Morn turned back to the plant wall and, reaching through the damage in the front wing, placed three crude fertiliser charges in a roughly triangular formation. If their activation went deep enough, she would sever the main loop, which would disrupt the entrance fields long enough for her to lumber inside and achieve her goal.

Except the dactyl was banking – it had more to offer. Morn instinctively lifted the farmour's arm to shield her eyes from the sun, her goggles filthy, and with her gun-hand released a fresh brace of shrapnel pucks. These popped left of target to poor effect. At this time she came to realise her suit's right foot was submerged in silt, and that the farmour was gradually toppling over. It was sinking, in fact.

The dactyl, unfazed by Morn's shots, was now inside engagement range and descending from a critical vector. Morn released the farmour's control handles and wiped her goggles clean with two fingers. She wanted to see the dactyl coming, not least because rapid arithmetic put her chances at slim to terminal. A moment later the machine released its salvo, as expected. Morn slapped the homing pigeon's release switch, heard the bird's anxious flutter as it departed on its grave mission to Southampton, and braced within her bone cage. At least her son Fallow would know she had gone down fighting. She gave a single soft prayer to the old ways.

The impact did not come. Morn opened one eye. She

opened the other. The machines had indeed adapted. For they had not shot her this morning – they had taken measures to capture her. The whole farmour suit was gummed up with a viscous substance not unlike tree sap; this substance sagged heavily from the bonecase and gearing; it had Morn woefully stuck. It stank. She took the handles once more and attempted to move the suit's arms and legs, but their reticulation was gone, and the strain cracked the casing around several key joints. Outside the cage, the wheelers were massing again, and above them the dactyl had returned to close surveillance. Morn unstrapped her waist and made certain her scramknife was secure in her boot. She released the farmour's locks, untied the wire cords around her waist, and stepped out of her stirrups on to the exit plate.

'Lioness,' came a genderless voice, cold and level.

Morn pushed against the ribs and with her other hand released the leather bindings that secured them. Like this she was a captive indeed. Or at worst, she was set to pass on. Make no mistake, Morn was not here to go quietly. Like her father, her mother, her siblings and her wife before her, Morn would resist the machines to the last, and was confident they knew it. Every quanta of data they held on her would explain who she was. In her many disruption lessons she had seen their minds at work. This very instant she would appear to them in hot-reeling statistics, a riot of angry binary. She hoped she posed a credible threat.

Morn stepped out of the farmour. The wind was bitter, and the sheepskins flapped from her shoulders. The machines surrounded her.

'The war is complete,' came the flat voice.

Morn realised the voice was emanating from all of them. In other circumstances it could have been the sky itself addressing her. She fixed her boots in the silt and placed a hand on the farmour's superstructure. Interlaced bone, rusting pins, toughened hide. Small reassurance for a woman whose entire adult life had been angled in defiance of the thinking machine.

'Not for us,' Morn said.

'Is that why are you here?' came the voice.

Morn did not reply.

'You would call this a sad place to perish for nothing.'

Morn lifted her chin, defiant. She was calculating, and she would perish for something. She abhorred these machines because it was her purpose to. There was nothing else left. They had made sure of that.

'Do you wish us harm?'

This was a solitary wheeler, ranged close and apparently breaking accord by speaking to her individually. It had a bright voice, possibly some reflection of its previous life. Perhaps it had once been an automated carriage, or courier, or, perversely, an ambulance.

'I do,' Morn told them. 'I pray for your annihilation.'

'Impossible,' came the whole group's reply.

Morn gave the machines a wry smile. The effects of the leaf were potent, yes, but more likely this defiance arose from the certainty of her death, the release it might bring, and from knowing she would destroy at least two or three of them as she went. She straightened, letting go of the farmour. It sagged lower. Despite the gum holding it together, it was still disappearing into the silt. An aeon hence, it would make for an interesting fossil.

'It is done,' said the machine voice. 'Please accompany us.'

Still Morn did not move. She knew what became of those who went. The machines attempted to mimic them, creating chimeras of metal and dead flesh before sending them back to the human camps. Such monsters had sown enough horror and dread in her time, yet had never once convinced them. She did not want to meet the same fate. She did not want to return to Southampton as a half-woman. For Fallow, her son, this would matter; more than for any other, for it would fall upon Fallow to deliver the killing blow, the removal of her fused spinal column, and later to oversee her scattering along the coast.

'Come with us,' the voice insisted.

'I won't,' said Morn. For they were toying with her, and she was not game. Fleetingly she questioned if, now that the war was over, there was precious little else these machines could pursue. They were dismal, in their way. With no one left to serve, no roles left to supplant, what else existed for these machines to do but go on mining the Earth's resources and making each other? It was the triumph of narcissism. It was a doom spiral. It was the worst vestiges of human nature imprinted on to them.

So no, Morn's war was not over. These machines could strip and denude her as they had her people, their communities and their colonies. She stood there at some sacrificial altar of labour, and she would go willingly as the lamb.

Morn knelt and unsheathed her scramknife. It began to rain acid from the toxic clouds above. She smiled. She went to them.

Chapter 1
Mornington household,
England. 2010.

There were two rules that children were expected to observe in the Mornington household. They were passed along with reverence, whispered at bedtimes and repeated when necessary.

One: you must never wake your father when he is sleeping after work.

Two: you must not speak while your father is watching televiddy.

Miranda – at twelve, the household's youngest child – had piously observed these rules for what seemed like all her conscious life. The first rule was adhered to by default in many ways, given that her father was either in work or in bed. He was a government scientist, or so Miranda understood, and also sworn from discussing his role with anybody either at home or in the village – so she and he found little else in common or to discuss, their intellectual gap apparently too great for him to bridge. The second rule was, in effect, needless also: following their mother's weekday dinners, Miranda would help to load the dishblitz before retreating to study in the quietest corner of the house, where her elder sister June could not find and torment her about the colour of her hair, or the quality of her skin, or the periods she would never have; and where her older brother Marcus, the middle child, would never venture at all, having discovered in his mid-teens the pleasures of occupying the same space as his family, yet living in parallel to them.

It was there in the study one night, as Miranda practised her Mandarin poetry recital, studiously ignoring the electronic telegrams arriving from friends on her personal viddy, that Miranda did something untoward, out of character, even insubordinate. She stayed up later than her mother and her father, listening intently as they carried out their strange night-time routines, and she read literature smuggled home from an area of the school library that was forbidden to youth of her age and sensitivity, and *especially* those of a curious disposition. The book she read this night was *Lady Chatterley's Lover*, which it was said was representative of a diseased or depraved mind from a gladly abandoned generation hence. To a twelve-year-old such as Miranda, however, the book was rebellion manifest. It was pure and it was illicit. She read into the early hours, devouring passages despite not always receiving their meaning. The very poetry of the thing was arresting enough. Never before had she been captivated by words placed alongside each other in these ways. And so it seemed to her a pity that she should eventually have to succumb to the need for sleep.

Miranda woke in the study chair in real and deep blackness. Only the leather beneath her hands was familiar. The air was cool and damp, having gone unheated for some hours. And the televiddy was ringing through the darkness.

Heart a stone, Miranda went to the study's flickering televiddy panel. Its clockface displayed two o'clock in the morning.

The caller's ident was withheld. Hesitantly, Miranda lifted the receiver.

'Hullo?' she said.

'Kip Mornington,' came a man's voice. Nothing more.

Miranda watched the screen. There was no discernible figure, only a dim silhouette against a light background. She rubbed her arms, which had broken out in goose pimples.

'Kip Mornington!' insisted the voice. Miranda wondered if it sounded somewhat accented. Empire, perhaps. She had gleaned that her father occasionally worked with men of the Americas.

'My father is sound asleep,' said Miranda. She swallowed. 'It's awfully late.'

'Then for heaven's sake wake the man,' said the voice. 'This is *urgent*.'

'I won't,' Miranda told him. 'I'm forbidden to wake him.'

The voice gave a low sigh. Its owner had evidently covered the input. He returned and said, 'Child, if you do not fetch your father this instant, there will be hell to pay. This is of critical importance. This is about your father's work.'

'You don't understand,' said Miranda, telling herself she would not dare apologise to this man for the rules of their household, or for abiding by the best wishes of her parents. 'I cannot.'

'Go and wake your father *now!*' hissed the man.

'Good night to you,' said Miranda, and for the first time in her young life she enjoyed a thrill of righteousness as she terminated the conversation and closed away the televiddy, and took herself off to bed.

Only Miranda's mother was in the sitting room when Miranda skulked downstairs sometime after nine o'clock the following morning. Her mother was seated on a Doncaster chair, back very straight but eyes downcast, listening to a government-mandated relaxation record at low volume. Miranda knew her mother's expression and posture well enough – it usually came upon her after a quarrel with Miranda's father.

'Mummy?'

Her mother could not bring herself to look up. In fact she stared out of the window to the corner of the garden where two great oaks were entwined in slow death.

The silence now was heavy, and Miranda came to the hearth where she placed a hand and repeated herself.

Then there was a *click* as Miranda's mother's lips parted. 'If there is one thing I cannot abide, Miranda, it is my children lying to me,' she said.

Miranda felt her cheeks flush. Immediately, she understood this was not about her father. 'Who has lied, Mother?'

Her mother turned to face her. Her expression was hollow, the skin tight.

'You answered the televiddy last night,' said Miranda's mother.

Miranda nodded. 'To a very rude man.'

'Then you closed the televiddy.'

Miranda nodded the once. 'I did.'

'You are a stupid, *stupid* little girl,' said her mother slowly.

Miranda became very hot. She tightened her grip on the hearth. Her stomach was rising.

'Well?'

'But what has happened?' stammered Miranda.

Her mother addressed the televiddy in the wall. A fast double-clap brought it to full volume. The government news logotype occupied one corner, and on the main panel appeared a large, oblate white sack, draped around the tracks of what appeared to be the city's monorail service.

'This is your father's work,' said Miranda's mother. 'We are being told that this... *thing*... is what remains of a dirigible weather globe, operating at extremely high altitudes, and also that your father's department is responsible for the machinery that controls it. What they do not know, Miranda, is that last night the air conditioning in his machinery room failed, and his equipment overheated.'

Miranda sat down on the bare floor. It was as if the coldness of the tile was all that kept her from combusting.

'We know, of course, that this has nothing to do with the weather. When men in suits arrive at the door come dawn, you understand there is more going on.'

Miranda cleared her throat. 'Have you spoken to him?'

Her mother shook her head. 'Not yet.'

'Then how do you know it's Daddy's?'

'Because I was on the end of his foul mouth this morning,' her mother scoffed. 'Now you'd better run along and play. I would sooner you were out of my sight, at the very least until your father gets home.'

Miranda wiped her eyes. 'I was only following—'

'Out,' her mother ordered. 'Go on with you.'

So Miranda ran. She ran blindly into the woodland adjacent to the house, through a heavy tangle of trees and overgrowth, and down to the clearing and the wide-gauge tracks along which freighters many miles long ferried imported goods to New London from the port of Southampton. Here there came the temptation to scramble down the embankment and try to board one of these megatrains, so that she might flee to the city and find a new way to live; live amidst all those libraries, filled with staggering books and stories, and the museums that contained what they had left of the old days; live along with the largest temples of the new. She thought about what it would be like to lie atop a megatrain's cargo pod and feel the wind around her body. What would they say to a twelve-year-old without papers or means? She had read Dickens, at least, and in that sense felt partly equipped for the life.

Still, the urge waned as it is wont to do when youngsters flee home with nothing but the quiet intention of returning. No freighters were scheduled to pass at this hour, in any case. Instead of lying there, with only clouds and insects for company, Miranda doubled back towards the house, where she found a thornless bush beneath which she would wait until her father's floatercar waivered into the grounds and came to rest by the outhouse, or his workshop.

Overtired from her late night, or perhaps flagging from emotional fatigue, Miranda kept this vigil until she fell asleep with her head in a growth of emerald moss, and slept there through the day's warmest hours. She only found herself waking as the wet sound of her father's floatercar filtered through the trees. Beyond their hamlet, there were no other habitations for miles around, and it was unlikely to be the postman, or the doctor, or the man who tried to sell them televiddy cartridges. In any event, she recognised the timbre of its motors.

Her father moored his craft by the outhouse as suspected, but he did not step out, or turn it off. He sat for the longest time at the controls with his shoulders rolled forward. The fans whined as they cooled. The stabiliser jets hissed and squirted as they kept the craft inches from the ground.

Miranda had a knot in her throat. She pushed herself out from beneath the bushes, swabbed down her dress, and went to the driver's port. Her father did not see her – he was staring into the distance, though there was nothing but the outhouse wall before him. His eyes were red and his mouth hung slack. She tapped on the window; he startled and his expression shifted, grew a shade darker. He barked something at the window in such a way that minute flecks of spittle patterned the glass. Miranda stepped back. The craft drew itself down. He stepped out, set down his briefcase and folded his arms. He smelled of whisky.

'Do you know what you've done?' he asked. And with that he turned and marched towards the house, leaving Miranda bereft, adrift on a million-mile ocean.

• • •

Their dinner was a turgid and bleak affair, with each of them pushing cooling food around their plate as though waiting for the world to end. The first utterance came, in the end, from her father, who sighed solemnly and began to speak without intonation.

'Four years ago my research position at the meteorological institute was defunded,' he announced. 'I was rendered to work for the government's extraordinary projects bureau, where my role ever since has been to oversee the development of an N-class orbital weather platform, whose auxiliary functions afforded the capture of highly classifiable intelligence, and, at a later time, the creation of micro-pressure systems fully controlled from stations on the surface.' He stopped briefly to look at the viddyscreen on the wall, which was flashing an ill green colour – offline. Miranda, in that moment, did not recognise her father.

'At around twelve hundred hours this morning, the computers that oversee the weather platform's navigation overheated. Skybound instrumentation began to receive conflicting messages, and the whole system suffered an embolism, so to speak. Shortly thereafter, critical heat levels caused the computers to shut down indefinitely, leading to the fatal loss of our asset, as you have doubtless seen on the news. Ordinarily this might incur a rap across the knuckles, an expensive lesson learned. Unfortunately, however, my appointment at the bureau coincided with the parallel trial of an experimental machine that, well… it transpires that my employers engaged a machine to mirror my entire bloody *job*. Unbeknownst to me, I have been pitted against an artificial thinking machine whose sole purpose is to manage a second, identical weather platform, operated from a partitioned network. This infernal thing was programmed to do much as I did – including keeping an eye on cooling. So when this morning the air conditioning went awry across both partitions, the machine was able to immediately activate several fail-safes, including those I would have operated myself given fair warning. The machine's weather platform is still operational at high altitude, unlike mine. And so the machine has, over time, been proven the superior task manager. I have been bested.'

'Dear God,' Miranda's mother said. 'Kip, that's unthinkable—'

'No,' he told her. 'It is the future.' He looked to Miranda, who was weeping quietly. She could not respond; saw now her part in this.

'In around fifteen minutes,' her father went on, 'men from my bureau will be arriving here to perform what they call a deep cleansing of the library and my study. From tomorrow I will be a civilian. I will have no research to my name. I will have no state transport. My life's work will be in their custody.' He settled his cutlery, with which he had been gesticulating, and stood up from the table. 'Please excuse me,' he said.

Miranda watched him walk to the fireplace, where he took down from the wall a large iron poker. For a moment she thought he might strike her with it. Instead, he went calmly to the green-glowing televiddy and, with a single, almost graceful swing, transformed its screen into a shoal of diamond fish.

Chapter 13
New London, Earth. 2029.

New London was burning. Behind Kip Mornington and his personal guard, all mounted on ironclad horses, the mob ran as a river to the fringes of Hyde Park, where thousands from all the counties of automatic England had gathered. With the mob came household appliances for the unlit pyre, by now a hundred-foot-tall pyramid at the heart of the green. These offerings were held aloft, a great torrent of metals and plastics, and Kip appeared delighted by the spectacle. This was more than a movement: it was an army. His army. And the first act of war was unfolding.

Behind Kip's mounted guard, the first daughter Miranda's motorcade crawled through the throng. She herself stood in the bed of an old farming vehicle and, like her father, was hemmed in by men and women sworn to protect her. Their greatswords, looted from the museums of the city, caught the light from smaller fires taking hold in terrace windows and shopfronts. The air was thick and burnt, and she held a damp cotton rag to her mouth. She watched as ash fell across the city, white flurries catching the sunlight. It gave the proceedings an air of grim celebration.

Miranda was not necessarily proud of her father's actions. She resented the pain that had preceded this day, much as she admired the acuity of her father's prescience, the single-minded drive and desire to fight that had ultimately cost him his marriage, his estrangement from June and Marcus, and arguably caused the death of Miranda's mother. Beyond this, Miranda was also in awe of her father's figure as it bobbed rhythmically before her, and overwhelmed too by the nature of his leadership. She had been strangely moved by the pure will mustered by these people around her, drawn here together by the idea that marching on Hyde Park might allow them to intercept, and so head off, a darker dawn.

Did Miranda believe in the cause? Did she really believe that domestic and industrial machines were set to replace and diminish workers on a scale far grander than that seen in the Victorian era? Was it really the case that they must reject them in all their forms? She turned to regard the seething mass of people in pursuit of her father, and realised that even to consider the question was irrelevant. The tide had shifted, and the mood had already swung. The labour force was now the armed force, and in turn it was the unstoppable force; and in any case, the incumbent government had demonstrated its withering regard for her father's ideas of a new cooperation, a form of social welfare whose central tenets put the new machines to work in ways that benefitted all. Contrary to predictions, the reins of industry had not been handed down, only consolidated and concentrated at the uppermost levels. A promise of fairness – the end of scarcity, rations and mass dismissals – lay smashed. Now the city was burning, it was much too late to go back. And Miranda's father was leading the torchbearers.

Presently, the pyre came fully into view: a colossal structure that dwarfed the ancient trees around it. Miranda turned to one of her bodyguards and asked when they would light it. The man, who had garbed himself in several pieces from a looted suit of armour, pushed back his helmet visor and grinned at her. He was one of her father's most trusted counsels – the same man who had replaced him at the research institute all those years ago, and whom he had nicknamed Merlin.

'When it's good and ready,' said Merlin.

'And there will be fighting?' said Miranda, aware that coaches loaded with forces sympathetic to the state and its sweeping laws of automata had been halted on the hyperway to London from the north.

'If there is, we'll bloody well choke them into the soil,' said the bodyguard. 'Their numbers won't stand.'

Miranda sighed and touched her face. She felt her worried expression in the lines around her eyes and brow, and bowed her head.

'The city will recover,' added Merlin, by way of reassurance. 'It has seen much, much worse.'

Miranda understood this rationally. Yet the rhetoric of civil war had been on her father's lips for a long time now. Even last night, in the public house, she had heard the blind hatred in the jeers of her father's supporters. As he made his speech, she had seen their focus and belief. They mob had come to believe in something, calcified around it, and that something was her father.

'Halt!' came a cry from the front. The motorcade did so promptly.

'What's the matter now?' asked Miranda. A state of hyperarousal seized her, eyes flitting madly from guard to guard.

One the bodyguards began to laugh. The other soon joined him.

'A thing of beauty!' one of them cried.

'A day to remember!' came another.

Moving across the crowd, as though skating on its surface, was a vast fibreglass dinosaur. Miranda blinked. It was a museum piece, in all likelihood. In coursing here, the mob had looted and ransacked the city and brought many of its icons with it.

'No,' said Merlin, tugging on Miranda's arm to turn her away from the spectacle. 'Not *that* old thing. See, look – over *there*.'

Miranda leaned on the cab of the vehicle and pitched herself up. There was no problem after all; or if it counted as a problem, it was a good problem to have. It seemed the crowd was so densely assembled around the pyre that further progress was impossible. Now only her father's horse moved through the crowd ahead, the mob parting and surging into his wake, his horse's tail bouncing. Miranda could see it all from there – the pyre and the faceless crowd of thousands – and the air itself was electrified. The sun above the city was deepest red.

At the base of the pyre, her father pulled up and rotated

his horse, giving it a moment to adjust to the spectacle of his London at arms. The guards fanned around him. For the first time today Miranda saw his face, and for the second time in her life she did not recognise him. She was Miranda the young girl again, seated at her parents' dinner table in her childhood home. She was listening to him admit defeat to the machine that, in hindsight, had proven to be the catalyst for his change.

Except her father was not defeated. He was stubborn. And Miranda was sure the pyre was about to be lit.

'Hullo…' It was her father's voice, reverberating. He was wearing a microphone, which surprised her – at home he insisted on voice and paper, as he could be surveilled through electronic equipment. Again he was cast as a stranger.

The crowd roared, and Miranda's skin prickled.

'All this way here,' Kip Mornington told them, his voice tremulous, 'I was afraid to look behind me. Though I heard you, I would not allow myself to believe.'

The crowd roared.

'Please,' he said, and even at such a distance Miranda imagined he was trying not to smile in wonderment. 'Please. I only want us to consider what we have done in standing together. In solidarity we form the greatest of unions – and yet each of you is still worthy of more than being a figure in a crowd. I – I am no leader.'

At this, someone handed Kip a burning stake, wreathing him in dark smoke. Miranda's stomach tightened. It was happening. She felt sure, then, suddenly and sickeningly, that this could be wrong, a mistake, and that some inexorable slide into madness would follow. No matter his protestations, it struck her that her father stood as a revolutionary in the eyes of the mob; in her memories her mother had used 'terrorist'. Yet she could not decide which of these she believed herself. The bonds between Miranda and her father were so tight as to make the distinctions soluble. Miranda was proud, and frightened, and restless. Her father stood out there as all the things he was said to be.

'Today, tomorrow, and always,' said Kip, 'we will work.' As he lowered the stake's burning end to the pyre, the crowd returned these words.

'Today! Tomorrow! Always!'

The fire took quickly. The flames tore up the pyre. Even as far away as Miranda and her transport, there came a tangible wave of heat, as though an aperture into the very bowels of the earth had been opened and quickly shut. Instantly the sky darkened, and the mob's various weapons and armours took on an orange aura. The pyre's smell was noxious.

'We are the workers!' called Kip. 'We are the breakers!'

'We are the workers! The breakers!'

And it was then that the tumult began. A gasp: Miranda's focus pulled to a mass of shifting bodies to one side of her father, men and women toppling like skittles and the awful silencing of chants. Soon it was screams that were audible, and the reason visible: an armoured government unit was loose in the crowd, with motorised foot-tanks rushing her father's position.

The guard fell about him as the tanks closed in. She saw their operators – men strapped inside steel cages – and understood that their target was set.

'Get her inside,' uttered one of her bodyguards, meaning Miranda, perhaps reading the situation similarly. Merlin took her arm. She shook him free and continued to watch. 'Inside!' hissed Merlin. But the tank unit was carving out its route to her father.

Just as quickly, the mob realised their strength. No longer rooted, they began to resist. As the chaos spread, Miranda saw two tanks go down, and the mob pile in to suffocate their operators. Surely enough, metal offcuts and panels and wiring looms came flying.

'They'll tear us to pieces,' said Merlin. 'We have to go.'

Miranda wasn't listening. Misplaced pride was now hot fear. Her father had seen what was coming, and had ordered his guard about him.

'I'm going,' said Miranda.

She vaulted the transport cabin and slid down its bonnet. Her bodyguards were screaming, but she was quickly into the crowd. She jostled and fought to stay upright; there were concussive blasts and fresh waves of heat. The foot-tanks were incinerating people. Closer she went, loosened of regard for politeness or polity, and tripped upon the smouldering body of a young boy, thirteen at most, and saw in his poor pale face, the only part of him untouched, the madness that had descended: the thing she had feared most come to life. She went on, towards her father, and understood it was both pathological and futile, and went on regardless; to be with him, as if to reason with him, so that he was not alone.

Too late. It was all much too late. The single remaining foot-tank made short work of Kip's guard. There was a heavy stench of horseflesh, and a single shot rang out from the tank's shoulder. She watched her father's own horse stumble then topple, Kip still on top, and the two of them as one being swallowed by the crowd.

The mob became a formless rage. As they tore into the foot-tank's armour panelling with bare hands, Miranda saw the operator's last expression – a rictus of surprise and loss, this being a young conscript no doubt, no true hatred in him yet – and then a mist of dark fluid on his window port, and the celebratory jeers, primal, of her father's avengers as they dismantled the tank and the operator with it. Eventually she reached the horse, whose enormous bulk the nearest men had shifted. Her father lay with eyes closed, at peace, chest rising but a bloody foam at the mouth. Crush injuries. It was not the shot but the fall; it was the weight of his charge. He lay shattered, held intact only by the clothes he wore.

'Daddy,' she said, falling across him, and only some of the gathered heard her and noticed. 'Oh, Daddy...'

'He's gone, little one.'

This was Merlin, there with her now, and the speed of her grief was dazing: it rushed out and over her body as a coastal wind in harshest winter. Her father was just there, speaking in a manner she never imagined he could, and now this. She lay shivering on the paving beside him, and thought of what her mother would say if she were there to see. Or if she was there regardless, looking down on them as her father insisted she did.

'What's her name?' somebody asked Merlin. They had linked the crude uniform of Kip's guard to the overalls she wore, and were right in their summation: the cloth and patches were identical.

'She is Miranda,' said Merlin. 'His second daughter.'

Hands quickly enveloped hers and pulled her to standing. Miranda swayed, and they steadied her, and their eyes studied her.

'What is your name?' one asked.

'Miranda,' she said quietly. 'Mornington.'

'Mornington! Oh, lamb!'

Miranda did not answer. She could not answer.

'She's one of his daughters!' cried another. 'He just said!'

'Whose daughter?'

'His *daughter!*'

Without waiting, the group held her aloft.

'His daughter!' – this time in unison. 'Mornington!' they shouted. 'His daughter! Mornington's daughter! Mornington!'

And rapidly their chant spread, and spread, and spread, until it seemed the whole crowd was chanting her family name. But Mornington being long and harder to say, the chant evolved, and presently the word was shortened, and now they sang together and louder, more fluidly, and she surveyed them all – this great heaving mass of men and women and children – and heard how all of them were chanting a word that could have filled the heavens.

'Morn! Morn! Morn!'

Epilogue
Southampton, Earth. 2070.

Fallow was down in the leaded cell, unwilling to test his luck. He had been down there since his mother set out from the city in her farmour unit; he had been unwilling to say goodbye to her also. It was doubtless selfish in the eyes of some, of course, yet Fallow did not want his final image of her to involve her frailness inside that skulking beast, skins flapping from its mass as she crossed the flatlands towards the ocean, with the filthy homing pigeon fluttering in her shoulder-cage. Fallow wished instead for a partition of silence: no news of his mother at all, no update on her progress overnight, and so no confirmation of her inevitable demise. Last dice rolls aside, his mother was stubborn and obstructive, and Fallow was unable, even as her son, to persuade her that the plan was suicidal. The moment it would be relayed to him was a moment he wished to postpone for as long as possible.

It was suicidal, though. No mistake about it. His

mother, with the tentative blessing of Southampton's local councillors, had undertaken to breach the machine nest, perform a covert operation tantamount to stealing their eggs. Given the nature of such an assault – close to full-frontal – the odds would be heavily stacked against a full detachment, never mind a single woman wearing analogue armour. In the gaping quiet they shared as Fallow prepared her bodysuit, helped to charge the scramknife she would use as a last resort, she admitted as much to him. Her concession was only intended to smooth her passage, however. Fallow knew it made no odds.

Twenty or more hours into Morn's mission, Fallow found himself pacing the room, agitating for fresh air while knowing that if he were actually out there, up there on the city wall's ramparts, he would only be awaiting the pigeon released if her farmour unit went down, or if his mother's tether to this earth was severed eternally, or both. There were so rarely birds in the sky these days he imagined the sight would be equal parts biblical and devastating: a mote of white and dun set against the blackwinter.

The imagination was a madness. Intolerable, endless madness. If he were to bear witness to that bird, would he be the one to catch it? Hold it to his breast, confirm its provenance? Fallow thought as much – he had hand-reared and trained his mother's death-bird, and in any case, it was expected of him to perform this as a duty. The task was simpler than the period it presaged: with the bird's arrival would begin the awful wait for his mother's chimerical remains to stagger back into the camp, whereupon the city's daughters would snare her and Fallow would arrive to deliver the *coup de grâce*.

Morn had not spoken to her son about this in the slow hour before she left. The scouting engineers had been busy modifying her suit; she was with the battle group commander, stationed inside the local post office. Then she would have been meditating.

Should his mother's last act of insurgency fail, which in all probability it would, they would need to begin siege preparations. The city was already dug in, already operating rations. There was nothing the machines could not have gleaned from millennia of successful campaigns. There was no cause for imagination or innovation: the playbooks were written and encoded. Southampton could be sacked, turned by decree into a fresh mountain of bones. The heads of fallen defenders could be slung over the city walls to traumatise their loved ones. Water supplies could be poisoned. Incendiary bombs could be launched. Napalm strikes could be summoned from orbital delivery systems. Nuclear holocaust was no less an option than it ever was. Mechanical rape was a means to control and subjugate. It went on, and on, the unending horror of it – the multiple, layered horrors of sapiens history made stark, available as mere tools or processes or points of reference to the machines. Who knew what insatiable, unsayable impulses would decide which mode of death would be selected come the true end, rapidly approaching?

There'll be another way, Fallow told himself. His grandfather Kip would have wanted that. That stupid old woman would realise her folly and turn back before the coast, and with her strategic mind she would help the city forge an alternative defence together. Necessity and invention. It was that or extinction.

Fallow sat in the corner of the cell and imagined what it would be like to be a prisoner here. In the face of their enemy, committing crimes against other humans seemed an antiquated concept now. It was a wrench to know it still happened.

Later the knock came. Fallow stood up in the corner but continued to face the cell wall. For some time now he had analysed the marks scratched there – ancient football slogans and hatched day-markers, and behind the old web of a long-departed spider, some ultra-nationalist symbols, the last dying screams of racial tension, more things made suddenly irrelevant, or at least partially hidden, by the larger threat. These markings were fixed in his attention as the family guard filed into the room. He counted three sets of feet. One of the guards cleared their throat.

'We've had word, Sir.'

Fallow turned. Four guards, not three. Two men, two women. Their expressions were unreadable. Practised, he supposed. To bear news of this kind was hardly a novelty for them. More of a grim tradition, with the war this far gone. One of them had a wet canvas bag held up to his chest like an offering; Fallow knew it carried the remains of his mother's pigeon. Sometimes the death-birds didn't land on returning. It was said this was because they intuited grief. As if the birds did not wish to be the messenger, omen. When it happened, someone was usually tasked to shoot them down.

'Do you think it was quick?' Fallow asked them.

'Sir.' The eldest guard stepped forward. 'Would you come with us?'

'Why?' said Fallow. 'To be told what? I already know what's happened. I'll get on with it. Come for me when her body reappears.'

'Sir, please,' insisted the guard. 'You must.'

'No,' said Fallow. 'I told them I wanted my own time with this. Run along. Tell the council I send my condolences. They have lost a queen.'

He clutched his stomach. His eyelids felt heavy. He wondered how else to process it. His stepmother having already gone had prepared him for a fresh turn of grief, but this was still enormous.

'The bird was not all that returned,' whispered the old guard. He wiped his forehead. It was humid in the cell.

'You mean to say her body's back already?'

'No…'

'Why are you being so cryptic?'

'We were asked to collect you. For an audience. That's all we know.'

'Fine,' Fallow said. He picked up the chamber pot and marched out before them. There was a waste processing unit mounted in the wall opposite the cell; Fallow tipped out the contents of the pot and held his breath as he walked away, so as not to scent what movement had inevitably stirred. The guards filed past, and he hung there against the wall a moment, watching. None turned to the other. They were set in formation.

'I'll need someone to check out a gun from the armoury,' he shouted after them. 'Large calibre. I don't want to recognise her face – not mounted on a monster. And I want it to be quick.'

Up top, putrid yellow rays of sunlight splintered the blackwinter. Fallow staggered along the land-facing wall top, shielding his eyes. He looked out over the coarsened wasteland of the South Downs, Eastleigh, and farther to the left, all that remained of the New Forest. Recently, the machines had found a means to petrify and process vegetation for their own mysterious ends, and their work had been alarmingly rapid. The M3 motorway was a brown glass river that ran into a sinkhole that had recently grown to swallow the entirety of Southampton Airport. Tunnelling machines were responsible, was the general consensus – two of the city's most trusted scouts had sighted something like the arches of an iron leviathan as it surfaced and dove once more on the horizon.

Lucky, Fallow thought, that the city walls stood on foundations dozens of metres deep. Which made it feel all the more wasteful that his mother had left at all.

He had been in the cell for the better part of two days, and had only slept for a fraction of that. His eyes were gritty, his vision narrowed. It was windy, though the landside was always the city's leeside: the coastal defence wall over Southampton Water took the brunt of the heaving weather, even now there would be someone trying to refill the mortar down there.

The guards had told him to go to the old phone box in the square, but Fallow asked for ten minutes alone first.

Now he stood on the wall and held his hips. He considered his mother's voice, the croak of it, the means by which she inflected certain words – she could lisp, or mumble, or stammer. She carried her trauma in her voice.

Fallow descended the staircase. The wrought-iron handle was cold, burning his hand.

At the foot of the staircase was a woman in a well-worn hazardous materials suit. Her face was perfectly oval inside the hood. He vaguely recognised her from the sciences encampment at the university; he had done some reading there in the early days of Southampton's self-incarceration. She was not wearing breathing equipment.

'We… Fallow,' she started.

'She can't be back already,' said Fallow.

The woman shook her head. 'She is not. There was, however, an important development.' She gestured with a low hand. 'After you.'

Fallow walked with her. They were going to the main square, the speakers' stages. He saw a crowd was forming. There were cheers and singing. An old marching song, supposedly sung in the first days, when the battles were more easily entered into.

The crowd parted as Fallow approached. The crowd silenced at knowing his face. In the spaces between them, Fallow saw the first hints of what lay before him. Pewter casing, waning lights. The curve of a gyroscopic ball. It was a machine – a wheeler.

Fallow did not hesitate. Somewhere amidst the commotion, the woman in her protective suit had taken his hand. She stroked it. He approached and knelt to the wheeler. It was a fully grown machine, soiled by travel and blemished at the usual contact points.

'What is this thing doing inside the walls?' demanded Fallow.

The crowd stared. The woman knelt beside him. She opened her hand: there was a knife across her palm. Circuits snaked across the blade's surface. He recognised it.

'Your mother's scramknife was embedded in the machine's core nervous column,' said the woman. 'The knife was broadcasting a message when the wheeler arrived.'

'What do you mean, a message?'

'Coordinates.'

'For where?'

'Fallow.' The woman was scowling. 'Your mother has turned this machine. It is an informant. It has told us where to hit them. Every node. Every terminal.'

'But how?' asked Fallow. He was agog. The wheeler lay prostrate with seemingly no energy or desire to right itself. He could not make the link.

'From cursory analysis, it appears your mother found a way to encode the scramknife. We are reverse-engineering the command strings, but it—'

'An infection?'

'No. Not an infection. Or at least not with virality – the machine would otherwise corrupt the rest of its local network, and in any case, they have learned well enough how to guard against such an attack. You will remember our attempted glitch-bomb – any infection is contained, the hosts extinguished within milliseconds. For them it is a cold logic. Quarantine is not an option.'

'So what? A lucky malfunction? Did the knife damage it?'

'Again, no. They are well shielded against physical penetration. Instead, it seems... I can only describe it as more of a persuasive technique. A string of queries. The memory module contains an abnormally large amount of encoded data.'

'Questions? She *confused* it?'

The woman looked around her. She leaned towards him and quietly cleared her throat. 'We can only go from what the data recovery team has gleaned thus far.'

'Which is...'

'Which is that your mother gave this wheeler a story. Lady Morn delivered a payload of stories, in fact. Her story – your story, of course. But also our story. And so I would have to say the machine empathised. It felt us all, at once – and it was compelled to help.'

Fallow closed his eyes. 'And now?'

'We listen. We take notes. We prepare an assault.'

Fallow shook his head. 'It could be an ambush. It could be lying, to expose us. The machines know us. They know what we run on. They understand nostalgia and sentimentality and—'

Fallow was interrupted by a great and sonorous thud that echoed deep into the city. The crowd scattered in response, some clearly shaken and gasping. The woman with Fallow stood to her feet. Fallow did the same.

'What is that?' asked Fallow. Yet in his stomach, he already knew. Through a smoking gash in the main gate strode a suit of farmour, glistening with marsh vegetation and rich, coppery mud. The unit's protective ribs were smashed. The pigeon-cage door clattered open and closed. The thing drew itself across the floor, clanking and rattling and buzzing at its joints.

Fallow went to it. His mother was inside, shivering. He looked her up and down. For evidence of machine tampering – the faults and flaws. Distorted limbs, or unsewn skin. Unmoored sections. When it came to chimera, there were a great many tells, all of which led to the same conclusion, and so the same result. But there were none evident here. Either the machines' handiwork had vastly improved, or this was really his mother. This really was Lady Mornington.

'Mother,' said Fallow.

Morn held out a hand. She was frail, exhausted. Dehydration had yellowed the whites of her eyes.

'They spared you,' said Fallow.

Was that a flash of a smile? Morn pursed her lips and shook her head. She said they did not. She said no. She had the strength remaining to pull Fallow into the smashed fascia of the unit, and so into her.

'They feared me,' whispered Morn. 'Actually, dear boy, they feared me. For in me they saw a machine with human parts.'

PART III

SEMOLT FIELD NOTES

Welcome to Scotland Yard's digitised archives. You are accessing evidence files from the **Cold Veil case** of **2032**. This case is classed as *sensitive*. Tap **here** to go back, or **here** for a background.

>

Thank you. You are now viewing a case overview.

- The Cold Veil uprising, 2032
- Attack on Birmingham
- Attacks elsewhere in England
- Key belligerents and subsequent trials
- Laurel M. Brace (English science fiction author and anti-technology militant, 1950–2032)
- Theories on the death of Laurel M. Brace
- *The Cold Veil* (novel; proscribed under the Terrorism Publications Act, 2020)
- Legacy in English lawmaking

>

Thank you. You are browsing the collected personal effects of Laurel M. Brace.

>

Thank you. You searched for 'Angelika Semolt'. There is one (1) folder in this record: **Semolt field notes**

>

Semolt field notes

Context: handwritten correspondence sent by **Angelika Semolt** to **Laurel M. Brace** concerning a third activist, **Remi <surname redacted>**, before a **week-long Luddite-inspired uprising** in **2032**. Semolt was arrested in London four days after the so-called 'zeroing' attack on Birmingham, during which ninety-two people died and 58% of the urban population was displaced. Semolt was later convicted of multiple offences, including murder, attempted murder, possession of firearm with intent to endanger life, unlawful collection of information for terrorist purposes, possessing a document containing information likely to be useful to a person committing or preparing an act of terrorism, and weapons training.

To start reading the Semolt notes chronologically, go **here**. Or tap **here** to start a new search.

>

Curator's note: These pieces were transcribed from graph paper found in a folder among Laurel M. Brace's

possessions. While each piece is numbered for quick reference and easy comprehension, we believe many more segments to be missing or destroyed.

#1

Despite her cold leads in the past, I recently renewed contact with our sympathetic doctor friend in the north. She described another potential project: Mancunian male, late thirties/early forties. This man's wife ('Joan') recently called the doctor's clinic with concerns about her husband's detachment in recent months. Emotionally flat/sexually disinterested/increasingly absent from the family home. A young daughter, Martha. I began a trawl, with interesting results. Zero pornography use. No credit card debt. He buys sleeping tablets from the States, likely with well-concealed crypto. A dalliance with St John's wort (usually typical of someone cognisant enough to self-diagnose an issue, yet too proud to seek intervention). Crucially, he is a reluctant technology user. Minimal mobile data/messaging use. Limited social media presence (with past accounts purged). Pre-Scrappage petrol car. No other domestic autom. Voted against UBI, sadly. More interesting is his acute aversion to all forms of news media.

To my mind, this one might be saveable. What do you think?

#2

Hello Laurel. Apologies for delay in response – it has been an intensive few weeks in the lab. It will be something to leave this place and these callous robots I work around. Today I watched a malfunctioning arm crush a whole colony of mice, then continue its routines as if nothing happened.

It was disappointing to hear of the Bristol railway operation not going to plan. The path is winding. What matters is that you saw success with the electromagnet – a partial blackout is still a blackout! I read with satisfaction of stranded passengers and 'lost productivity'. How long before the public begin to make links? Do they not see it is *all* lost should this shift go unchecked? I wish you fortitude with the next test. The movement sustains.

Re: our friend in the north. The Mancunian's name is Remi. With your blessing I pursued the good doctor's lead – Pietro sent the fox up there a fortnight ago. Her data and tissue samples confirm my initial suspicion: Remi needs saving. I should add that there is mounting evidence of trauma – cause so far unknown, but conceivably linked to his media consumption (or lack of – see previous note). I ran Remi's saliva through the lab after hours – nothing untoward/hereditary in a physiological sense. I had Rupal collect a blood specimen, also clean. Otherwise his main ailments are the common produce of this country: anxiety, paranoia, insomnia. Remi's wife Joan has called the family doctor several times more. She told the doctor she is forbidden from telling Remi the date and time, or from discussing anything that might suggest the influence or exertion of forces acting beyond the family home. I had Rupal make several audio recordings, as this seems extraordinary to me. Nothing yet – except perhaps to note that Remi's daughter has stopped calling him Daddy.

#3

Let me fawn: my latest read of your novel unlocked a new
pathway. Miranda's transformation into Morn is one of
choice. In dire circumstances, she *chooses* to follow in her
father's footsteps. She chooses without coercion. Through
this, I understand once more that our new colleagues *must
choose* their own way with us.

I am still working with Rupal's dataset to produce a
richer profile of Remi. I would say he is reluctant to confront
his past, except to reinforce his perceptions of it. There are
no photographs in the house. He does not use a computer.
He does not read books. He continues to studiously avoid
the news – a disinclination I am convinced could prove a
vector for persuasion. Part of me wishes to visit the north,
to see him with my own eyes. Some weekend soon.

#4

Small one. Did I ever mention the behavioural psychologist I
used to see? We recently spent an evening reminiscing. He
is interested in your project, though does not comprehend
its full ambition. I sent him a copy of your book. Should he
prove sympathetic, we may have an opportunity to enhance
our profiling techniques.

#5

Remi's mother-in-law died. I was listening through Rupal
when his wife received the news – Remi did not react to her
pain at all. There is a huge backlog on the coroner's side,
which will drag out the process. When it comes, I expect

the funeral will be an interesting performance.

Remi is rarely home at the moment. His wife seems ill, but is putting on a brave face. The daughter, Martha, is incredibly sensitive to the mood of the house. If Remi sleeps, he does so for two- or three-hour stretches at best. His avoidance of the news is disciplined, but occasionally he is caught off guard, and quickly becomes aggressive.

(Being honest, I have come to regard Remi as a sort of estranged friend. There is an intimacy... hard to explain. I had an unnamed sample returned for cataloguing that smelled of him. His sweat, perhaps. A private smell. I have the vial here now.)

Despite all this, I would contend that Remi's family is otherwise unaffected by the state of things. In his avoidance of current affairs, Remi is almost wilfully detached from what is happening around us. And yet he is seeing the way, even without realising the true cause of his ennui, because the machines encircle him, and their strength is what ails him. I would like to push. I want to know which way his heart tilts.

#6

Grateful for your response, as ever. Satisfying to know you are invested, given your busyness, and the scale of the challenge. I *did* read your *Times* column on the truck drivers' strike, yes. I found myself thinking, if only they knew your *nom de guerre* – never mind that you finance the logistics! Peace and solidarity to all of them. More soon.

#7

Curious: I discovered that Remi has taken up jogging. It
has come from nowhere, as far as I can see. It can be hard
to know whether to instruct Rupal to stake out the family
home for truths told in Remi's absence, or to follow him.
In fact, it disturbed me so much I finally made the trip
myself. The air was claggy and made me sweat. On several
occasions I sat on benches as he passed by; I knew most
of his routes and knew his timings, and he knew nothing of
me. I was a ghost. My God, it was something to sense the
air disturbed by him. Tense, yes, but how could he know? I
have spent so long analysing him that sometimes I question
if I love him. Can you mistake pity for love?

#8

Forgive my brevity, I am just too despondent to explain
in full. Today was Remi's mother-in-law's funeral. Remi
disappeared shortly after the wake. I should have heeded
the warning signs. Paid more attention. His mother-in-law's
funeral went as expected... except his behaviour has given
me good cause to believe he was somehow mourning
for the wrong person. Does that make sense at all? All of
his behaviours... his erratic search engine history... One
alarming example: in the dead of night there was a string of
manic queries for children's coffins.

Perhaps some people are not for saving.

#9

Me again. I am unsure if I should send this. Rupal transferred more footage. Some hours after Remi left, his family home was gutted by fire. I cannot say if his wife or daughter escaped. There were police and fire crews present for some time. I feel ill. I don't know what to tell you. You can destroy this. I just think you should know.

#10

Hello Laurel. I count at least three months since I last wrote. Where has it gone?

I wondered: have you any tattoos? My most recent is a pigeon. It was inevitable, I think. I have obsessed over that image of old Morn out on the coast with her homing pigeon for so long. My tattoo goes from shoulder to shoulder, wings fully out. Its head is regal. The linework is poor and it has healed patchily because I find it hard to sleep on my front, but there it is, outstretched on my back, free and ready to return me, should everything grow too heavy. I did not mind the pain so much – it feels like a reset, it can be numbing. One day I should like to show you.

I try not to dwell, but I am still sorry for what happened with Remi and his family. That terrible thing. I wanted so badly to bring him to the truth. I know you said you would look into it – did you learn anything? In the meanwhile, I continue to search for new colleagues.

#11

Laurel, do you still read these?

Work has been so busy.

#12

Please respond when you can.

Curator's note: Brace's collection included a significant number of redacted or partially burned materials following this note. Linear numbering continues.

#13

Laurel, it has been such a long time. Where to start? Perhaps with a favour... please forgive the writing, my hand is shaking. Do you remember the Mancunian I told you about, all those years ago? Remi, the dissociating man? God, how to not be flippant in this. He surfaced. London! Here! I can scarcely accept it. Being so analogue, as he always was, he slipped easily from the grid... and yet he was drawn to us. Drawn here. Rupal found his flat. Did she show you? Did you already know?

What has changed? Better to summarise what has not. He is a lonely man, recovering from some sort of addiction. I like to think he now understands better than ever that the world made around him is not the world he wishes to occupy. With your guidance I aim to guide him to the revolution. If London is a manacle, and the world a cage, then we remain the keys.

#14

I have been working with Pietro on the first-wave plan for Birmingham. Your consent made it much easier: it was such a huge relief to hear from you. The reckoning is close.

Remi works in central London as a courier. We flashed his navigation bug and now receive regular updates on his movements. His transit data is too erratic for pattern generation, though strangely beautiful when visualised. There are, however, some defined and repeated behaviours you may want to analyse yourself – I dead-dropped some footage and observations separately, along with my proposed strategy to expose him to the truth of the matter. My hunches were correct, is the point. Remi has barely recovered from a significant traumatic break. He has no social life beyond his clients. I would call it a self-imposed exile, and I have some ideas. Say the word and we can begin.

#15

Laurel, thank you for reviewing my new work. I had ascribed Remi's repetitive actions (the cooker especially) to obsessive compulsion – making certain the hobs were turned off. Your insight is alarming yet persuasive. Clearly I have missed so much – not least the lack of gas services in his flat. You honestly think he attempted to kill his family this way? I had never considered it, despite the coincidence. The thought is nauseating. At the same time, he would surely have been arrested, and there is no evidence of that.

#16

It is hard to shake this feeling that Remi is already part of our cause. He simply does not see it yet.

#17

Did you plan for this to be so perfect? All those years
ago – did you suggest it to me, somehow? Give me the hints
I needed to join the dots? I cannot see the whole picture. I
cannot see how it was put together. Yet I accept that you can.

If what you say about this engineer Greenley and Remi's
daughter is true, then I am awed. The pieces fit. And now I
know something of your masterplan, I am anxious to enact
my part.

Your proposition to use an abridged version of the book
is perfect. It will, to Remi, seem like serendipity.

I also agree that we should use fire as a trigger. Let
us illuminate what he has repressed. If you are right,
a fabricated news report involving a fire will induce a
shutdown, potentially retraumatise him. We can then step in
to help stabilise him. Give him purpose.

I suggest using Rupal. She gives him the space and
agency to choose, to volunteer himself. By the time her
betrayal is evident, he will have read the critical sections of
your book, and we will have begun the process. That is the
power of the novel.

#18

The ambulance did us very well. I must say that Remi being
in the back and so close to me was a surreal experience. I
had to restrain myself from stopping the vehicle and going
back there to touch him. Like a dream. I caught myself
being prickly with him. It annoyed me intensely that he
does not know the extent to which I have involved myself

in his life. The ways I have tried to save him. In the end this frustration was all too much, so I had Pietro hood him until we arrived at the warehouse. God, why am I writing this? He is with you now. He may be a monster, but please look after him.

#19

As you predicted, exposing Remi to our dataset caused him to attack various items of technology on returning to his flat. He has started to hate, and so we must take care to guide, not instruct. We must set the parameters from afar – his reality is already so warped.

Sometime later, Pietro and I took the ambulance and collected Remi outside Rupal's den. Let it be known that Rupal was heroic in her sacrifice: Remi truly believed her to be his co-conspirator; he read the abridged novel, as well as the planted paperwork, and he plotted an escape.

Now you have him, what will you do? How long will you hold him in the cell? Keep me updated. I feel bound – to him and to you. It has been too long since I heard from you properly, and I cannot bear to miss out on his development.

#20

Did you arrange my meeting with Remi? It was a surprise, and good to spend real time with him after so long. It felt like destiny, he an old friend.

Clearly your teachings are starting to sink in. He does accept that Martha is alive. He accepts to a lesser extent that in a broken-down state he attempted to murder her.

He fails to remember any of it, frankly. He said, 'If I really did all this, it was because I saw the way things were going and didn't want her to suffer the future.' He told me he used to look down at his own hands and not believe they were his. He was convinced in some way that Joan and Martha were fakes, copies. Can you imagine?

What is truly interesting is the distance now between them. He will not speak about Joan. He misses Martha dearly. He understands the folly of his early fatherhood; he never trusted Martha to find her own path. At the same time, he recognises the magnitude of her being alive. His face when I said she was working for a robotics engineer in the north – his whole demeanour changed, so that he was rocking forward, straining. I told him that Martha is being exploited by Greenley, whose long-term aims can only result in oppression, death. And Remi would not blink. He was so angry I felt his chair trembling through my feet.

#21

Your advice, please. Despite his growing knowledge, I worry Remi does not yet signal any of the emotional investment needed for him to act on our behalf. Self-preservation? Or something else? It is hard to discount psychopathy, actually. Hard not to feel afraid of a man who can make an attempt on his family, as apparently he once did, and have no recollection of it.

I resent him, I loathe him, I am ashamed of him. And still I care deeply for him.

#22

Remi responds well to the lectures you recommended. Thank you. On the other hand, I am not sure he is convinced of the need for direct action. It pains me to suggest he does not hate *enough*. I will concentrate matters by sending him some personalised testimonies from the States – our colleagues over there are willing to chip in. The autofac riot accounts are harrowing, and our sisters' stories from Detroit are a powerful primer. (How utterly cheap humans seem in the face of profit. I stretch out my arms for the oncoming reboot.)

#23

I find it fascinating how people like Remi, pulled from denial, can adapt and begin to flourish under the truth. Initially, he was reading up on the enemy's data collection tools and how they can be used to snare people (perhaps we needn't overanalyse this, given our tactic of demonstrating them *in extremis*). More lately, he is interested in the supply chain of autonomous weapons systems – what can be done to disrupt the flow, etc., but also what might replace it, and how we intend to live in the zero years beyond.

We also spoke a lot about how something 'engineered for the good or the safety of people' can easily be turned against the people. He appreciated the simplicity of this, and without prompting mentioned Kip Mornington's death scene from the novel.

Sometimes when Remi smiles you can see all of his sadness at once.

#24

We arranged a small social gathering to remind Remi that he is part of something. Just a pub, well out of the city. It helps us all sometimes, given our lack of digital contact. (Remi says his hand aches from all these handwritten notes.)

After wine, Remi and Pietro debated universal basic income. Pietro won, easily. Remi sat stupefied by Pietro's argument that it was too late, that the die was cast. He suddenly saw with clear eyes that the referendum on UBI was where the fork truly occurred, and that no profusion of utilitarianism or machine-friendly co-ops like Greenley's could now reverse the military–industrial pursuit of automation, the most basic capitalist structures being sustained indefinitely. It is all very well running a co-op with machines on board, but sooner or later you will be bought or aggressively taken over, rolled into the death business. It was then that Pietro said to Remi, 'What will happen to your daughter?'

I felt for Remi. It was obvious to him, and it had always been. I reassured him that it is healthy to have your mind shaken. I told him to read your book again, to be ready.

He asked what comes next, in the after. The zeroing. 'Hard labour,' Pietro said. 'The people all together.'

#25

A breakthrough. With only subtle suggestion on my part, Remi asked to join a small protest expedition to Bristol, in support of drivers being made redundant by a haulage firm going auto. Remi's willing impressed me, despite his reluctance to engage in casual conversation (while much warmer in general, he easily lapses into himself). Still, certain pathways are clearing. He appeared genuinely saddened by the plight of these men and women, whose livelihoods and futures have been coldly stolen. He was overheard telling his confidant, a much older recruit named Benjamin (is Pietro managing him, by the way?), that it was hard to argue for automation in the face of homelessness. We have never encouraged this line of thinking. Clearly he is thinking beyond the curriculum.

Remi came through on the day, too. The plan was to have a small squad hang a protest banner from a bridge over the city-bound M5 motorway, so that commuters would see it. When the group crossed the bridge from which they intended to hang the banner, Remi saw they had nothing to secure it to. He stepped up and suggested they instead pin the banner to the slope of an adjacent field using some of their tent pegs – again, perfect. I asked Rupal to sabotage the banner fairly soon after the team left, so that they could see the effect without being able to act. Rupal did as instructed. With three pegs released, the sheet came away and drifted across the motorway carriageway. Almost immediately, three manually driven cars swerved and collided with a stream of automated traffic: nine cars in total were damaged, with only minor injuries. Latterly a driverless lorry jackknifed and almost perfectly blocked the westbound carriageway. Remi responded facially but did not speak. Nothing was asked by him. No explanation was given.

In my opinion, the threat of harm, particularly with

regards to your cell at the warehouse, continues to outweigh Remi's moral imperative. He closely associates punishment with failure. But more promisingly, he is scared to let you down.

(Re: the motorway – traffic tailbacks lasted five or six hours. Miles long. Small and often is certainly disruptive. After Birmingham, we will surely paralyse England.)

#26

Last night we spoke at length about your book, Remi and I. He has read it three times now. He does not understand why we use drones like Rupal if we are so set against automation. I told him hypocrisy is a powerful weapon. Use their tactics against them; the end justifies the means. He accepted this and said he felt for Miranda. Her decisions were made for her – 'She was swept into her father's wake.' Remi said this with no irony, considering what happened to his own daughter. I asked, 'Doesn't Morn choose, in the end?' He scoffed. He said her father's own choices had annihilated hers. He went quiet for a long time after this. Later I asked him, 'What drove Morn to fight the machines?' And Remi said, 'Hate.'

#27

I strongly disagree that Remi's progress is slow. He has not believed in anything much before now. It might well be taking months, but he is emerging as a worthy candidate.

A thought struck me, actually. Remi insists that his attempt to 'save' his family was to protect them from the future we ourselves are resisting. The parallels between him and Kip have been there all along. I maintain that he was always preparing himself for our war.

#28

Laurel, I cannot stand what you have had done to him. To his face. I simply cannot forgive it. I wish I had never told you what he said to me about your book. These means are beyond cruel – like something they would do to a dog in my lab. You told him we were *cleaning* him? He was learning the way! What choice have you given him now? He flinches at every little thing I do! His cheeks haven't stopped bleeding!

Is it because he didn't get your book like some of us do? Is that it? Is this about your ego? Or did you have those wicked machines mutilate Remi's face to test me as well?

#29

Remi will not speak except to relay your threats against Martha, should he stray. You honestly did this? He has vanished, you can tell. It is all unravelling. I told him we would be liberating her – what does he believe now? What does he think when he looks in the mirror at these awful new scars of his, at this stranger's face you've had carved into him?

This is not why I came with you. I do not accept that different recruits demand such radically different stimuli. I believe in this cause. I believe in a better way. Respectfully, however, blackmail is not the answer. Nor should it be a foundation of the zeroing.

#30

Pietro is worried about things. About your plan. About Remi going rogue, telling someone. Pietro said he was going away to think about it. It is all so big. Honestly, I do not understand my part either. How many more of us are ready? You say you have raised an army, but how can we know? You never let us communicate with each other. You control who we talk to. You control everything.

#31

Remi came out of the infirmary. He came directly to my flat, which he knows is forbidden. He is not the same man. You have broken him. I cannot read his eyes any more. I cannot see inside him. And yet he swears loyalty; he tells me he is in, says he wants Martha to know. Know what? I want to ask him. What Laurel Brace promised she will do to your daughter if you fail her?

   Respond to me, at least this time. You owe me that.

#32

You bitch. Is this how you wanted me to feel? Is this the game? I have given YEARS to you. I give my blood. The least I deserve is a fucking reply.

#33

One week. Accept this message as my final word. Remi is partnered with the old man Benjamin for their trip to Greenley's allotments. They will take my car, which I have rigged with a backup unit. I have supplied a pistol in case things get hectic. The plan is for them to drop me in Birmingham and continue on in the second wave. They tested their shorter on a residential substation in Greenwich – it blew every last fuse in a forty-seven-storey tower block. When the men get to the allotments, there will be no danger of failure. Pietro is missing, so I cannot get the full measure of Benjamin, but he seems involved. Remi has rallied somewhat: he tells me he wants to wear a Birmingham City shirt because he has read about hiding in plain sight.

Why am I even writing to you?

#34

Remi, Benjamin and I leave for Birmingham this evening. You will not hear from me again. Let this be known: the workers are bigger than you. I would spit in your face if you were here. I renounce you. You fucking bitch! I am going up there in spite of you. I am doing this for Miranda and Remi's daughter and all our children. They deserve a better future, and they deserve better than you.

Hope I don't find you in the after. None of us will need you by then.

**[Collection note: correspondence ends.
Tap here to read again.]**

PART IV

MARTHA

1

It's Martha's turn to deliver a bag of limbs. She leaves the allotments early for Manchester, collecting the rucksack from the shed above Greenley's lab. The rucksack weighs a lot, so when Martha boards the train she's glad to get it into the luggage rack, relieve her back. Gladder still that no fingers or toes, with their silky synthetic skin, are poking out of the rucksack's broken zipper.

Despite the train's aircon, Martha's hair sticks to her forehead. She undoes her military blouson and flaps her top to get air on her skin. Early summer in Dillock means muggy days under dark cloud, so even when it's not raining you're dreading it. The hills don't help, this being a market town in shadow, seated beneath vast moorland whose burned-back and nude-peat plains absorb the rare light.

The train leaves Dillock late, chuntering out of the station with a cheery peep. It shouldn't matter, given the time and money owed to the allotments; just last week Greenley was moaning that their creditors were 'starting to take the effing biscuit', leaving Martha to cringe at his neutered swearing, unsure how to react. Greenley's partner Sharon still chided him for it, like Martha wasn't seventeen, see, or a functioning adult.

Well, today she'll remind them what she can do. She sits there listening to a salvaged Minidisc player, a 'Best of the alt-noughties' compilation made by the foster brother from whom she'd stolen her first kiss. As the train hums along, the music places her again in the foster home, all jam sandwiches and sugar soap and blue paper towels, and she remembers the outline of this boy's face, his gawky arms and slender calves, his too-big hands, his jaw and eyes in isolation. She smiles thinly: they'd flit between each other's bunks come the early hours, sure they'd never alert anybody to the smell of her black-market cigarettes if they only leaned far enough out of the window. He was a kind of love, that boy, taken from Martha and placed into digital rehab, then erased forever when she was moved to the next home. She always feels she didn't steal enough of him. She closes her eyes, lest she stare into the same hole she burrowed into in the months following her mum's death. Minor key, swelling strings. Seventeen now (going on thirty, according to Greenley), but only eleven then, which made it six years in care. A long six years, they've been – puberty navigated alone while she was shunted between state facilities and volunteer carers filling holes in the social net, some with better intentions than others. All those meetings with pro bono counsellors, therapists who'd travel over from Yorkshire, down from Cumbria, from all over the north, to spend time with her. Those rare treasures who listened, who sometimes took Martha's hand and squeezed it, told her it was fine to cry, even though she never really could. People who taught her to accept that friendship could be transient; that some friends will go willingly into the dark, and that others could need saving from themselves. People who explained the hidden costs of loss, a harsh lesson for Martha to learn so early. And people with whom she shared her mother's absence. Most importantly, they were real, unlike her father, who was dead to her a long time before. ('I don't remember him,' she told one counsellor. 'I never had a father.') Because the bastard had been a no-mark, a waster, a fuck-up, best she can tell. When she was seven he'd had a breakdown and vanished. Her mother insulated her from the worst of him, and the gap was easily filled. Change the tune and *snap*, the waters close over.

Now Martha's journey gets interesting: dense trees around a derelict industrial site, currently a squat for a group of textile artists. 'Another co-op is not competition,' Greenley told the allotments crew. Beyond the railings and wire, colourful patchwork flags hang from a rotting roof – a taunt to the drones, the sky-eyes network overseeing the country. Here the train moves to full pace, and the last of spring reveals itself in cool greens and strong-growing weeds, vast empty fields, automated dog walkers at perfectly spaced intervals along the brook. She flicks the playlist on – classic nineties to early-twenties ragepop, rough beats, some bloke yelling, 'Impotence! Impeachment!' over and over.

Then the sight Martha loves most of all. As the train starts across the Fiddlehead viaduct, the trees thin and the land tapers quickly away. Look down and follow the steep slope into the elbow of the valley, the dashed lines of mixed electric and petro-traffic. Turn to the opposite side, where the allotments – their allotments, Martha's home – slide into view. Proud as punch, Martha is, with all of it there to see: the vegetable patches, her self-painted shed – tiny but cosy and hers alone – and the various machines, growing canes, the goats and woodpiles and tool sheds. There's Rolly, working on his vintage motorcycle. Here's Sharon on her rounds, a handful of pulled weeds by her side, cigarette smoke rising from beneath her hood. All around Sharon is the uncanny green grass of the allotments, luminous on the slope. And there, stitched into this slope, are row upon row of limb-trees – the allotments' core produce and source of income. Next to the limb-trees, trenched into the fields, run the tracks for the co-op's fleet of 'hands' – a set of two-part robotic units, designed and engineered by Greenley, and whose nickname really ought to be arms. The hands move up and down the field, tending their crops. Martha's hand, the one she maintains, is farthest to the right. It's currently at the end of its trench, where it rotates, extends and arches in a fast, fluid motion. Elegant things, the hands, and uncannily precise. The hand's manipulator case hangs above a limb-tree. Suddenly the manipulator flowers into an array of surgical steel, and it plucks away the tarp. Martha conjures its noises, acutely sharp and sonorous. Beneath the tarp lies a set of untreated, unsheathed limbs whose surfaces carry a lambent glow. A bush of pale fingers, and two male feet, soles up, held aloft on two partially developed legs, unlikely flagpoles standing there absurdly. Martha grins to herself as the hand sprays them with growth hormones, and then the allotments are gone. Fiddlehead viaduct recedes, and the train enters a run of red-brick tunnels. Martha sits alone with her rucksack of limbs, and her music, and the taste of that first kiss in a foster home proving elusive, one too many memories away.

At Manchester Piccadilly, Martha ambles along the slippery platform, cutting an awkward figure with a rucksack almost the height of her. Despite a sort of fragile peace, rigidly enforced by the panopticon, plainclothes police still perform random searches and explosives swabs on the main concourse, so Martha doesn't hang around trying to find the platform of her connecting train to Crewe. It's late in, so Martha decides to lug the rucksack up to the mezzanine level. People-watch, take some photos. Get proof she did this alone, again, despite the others secretly doubting her, and also to record the time in case there are issues with Greenley's service level agreement. Take photos because city life distracts her, and viewing the place through a screen is one way to filter the noise.

'Nerves do us good,' Greenley told her that morning. 'It's okay to push yourself. And we trust you. We do trust you.'

His insistence had made Martha's palms clammy, too. Frankly, she thinks she's already proved herself. She wonders what it'll take.

The train Martha needs, due from Birmingham, doesn't show at all, so she hops aboard the ultrafast London service, messaging the client with news that he should meet her at Macclesfield instead, and that she doesn't know what's going on. She's one of the first on the train, easily finding an empty pair of seats, and places the rucksack by the window.

It isn't far to Macclesfield, which means she can still make the drop and scoot back to Dillock in good time. She updates Sharon and crosses her arms, no distractions.

Just before the train leaves, a woman asks to sit down next to her. Martha hutches up reluctantly, propping the rucksack on her knees. The woman is flushed, as though she ran to catch the train, and her hair is wet. She draws a bottle of water from her bag, along with a pen, a well-worn paperback and a pillbox. The woman asks to use the armrest. Both of them looking out the window as the train slides along. Moments later, the woman starts counting out tablets and arranging them neatly on the seatback's fold-down table. She leaves them rattling, all different colours and shapes, different markings. Martha glances into the woman's open novel, and is taken aback to see a smaller booklet hidden inside. The word CHEMO stands out immediately.

'You okay minding my things?' the woman asks, sensing Martha's interest. 'I'm absolutely busting.'

'Course,' Martha replies, embarrassed. The woman's face opens out as she smiles. Martha smiles back, follows her passage to the toilet, and looks down at the bottle. She thought she'd seen something: the words LOVE and APPRECIATION are written around its sides. She turns away, guilty. The train is passing a scrapyard full of nearly-new diesel cars. Then the woman is back, and Martha pretends not to notice as she takes her tablets one by one. Tap, swallow. Tap, swallow.

When the train reaches Stockport, the woman gathers her things. She smiles at Martha again, but Martha can't reciprocate. She knows now where the woman is going – knows better than most. Because in this woman Martha has found an abstraction of her mum, who also came to Stockport and the Christie for chemotherapy. The same mum who lay on her side with bedsores and dry lips, legs lost in wires, with the smell of death blooming in the most innocuous things – the cups of tea and chocolate boxes, the single white orchid, fake, on the windowsill. Cuddling her mum in the hospital bed until a nurse came in to say, 'Sorry, the beds are for patients only,' only to backtrack on seeing how Martha had moulded so perfectly to her mum's shape.

Martha wishes the woman good luck. She hopes it means something.

'Ta, poppet,' the woman says, and leaves.

Martha returns the rucksack of limbs to the empty seat beside her.

Love and appreciation.

2

Macclesfield railway station, and outside to a nondescript electro-converted car. A quick flash of headlights. A man, small and portly, slipping out.

'Doctor Abbas,' he says, hand out.

'Hiya,' Martha says, keeping her hands in her blouson pockets.

The doctor scratches the back of his head. 'You're, uh, young.'

Martha turns her boot heel in the gravel. 'And?'

He glances over her shoulder. The body language of a decent man running on desperation. Dr Abbas, previously of Manchester Royal Infirmary: a fleshboy, skellyman, or one of the other less kindly names Martha knows from the town. In its last days the NHS ran entirely on the goodwill of its staff. Now, its volunteers rely on smuggling for even the basics.

Martha sniggers. 'You made decent time, anyway,' she tells him. 'Cheers for tweaking your plans.'

Abbas smiles weakly at her. She wonders if she appears

feral to him, hair tangled and smelling strongly of woodsmoke, her skin heavily freckled. Loose clothing so at odds with fashion – the nice things she used to wear. In truth, she may well be feral: she hasn't looked in a mirror for a long time, and whenever she catches herself in reflections – train windows, glass facades – she's leaner, more defined. Sometimes it's her mum staring back at her.

'Who these for?' Martha asks him, lifting the rucksack down from her shoulders. She settles it on her boot caps, so the canvas won't touch the wet gravel.

'You know I won't tell you,' Abbas says, opening the car boot. He rolls back the parcel shelf, wheezing slightly. He's wearing a hearing aid, old style. 'Patient confidentiality still means something,' he continues. 'It's not like you have a right to—'

'Go on,' Martha interrupts. One hand on her hip, a decent impression of caring less. 'I counted the lengths – you've got a kid's set in here. Poor bastard know what's coming? They gonna make it, or what?'

Abbas shakes his head. 'I'm not doing this. Sorry.'

Martha smirks. She slips the invoice from her money belt and hands it over. 'Greenley wants it paid sooner than last time.' She shrugs. 'I don't mind, to be fair. We should do them on the house for kids. He gets hung up on paperwork; be easier if we went in for crypto. Get a drone running deliveries and all...'

Abbas, still confused by Martha's approach, nods coolly. 'We're trying,' he says.

Trying to mend things that can't be fixed any other way, that is.

Then a hesitation, the unsaid things held back. Martha stares at Abbas and tries to imagine how well he would've been paid as a doctor before he went underground. Tries to imagine how many more doctors and nurses volunteer to keep the torches alight.

Martha unloads the rucksack into the boot cavity, where Abbas has opened a hidden compartment in the subfloor. The prostheses fit snugly when she lines them up. There's nothing grim about it, though it might look macabre to a passer-by.

'They're smart,' Abbas says. 'You changed your polymers?'

Martha shakes her head. Staring at the kid's prostheses. One is an over-knee replacement, right up to the thigh; the other a foot and partial shin. 'Maybe it's the light,' she tells him.

'And they're warrantied like usual?'

'Course. Four years. Greenley's looking at mobile servicing, but he says you can't get the staff.'

'No,' Abbas says, arching his brows. 'I only mention it because the last lot came on the back of a motorcycle, and we had to really scrub them down.'

Martha grins. Rolly, that must have been. For him, running deliveries is an excuse to hoon about on B-roads.

'You want a lift anywhere?' Abbas asks, quickly replacing the floor cover. 'I mean, back into Manchester? I'm due for a home call near Ancoats. Car's empty, except for these, so it's no hassle.'

Martha reties the rucksack and stuffs her pockets. 'Go on then,' she says. 'So long as you don't try feeling me up on the way.'

Abbas's expression locks up in horror.

'Only messing,' Martha adds, chuckling. 'If you tried, I'd cut your balls off and feed them to our goats.'

Then she waves to open the car door and lowers herself into the seat, leaving the doctor standing there, face a picture.

The doctor's car takes them towards Manchester on a congested route, northward into the city, the stratified city, through fortified suburbs whose boundaries stand walled and gated and sentried, and then up and over the recently electrified Mancunian Way, a confused retrofuturist monument to the nineteen-sixties and the early twenties. They're silent, both of them, their transaction having been made, their lives all set to diverge again. Silent and appreciating their mutual agreement. A few minutes of this, the doctor's nasal whistle, before the car slips into a juice-and-drop spot fifty yards from the railway station. Owing to the charger points installed here, it's now an unofficial red light zone, darkness afforded by railway arches of sooty brick. The diesel fumes have long since diffused, but in the right wind you can still smell the old trains.

'Right then,' the doctor says, as the car settles.

'Ta again,' Martha replies.

Abbas is reaching to pop Martha's door when a shrill alarm sounds from somewhere deep in the car. They both startle, lock eyes. Frantic, one hand tearing out his hearing aid, Abbas slaps his pockets and produces a series of small devices. These he places on the dashboard, the fourth or fifth in his hand. 'None of these,' he says, baffled.

'I think it's the car,' Martha says slowly, producing her own mobile and shaking her head. 'I know that tone from somewhere.'

'The car?'

'I don't... Hang on. I'm sure we did this in school. *Ages* ago.'

Abbas glares at her.

'That's it,' she says. 'Emergency broadcasting. I swear down that's the tone.'

'And there's nothing on your phone?'

Martha rotates the screen to him. Back to her, for a second shock. The screen has filled with red exclamation marks – Sharon, Greenley, even Rolly, who she can never quite imagine using a phone.

All of them are asking where Martha is. All of them are saying to get back to the allotments ASAP. All of them asking if she's all right, if she's seen the news, if Rolly can come and fetch her on his bike—

'Something's going on,' Martha says. And though Martha and Dr Abbas haven't seen the news, the car hears 'going on', and serves it to them. A flashing windscreen HUD – *URGENT.*

Martha pushes the door open. The alarm isn't in the car. It's coming from the city.

'Stream low,' Abbas says, and the dash projects an image on the windscreen, fuzzed then sharpening as the unit compensates for the dark arches beyond.

Abbas gasps: it's drone footage, that curious isometric. Night-time, and the craft obviously a long way up. Infrared mix. The camera is mounted in a fidgety gimbal, but the subject is strangely clear: they are looking down on a cityscape in negative. A large city in total darkness except for white-hot patches of things burning, encircled by a vast, unbroken line of streetlamps and car headlights. It's as if some regretful god has draped a circle of black cloth upon the place, lest they accidentally look at it. Dead motorways and lightless high-rises, shadows only hinting at infrastructure. Everything shorn of civilising lines and angles.

A headline ticks along the bottom of the screen: BIRMINGHAM ATTACK: FIRST PICTURES.

'What the fuck,' Martha says. Gutshot: that sparkling dread. 'This is Birmingham?'

'Look at the time stamp,' Abbas says, voice quiet. 'In the corner, see? My *God*. Look at the timestamp – this was taken in the early hours. How are we only just seeing it?'

Outside, something clips the open door, and Martha's attention is drawn away. Clusters of people are sprinting past the car, ostensibly towards the city centre. No screaming, no panic, just a mass of silhouettes, the tattoo of feet.

'My God,' Abbas repeats.

'What happened?' Martha says. She stands up and leans over the door. 'What's going on?' she yells at someone running past. A youngish lad turns and shouts, 'An't you seen? It's kickin' off big style, mate! Total fuckin' wipeout!'

Martha turns to Abbas, whose eyes are very wide. She nods once, and before he can say otherwise, Martha is gone with the crowd. For the first few metres she can hear Abbas calling desperately after her, but she doesn't flinch – extends an arm and waves over her shoulder without turning or glancing back. The surge is too intoxicating to resist: the sense of being in a movement, the sweeping and unknowable now, electric skin and a tumbling stomach.

The crowd is massing in Piccadilly Gardens, the heart of the city, most standing and facing the massive civic screens. Hundreds of people are packed on to the AstroTurf, some crying and shaking, almost all of them on phones. Martha gets in the thick of it, pushing through, nimble even with the big rucksack, until she breaks the line at one of the screens and comes before a new set of images.

Daylight, exterior: an enormous column of people walking up a motorway. A shifting mass of people covering all three lanes and the hard shoulder, pressed together so tightly you only see hair and shoulders. Beneath them a fresh headline: PRIME MINISTER DECLARES STATE OF EMERGENCY.

'What's happened?' Martha asks the woman to her right. The woman is middle-aged, well dressed, with a collection of expensive-looking shopping bags at her feet. Her phone is flat in her palm and projecting a bowl of light, inside which her family are gathered at the family dinner table, looking up and out into the city.

'They're saying it's a kind of bomb,' the woman tells Martha, not taking her eyes from the screen. 'It shut down the city's electrics. Lights. Roads. Cars. Hospitals. All of it. The whole thing. All the backups and bloody everything. The city just went out.'

Martha stares at the screen. The people marching.

'Where are they going?'

The woman glances up at Martha and tuts softly. 'They're refugees, sweetheart. They're going anywhere.'

Martha rubs her face. A pang of loss and fear, mixed with sadness. A numb thread of not understanding, and the wish she could. She has no family or friends in Birmingham, no real tether, so there's a distance. But most pressing of all is the sense of enormity. As if she finally understands some of the things her mum told her about living through the noughts and tens. The day her mum sat at home, for instance, playing truant from college, and saw two planes collide with two towers; felt, in some immature, ungraspable way, her cossetted world judder and rock from its axis. How her mum described a revised world taking form, shaped by the pressures of its new orbit. A country in which innocence gave way to cynicism, and the fascia of civilisation was picked at, slowly elided. 'Sometimes I cried my eyes out while I fed you to sleep,' her mum once told her, 'because you didn't have a clue. I wanted to hide it all from you, at least for as long as I could. I thought, this way you can't ever be angry with me.'

Martha has forgiven her mum that, though. Here, today, the world is still changing. The most perverse thing being that she doesn't fear its horrors, but instead she finds them exhilarating. A modern city with its plug pulled – the idea is unbelievable. But it captures her, quickens her.

She stands there. Shocked into quiet, then, like the rest of the crowd, and marvelling at the way Manchester has paused, holding its breath, to watch the people of Birmingham march north.

3

When the police arrive to disperse the crowds, Martha returns to Dillock on a heaving train, grateful for the lightness of the rucksack, but otherwise distracted, weirdly homesick and thirsty, and none the wiser on Birmingham. Terrorism, they said on the screens. Definitely terrorism. And now there's more terse chatter in the carriage, a vehicle-borne device being one possibility: a truck or bus or bin lorry or tanker, or something bigger. Maybe multiples, rigged up and synchronised for maximum effect. Maybe they used the old tunnels under the city. Before they left the screens, talking heads on the news were dismissing nuclear strikes but giving it all that about 'severe broadband electrical disruption' caused by something like an 'electromagnetic pulse', or 'hyperlocalised EMP'. Not that Martha can confirm anything now: her mobile has stopped working, owing to redirected satellites or stressed relay stations, or the networks being down altogether.

Martha closes her eyes, lost in her imagination. Without

realising it, she's trying to grasp the processes that even go into setting off a bomb. Is she naïve to question how someone could wake up and look at all of this – boring life, the fixings and faces, roadways and trees – and decide to reject it? Do they go out to jumble the order of it, or end it? Do they watch what they do? Do they live through the aftermath? Do they feel anything to hear children screaming for their parents? Does a bomb like this – whose damage is apparently confined to *things* – feel easier to trigger? What about afterwards, when the stillness, the debris, the absences, are all that remain?

The train reaches Dillock, inbound rain like nicks in the glass. Martha alights quickly, itching madly under the bag straps. Wind on wet fabric. A dampness, welcome on her neck and hairline, but not so much for the storm it's likely dragging in.

She walks the long way back to the allotments. Fast feet, leaning in. Worlds away from Manchester, or Birmingham, or any city, come to that. Without really thinking, she collects a carton of fresh farmer's milk from the town's vending robot, a cutesy cylindrical thing whose face was painted by the local school's competition winner, and more recently graffitied over by someone older and more profane. Then she crosses the farm's wet fields, long grass dampening her toes and shins. She could sit in with Sharon, warm up by the wood burner. See what else has happened in Birmingham on Sharon's little wind-up set. Hot wool and lemon verbena. A bit of sense talked into her – Sharon being good like that.

Over the last stile, Martha cuts down through the trees,

the railway line an intrusion to one side. The smells of decay and blossom and musk, the signature of some unseen creature. Deeper in, the branches shivering. There comes an occasional slapping noise from ahead. Martha exits the treeline on to Greenley's land, allotment city. The rain is getting heavy, and no one's about. Spidersilk is strung in bowing lines between structures. Gardening tools are wedged in the biggest growing patch, and nearby is a barrow full of soily cauliflowers and legumes, tilting precariously, its handles capped with heavy-duty gloves. The sound of rain on shed roofs, glass and fabric awnings, on the tarp covering Rolly's motorbike and the limb-trees, and on the corrugated plastic off-cuts and timber salvage. A gentle throb, in the low end, from the groundwater pumps. She goes between the sheds and under the wind turbine, whose blades cut silently. The solar arrays, mounted in trailers on the south-facing slope, are all facing due west; in the morning they will turn together to the east. In the growing lanes, the robotic hands are all turned off; they stand there in reduction, curled into themselves.

One of the sheets covering the limb-trees has come unfastened, and is lashing against the nearest hand's working arm. Each slap sends a fine spray in the air. The loosened sheet has exposed the limbs of a bush that should not be exposed – a clump of partially formed arms, a battery of skinned legs – pointing accusingly at her. She swallows and stands in the drawing-down light. Now the shush of pre-dusk, the softened lines and blueing grass. A low mist developing on the slope above, a ghost wall descending the bank. For the first time a chill, though it isn't particularly cold. The quiet here is so massive and contrary to the crowd she'd joined in Manchester. She goes to the hand, boots squeaking in the dew, and steadies herself with its cold wet steel. She grabs the loose flysheet, holds it taut. It's rubbery, almost greasy. Nowhere near as heavy as she thinks it's going to be. Up close, perhaps owing to the light, the artificial limbs are especially alien. With her other hand she touches one, just to see. A rain-glossed, half-grown arm, beige and hairless. Fingers without knuckles and form, but creased in preparation; same for the elbow. She uses one finger to slide droplets of rain from its surface. Finally, she pulls across the flysheet to secure them, zips it all closed. Maybe it's the time of day, her frame of mind, but the limbs had started to make her think of blast injuries.

'All right,' she whispers. 'Where are you all?'

As if in response, something snaps at the treeline. Martha's neck prickles. A movement – too low to be human, too fast to make sense of. She crouches, inches herself against the closest shed wall. Not scared, she tells herself. Interested.

A slender head emerges from thick bramble. A fox, long ears twitching in the rain. Autumn bronze and black fur, a thick brush. It's scavenging, probably. It'll be out of luck: there's no meat here except for a few vats of soggy synthetic. Then again, it could rifle the recycling bags, though Rolly will have seen to the compost already. As the fox sniffs the air, Martha holds her breath. She watches this creature, poised and long – and is suddenly rewarded when it springs forward and bounces around in the long grass, tail spraying fine droplets in great arcs. It's chasing a bumblebee, the sight of which alone would be magic, were it not for the tiny yaps the fox lets out as well. Martha covers her mouth to hold in her grin. Presses herself into the wood, trying to remove herself from the equation. The minute expands. The ground around the fox seems to be shimmering. Then, just as quickly, the bee is gone, or the fox is sated, and the spell breaks. Martha steps away from the shed, tenser than she realised, and on towards the fox.

It notices her coming. A white glint in the eyes. It holds Martha's gaze for long enough to blink twice, very clearly. Martha returns its blinks without thinking. A sort of conversation. The fox opens its mouth fractionally, black gum, a hint of yellowed teeth. A flash of plum tongue. Martha holds up one palm and waves tentatively. The fox dips its nose, then backs away. 'Wait,' Martha says. 'Don't.' But the fox has turned, slinks into the thickness of the forest, towards the dry. Its bob, brilliant white, is the last she sees of it.

'Huh,' she goes. A daze. The allotments no longer so desolate, and the sleeping machines less eerie in their silence. The others must have gone to the pub, she's telling herself. That, or they're clustered around a screen somewhere, like everyone in Manchester was.

Martha unlocks her shed door. She sits on the coir mat and kicks off her boots, massages her wet toes and stretches out over the sheepskins she keeps on the floor. On the walls she keeps pictures of city landmarks and long-closed gig venues. From the ceiling hangs an upcycled wind chime tinkling on the breeze. Soothing notes, the warmth of wood on wood. Since she moved to the allotments, Martha has felt more present, much closer to the elements, more aware of the air changing from month to month. It's one bonus of being up north, where they still have proper seasons: you notice the valley bloom, and later, as the ground frosts, everything die back again.

The shed has a small leak in the ceiling when it rains. Water drips from the central light fitting, down through a hardened silicon seal, and on to the sheepskins. Martha can scent it – mildew, a deeper smokiness. It smells of home. She pulls the blanket off her bed and stays there for a time, closing her eyes, listening to the restive chimes, thinking of the fox. The shed door creaks and taps against the frame. She remembers arriving at the allotments, bewildered and slight and anxious to meet the people who'd agreed to take her in. She thinks again of Birmingham, and all those people walking up the motorway. A word, helixing in her mind: *refugees.*

Right on the edge of sleep, Martha is roused by a voice on the wind. Greenley's reedy tones, at once loud yet distant. Raised, too. She's up, then, lest the others stumble on her lying down on the floor like this, cast their judgements. The paradox of being seventeen and hating that they see her as a teenager.

Looking out, however, there's still no sign. She goes towards Greenley's shed by way of the lab vent – a small outlet topped with a reclaimed red–clay chimney pot. Beside it, she realises what drew her this way. She squats and listens. They're all down in the lab.

Galvanised, Martha steps around the guy wires supporting Greenley's radio antenna and enters his shed. A new cable-knitted blanket on the bed he uses when he's too busy to walk the fifteen yards to Sharon's. Martha's eyes shift to the stack of hardback books on the floor: reference and esoterica. A couple of garishly jacketed fantasy novels. On the shelves, succulents and trays of giant cress. The large planter he sometimes takes outside for rainwater, has named 'Triffid' for some reason. Copper pots, a camping stove. A pinned-up protest banner screaming 'CO–OPS NOT CRISIS'. A set of mugs hanging on hooks – old trade union slogans, one featuring a crude impression of Margaret Thatcher with crossed-out eyes. A leather-topped mahogany desk for his elaborate ham radio rig, around which are pinned postcards from contacts all over the world.

Martha heads down the staircase. Damp concrete, no handrail. Tap-tap-tap. Her clothes still sodden. Then over the basement floor, where she's shocked to find the lab door sealed. Staring around at utility lights, thick with spider webbing, little moths dallying. Does she knock? The lab isn't usually closed, what with Greenley insisting there's no hierarchy on the allotments – at least when it suits him. But Martha allows her hand to fall anyway, accepting she isn't welcome for whatever reason. She puts her ear to the door.

'Only a bloody kid herself!' a voice insists. Lower register, that Lancashire *bluddy*. Rolly.

'It's a minor complaint,' another voice responds – Sharon. Then, with some finality, Greenley himself: 'You know we can't risk aggravating long-standing clients. As an attitude, it's not exactly disgraceful. I rather admire it, actually. But as an approach, it would be suicidal to allow it to happen again.'

Martha pinches the fleshy pad between her thumb and forefinger.

'Can't we just have a quiet word?' Rolly asks. 'She really flogs her tripe out for us—'

Crosstalk, then, and an angry response.

'I won't – I'll not have that,' Sharon goes, as if she's repeating a point.

Then Greenley, even closer: 'I think we're done here, aren't we? I'm going upstairs to try calling her again.'

Martha's eyes widen. She darts into the recess behind the door, just as it swings open. Through the crack between the door and jamb, she can make out the lab's stainless units, the rubber safety flooring. Cobwebs in her hair. A smell comes through: it reminds Martha of some crusty socks she once found on the floor of her foster brother's bedroom – dank and human. And right there, right on the other side of this door, is Greenley's sleeve, and the side of his face, head angled down.

'Oh,' he says flatly. And with a lurch, Martha realises her wet boot prints are all over the floor.

She covers her mouth.

'Sharon?' Greenley says. 'She's back already. Make sure she's in warm clothes. She'll be soaked through. We'll pick this up again tomorrow.'

The gap in the door darkens. Greenley is looking directly towards her. If he can see her through the gap, he's pretending he can't. If he has something to say to her, he's decided it'll wait. Then he turns and goes back inside. A moment later Sharon and Rolly exit the lab together, clomping up the stairs. Martha slips off her boots and tiptoes up behind them, her socks drawing up cold water.

'Shit,' Martha says.

Sharon's sitting on the edge of Greenley's bed. Martha has time only to drop her boots before Sharon launches Greenley's new blanket towards her. Martha catches it clumsily, brings it up to her chest. 'Sorry,' she says.

Sharon grins. 'For what? Not having the sense to wipe your feet?'

'I couldn't find anyone,' Martha tells her. 'I – I wasn't sneaking about.'

'Course not,' Sharon says, and winks. 'Hard to be stealthy now we got rid of the diesel gennies, eh? You'll catch your death with your hair so wet, mind. Go and get it dry. I'm doing a cheese and onion pie – I'll bring some over.'

'Am I grounded?'

'Grounded?' Sharon's grin widens. 'Earwigging as well, were you? No, love, you're not grounded. You just decided to be an arsehole today.'

Sharon knocks on Martha's shed door before she opens it, a grace note of respect where perhaps the men would afford none. Sharon can be matronly or motherly, yet mostly she seems to want Martha on side, uncynically, as a friend or confidante, a sister-in-arms. A good foil for Greenley at his most impulsive, come to that. For these reasons she speaks to Martha with care and thoughtfulness, and in times of need will fix Martha with kind eyes while allowing her brows to do the talking. With those things she can sympathise or empathise, smile or frown. Martha, meanwhile, is wary of the age gap, if not the gulf in their experiences. She compensates by listening harder, tempering her most stubborn responses. This is why she annoys herself when she catches herself laughing a bit too hard at one of Sharon's jokes, usually at Greenley's expense, but sometimes Rolly's too. Then again, a sharp tongue will endear Martha to many. And Sharon had quickly worked that out.

'Slice of this'll fix you,' Sharon says, tilting her baking tray. The pie is massive, a thick emulsion of cheese on its lid.

'Smells ace,' Martha says.

Sharon settles it on Martha's bed and slaps a midge that had settled dead centre on her forehead. 'Wait till you've had a bite,' she says, grinning. She sits down next to the pie and licks a finger to touch away the crumbs on Martha's blanket. She clears her throat. 'Look, this news today. Birmingham, I mean. Did you want to talk about it? Ask anything?'

Martha shrugs. 'It's not really… What is there to say?'

Sharon glances out of the window, then down at the pie. She stretches for a trowel in Martha's tool rack on the door, cuts a deep slice from the pie, and hands Martha the whole thing. 'Probably about fifty cheeses in there,' Sharon says. 'God knows you'll dream tonight.'

Martha tears off a chunk of crust and dips it in the filling. It's sharp yet buttery, and even better than it smells. 'Really good,' she says, nodding.

'So yeah,' Sharon says. 'About today. I suppose I wanted to tell you a story – not because you got home late, but 'cause I know you'll be feeling unsettled.'

Martha takes another bite.

'Going back a fair few years,' Sharon says, 'my brother was a roadie, right? Toured with metal bands, all over Europe and Canada. One afternoon he calls me from work, though not really out of the blue 'cause we constantly shared GIFs, memes, all that old-fashioned stuff. And I answer and I realise pretty quickly he's in tears. Absolutely in bits. So I'm all, Andy, what's up? And he's sobbing, the lad. Can't speak, just this stifled crying at me. So I ask him again, what's going on? Do I need to come get you? Do I need to call someone? I'm sitting there with my heart in my mouth, wondering what's happened. If something's happened to my niece. But no. He's been sorting through a vanload of hire equipment that's back in from London. Drums, amplifiers, guitars and all that. My brother and his colleague took the delivery and started opening the hard cases to do inventory checks. Make sure everything's there. But after the first couple of boxes, they're getting confused. Some of the equipment is caked in dust. Some of it has this weird sticky stuff on it. They notice holes and scuffs, and now they're panicking because they've signed off the return and will have to cover all the repairs. And then they realise where this stuff has come from. What's actually going on. The two of them in that cold warehouse, oh God, leaning on each other I bet. The silence. Because there are bits of people in the flight cases, Martha. Clumps of bloody hair.'

Martha stops chewing and puts down the trowel.

'I know,' Sharon says. 'I *know*.' She continues: 'There'd been a militant attack at a festival that week. God, Martha, to say you were so little. And I say an attack – I mean this was another attack. There were lots of attacks around then, almost enough to lose track. During the clean-up, some of the cases got missed, I don't know, a tragic bloody mix-up. Next news, the cases have turned up at my brother's warehouse, and he's got to deal with police and hospitals and find an incinerator for all this horrible stuff he's suddenly responsible for. He said to me, "It's poisoned me, Shaz. Never seen anything like it." And he wasn't wrong. None of us had seen anything like it, and imagining it was enough.'

'Fuck,' Martha says.

'There was a cruelty about those years that you won't remember. There has always been cruelty on this little island. Ask Greenley about the IRA when he was studying in London – had a run-in himself. Nail bomb. But this was personal. It was my little brother; that day it came home for him and for me, and we weren't even directly affected. It was all you could do to stay clear of the news, and then this happens. And you know what? Why I'm telling you all this? Because even when you were afraid, even when it turned up on your doorstep and rubbed your face in it, you had to believe it wouldn't be you. *Had* to. Selfishly, you had to believe it would be someone else. Or if it wasn't, that you'd fight. That you'd make it out.'

'I wasn't scared,' Martha tells her. 'Today. I wasn't afraid. I'm not scared.'

Sharon cocks her head. 'No?'

Martha shakes her head.

'Well, that's good. But you better know you can talk to me if you are. It's a slow burn, this kind of thing. Greenley calls it furtive, this anxiety about the world. You ask him – he gets so animated. People so easily stop trusting each other. Assume the worst... it goes on. And that's partly why he set up this place. Why we're helping people in the town. He came here and said, okay, things are really shitty, so what can we do for our community? Because at the height of the attacks there were reprisals every other day as well. People talked about civil war like it wasn't just nutters on each side. All these lost kids were getting into it – they were kids to me, anyway. Your age. Younger, actually. It completely gutted me.'

Martha knows all about lost kids; she swallows her first response. 'And this doesn't feel different to you?' she asks. 'Birmingham?'

'No. It feels big, sure, but no. Keep watching and we'll learn their names and faces and motives – that always helps. Seeing that humans did it… that helps you get your head around it. Maybe that's silly.

'Whoever it is, though, they're idiots. Black out the media and how d'you hope to tell the world what you're up to? Poundshop terrorists. Imagination, that's about it – I'll give 'em that. But that's it.'

'Yeah,' Martha says.

'Besides – we're in the sticks. Nothing'd ever happen out here. Nothing much.' She slaps her arm. 'Except these bastard *midges*.'

Martha picks up her pie again. Takes a bite.

Sharon smiles tightly. 'You eat that slow, pet. Save you on heartburn. And do me a favour, eh? Don't go bloody renegade on us again. Greenley's old ticker can't hack it.'

4

Martha sleeps fitfully in her wools. She dreams of explosions in the valley, a military jet on manoeuvres, burning hares running across the allotments. At first light she boils a kettle – half for the washbasin, half for her flask – and tries to revive her phone on the wind-up generator, without any luck. She remembers she keeps an old SIM card and phone in a drawer, the same way one of her foster mothers used to keep a single cigarette somewhere close. A control test: there if she needs it, that access to her past life, and sometimes it tempts her. But today she resists, because to use it would be to re-enter her old life without preparation, an old life with a different set of rules. *And in any case*, she tells herself, *it probably won't work.*

She's half into yesterday's still-wet jeans when Greenley walks past on his early rounds. She's fully dressed and stirring nettles in her flask when he returns to knock on the shed door.

'Hi,' she says.

Greenley looks gaunt and edgy. The bags under his eyes are especially pronounced. 'Wood store,' he says. 'In ten.'

'Morning to you as well,' Martha replies. 'Any more from Birmingham?'

Greenley shakes his head unsurely, then stalks off towards Rolly's shed.

Martha closes the door and pins up her hair. Pulls on her coat and wellies. The rain stopped in the early hours, but the ground is lustrous. She slops up towards the wood store, the flask a comfort beneath her coat, surprised to see a number of oily bubbles drifting lazily between the sheds, most popping on the solar arrays. When she looks across, there's a rotating device on Greenley's shed roof. Another of his little experiments, or distractions.

Martha is last in at the wood store, and while Sharon winks at her, neither Greenley nor Rolly give her the time of day. The men make a point, in fact, of not looking at her. Martha laughs weakly to herself and leans on the rear wall, the sole of a boot pressed against it.

To one side of her is a small table, an anaemic cake sitting on top. Four paper plates, a fork, spoon and a fan of paper serviettes decorated with nativity scenes. Martha considers eating it in one. She'd do it to spite them, had Sharon not made the effort to talk last night. She turns to the front, where Greenley is pacing.

'I wanted—' he says, then sneezes. He sits down on a broken pallet and begins to pick curls of damp grass from his boots. 'I stayed up late,' he starts again. 'You know how ideas can seize you. Well, my idea is that we really ought to pass on this month's profits to the Birmingham crisis appeal.'

It clicks for Martha. Greenley's eyes, his vagueness – he's been taking speed again. She watches for Sharon's and Rolly's reactions. They say nothing, though they do share a glance.

'Silence really is consent, you know,' Greenley adds.

Still no reply from the room. Rolly coughs into his fist, catches Martha glaring at him. He glares back from beneath his fisherman's hat. His hair and beard are more unruly than usual, and there are porridge oats in his moustache.

'In which case, let me spell it out,' Greenley goes on. 'We took some big private orders this week, on top of Martha's drop yesterday, which – thanks to her polite reminder, no doubt – has been paid for in full, with arrears, this morning. We've broken even on labour this month, *and* we've already covered Saturday's community meal at the church. We don't have any more health derms to pay for, either, since no babies have been born in the last fortnight. So, I'd sooner the hands' earnings go to the wider reaches. At least, this is what feels just to me.'

'So we don't keep the cash by for a rainy day?' Rolly asks. 'Order parts for another hand? Or finally upgrade the alloy printer? Buy a delivery drone—'

'Yesterday *was* a rainy day,' Greenley snaps. 'Besides, we don't need another hand. We don't. Growing profits for the sake of growing profits is an old way to think, remember? That, and we can't get near our production moulds at the minute. Our contractor was raided by the council last month – one of their other clients was caught printing a load of bloody machine guns.'

'Reinvestment, then,' Rolly says. 'Reinvest in the business—'

'That's the same as enterprise,' Greenley snaps. 'So no, for the reasons above. And stop calling this a business, will you?'

'Whatever.'

'I'm fine with doling out the cash,' Sharon says. She nods at Rolly. 'What's the matter with you?'

'Nowt,' Rolly says. 'Nowt is.'

'They're people,' Sharon says. 'Isn't that right? They're struggling. Don't pretend you've had some kind of empathy bypass.'

Rolly looks genuinely hurt by this. Martha finds it hard to work out his friendship with Sharon at the best of times, but something about the exchange seems a little too petty.

Greenley nods at Sharon. 'They are struggling. So I'll contact the institute and we'll do our bit.' Finally, he turns to Martha. The others follow his gaze. 'Anything you want to add, over there?'

Martha mumbles a no.

'Nothing at all?'

Martha keeps her mouth closed.

Greenley claps once. 'Then let's crack on with our day, shall we? Rolly, can you get the hands warmed up, please? Sharon, we've a new ankle design I'd like you to test on the impact deck – I'll explain the ligament system shortly. Between us, we also need to dig some potatoes. Lest we forget, we're still only six inches of topsoil away from total dystopia. Martha, I want you to re-sort the recycling baskets, please. There's far too much in the landfill bag, last I saw. But first, please stay here for a moment.'

Sharon and Rolly file out. Sharon watches her feet.

Rolly holds eye contact with Martha all the way.

Martha comes away from the wall. Listens to Sharon and Rolly in the wet outside.

Greenley stands up and closes some of the gap between them. Sometimes she forgets how tall he is. 'Adventure, was it?' he asks her, calm enough.

'I stayed in Manchester to see what was going on,' Martha tells him. No point trying for wriggle-room – Greenley has a certain way of seeing things. 'When the Birmingham alert came up,' she continues, 'my phone packed in.'

Greenley nods. 'Mine's been playing up, too.' He buttons his patch jacket and removes his glasses to rub his eyes, pinch the bridge of his nose. 'You realise, of course, that you were with a client. He knew you were underage, which already puts him in a certain position, particularly as a caregiver, and especially under our current… circumstances. What was he meant to do when you ran off with no means to contact us? When him contacting me directly poses such a risk to his work? How am I meant to trust that you won't go AWOL the next time we ask you to do a drop?'

'It wasn't like that,' Martha says. 'The drop was done.'

A loud crash rings across the allotments, rattling the walls of the store. Rolly dropping something, or one of the hands shorting out. Their biggest solar array has been temperamental for weeks now – maybe it's finally given up. Greenley shakes his head wearily.

'You didn't think we'd worry?'

'I'm a big girl.'

'You're also an ambassador for us.'

Martha rolls her eyes. 'Yeah, and not a drone.' She

pinches the fabric on one shoulder. 'I don't have strings coming off me.'

Greenley shakes his head again. 'I'm not saying you do, never mind *should*. And of course I realise yesterday was distressing – you might've lost track of things, you might have much been less inclined to... I don't know. But this isn't about putting reins on you.'

Martha's heckles are up. The store's lights are too bright. 'I knew what I was doing,' she tells him. 'I looked after myself.'

'Oh, Martha. You're getting the wrong end of the stick. We'd almost certainly be lost without your diligence. We simply need to talk about how to behave—'

'*Behave?*'

'Yes—'

'How I *behave*? Come off it. You want me to stay here twenty-four-seven like some pet Cinderella? You want me sticking around so your pet ex-con's got someone to gawp at, have a wank over? I can do this job with my eyes closed. I can *piss* it.'

Greenley's mouth is a tight O. There's sweat beading on his brow. 'Let's not be so aggressive,' he stammers. 'Rolly's a changed man. He isn't like that and you know it—'

'He's exactly like that,' she spits. 'You're all the fucking same.'

'Martha!'

She turns to go. She doesn't care where, or how, only that she's gone. But now there's someone charging back through the door – Sharon. Sharon with the brightness of the day behind her, and her breath short, and her eyes running. Sharon on top of Martha, and very nearly straight over her.

'Where is he?' Sharon pants. 'Where?'

Martha points confusedly back inside the wood store, as if he could be anywhere else, and Sharon barges past. Martha holds the door frame.

'You'd better get out here,' Sharon says to Greenley, in the kind of tone that only couples share. Except it's not a statement, or an order. It's a plea.

5

The air is cool outside. Under the close and silvered sky, two things strike Martha as wrong. The first is that Martha's hand is stripping itself down, which means Rolly has set it to self-maintenance without her say-so. The second is harder to define – a sort of rupture in expectations. Because when Martha scans the allotments, the outbuildings and greenhouses and stores – the objects she's familiar with and reassured by – there's something missing.

She looks harder.

No, not missing. Replaced.

There's a small car parked where her shed should be.

'Don't,' someone says.

Rolly is standing to her left. He looks boyish, almost lost. He says, 'You mind coming back inside?'

Martha can hear something lowing. It brings to mind animal traps and sharp wire. Blood and fur. In her time here she's watched Rolly skin roadkill, and dealt with it; part of learning the rural way. But occasionally, without telling anyone, Rolly will lay traps in the forest, and those she has never been able to deal with.

She doesn't want to go back inside, no. Not now she's noticed Greenley and Sharon standing around this car on her shed.

'What happened?' Martha asks Rolly.

He winces at her.

'What?'

Still wincing.

'Rolly.'

Rolly takes her sleeve and cups his mouth. 'Someone in it.'

Now there's this bright thread – she can see it, nearly – connecting her to the car. Reeling her in. The car is modern, electric and autonomous, and damaged beyond repair. There's bodywork missing from its front wing, and its bonnet is fully concertinaed.

Rolly holds his face. Pale and sweaty. A sort of slime on his chin. Has he been sick?

'I dunno what it's about,' Rolly says. 'Greenley said to keep you back here.'

'God's sakes,' Martha whispers. She sets off through the growing patches.

'Hang about,' Rolly says, coming after her. 'There's something else.'

Martha can see that for herself. The car windscreen is shattered, laminate film holding together the tiny fragments that cloud the interior. Both of the car's doors are gull-winged open, with Sharon's boots and backside protruding from the near side. Opposite Sharon, glimpses of Greenley's creased brow, frantic hands.

Martha's almost at the bonnet. This close, it's obvious her shed has been demolished, its remains lifting the car clear from the ground. One of its front wheels is still spinning, electric motor whining at a low pitch. The smell of burnt coils catches in her throat.

'Sharon!' Greenley shouts. The moaning again, followed by a bout of groggy coughing. Greenley has a man's head against his breast.

Martha comes round the car, behind Sharon, and Greenley finally spots her in the gap between Sharon's hip and the car's door frame.

'Sharon,' Greenley says, and signals to Martha.

Sharon looks over her shoulder. Slowly backs out of the car. Her face, when she stands, is twisted, embarrassed. In the seat she was covering is an old man wearing a camouflage jacket. Some of the old man's face is missing – Martha can see his teeth through his cheek. It could be the shadow, but his right eye socket seems to have slipped down his face. A section of white hair is attached to a pink flap that hangs limply from his forehead.

'Is that blood?' Martha asks. Not the right question, necessarily, but all that comes to mind. A fizzy sensation in her mouth, like she's going to be sick.

'Get her out of here,' Greenley hisses to Sharon. Then, shouting over the bonnet, 'Rolly! What the *hell* are you doing? I told you to keep her back there—'

'Is he dead?' Martha asks Sharon. 'Is that old man dead?'

Sharon takes Martha's arm, turning her with it. She steps around and pulls Martha into her. Tobacco smoke and camphor. 'I don't want you seeing,' she says.

'How did he die?'

'It's, oh love…'

Martha looks back to see Greenley sawing at the injured man's seat belt with his Swiss army knife. The injured man's breathing really isn't right. Something clogging the pipe.

The old man, the dead man, stares on at the occluded windscreen.

Then Greenley has cut the injured man free, and Sharon runs to assist. The men roll out of the car in their strange embrace, the injured man on top of Greenley.

Martha is frozen, watching it all unfold. The old man in the second seat is in full view now. A small gun, a pistol, is balanced on the peak of his knee. His hand a little lower down the thigh, like he'd rested the gun there to check his phone, or change the route, or explain something in gesture with two hands for clarity.

'Martha! Hurry!'

This was Sharon. Martha snaps back and goes to her. Together they roll Greenley away from the injured man. The injured man is wearing a blue football shirt, dirty across the gut. He must be mid-forties, early fifties. There's a stud of dry blood under his lower eyelid. His face is puffy, heavily scarred around its edges. His eyes are half-closed and rolling back. His left leg is bent the wrong way at the knee. When she leans close enough, she can make out the crest on his shirt's breast. Two globes, a ribbon. Birmingham City FC.

'The attack,' Martha says. 'You were in the attack.'

'He's slipping,' Greenley says, waving his phone over the man's neck and torso in some vain attempt to scan for ID, for an insurance derm. 'Sharon, check his wrists, will you? I can't find a thing.'

'Rolly!' Sharon screams. She starts squeezing along the man's left wrist. Then the other. 'Nothing in either,' she says. 'For heaven's sake!'

Finally, Rolly comes running. He arrives the wrong side of the car, pointing at the dead man.

'Why the fuck's this old one dressed up like paramilitary?'

Martha steps away, unsure where to look. She has her hands at her sides, useless and awkward. Without the injured man's derm, they can't access the emergency services. Without a derm, he's on his own. No one takes that kind of risk any more, or so she thought. And she should know: they've spent the last few months making sure everyone in the village is chipped.

'We need to check for wounds,' Greenley says.

'Let me,' Sharon tells him, and starts cutting at the football shirt with the Swiss army knife. The injured man's skin is mottled. Unbroken skin, but a welting bruise on the ribs.

'Internal bleeding,' Greenley says, touching along the injured man's abdomen. 'Sharon, here – press here. That feel hard to you?'

Watching Sharon push her hand into the man's side, Martha steps forward. 'Pass me your phone,' she says to Greenley.

Sharon and Greenley stare up at her.

'Does it work?' Martha says. 'Because mine's still knackered.'

Greenley blinks.

'Phone,' Martha says. 'Just let me try.'

Greenley unlocks his phone and tosses it to her. Martha

immediately pulls up Dr Abbas's number. In three or four bells the doctor answers with an impatient rasp: 'What the hell are you *doing*? I told you no more calls! I've paid up, damn you. We're settled. Now *piss off*.'

Martha swallows. Probably it's audible. She says, 'It's me again. The girl.' The line's breaking up and she's watching Greenley and Sharon and Rolly as they work to sustain the man. The rustle of the trees and the man's sticky breathing.

'Where's Greenley?' Abbas says.

'With a man,' Martha tells him calmly. 'He's in a state.'

'What man? What d'you mean, there's a man?'

'Messed up. A man. Two men crashed on the allotments. The car, I mean – it crashed. One's dead, and the other has no derm.'

The line goes quiet. The doctor sniffs. 'Are you in danger?'

Martha looks at the car. Wisps of smoke from the bonnet. Back to the injured man; his strange, scarred face. 'I don't think so.'

'There's a response from the injured man? Nothing obstructing his airway? You've checked his breathing?'

Martha snaps her fingers towards Greenley. Greenley looks up, surprised by her boldness. 'Is he still breathing?' Martha asks. Greenley nods tersely. 'Yeah,' Martha says. 'He's in and out. In and out, yeah. His breath is rattly.'

'Okay,' Abbas says, 'then I'd like you to describe the patient's injuries to me. Quick as you can. Don't overthink it – say what you see.'

Martha takes a breath. *The patient.* 'Um… his left leg is twisted round at the knee. His foot's the wrong way. I think there's some bone poking out of his shin. He has these blotchy red bruises down one side. His face is messed up. He looks sore all over.'

'Has he vomited blood?'

Martha squints at the man. He looks sort of unfinished – an impression of someone, a draft. 'No,' she tells Abbas.

'But the bruising's visible?'

'Definitely. It looks like burns.'

'So, I'd ask you not to move him. Don't put him in the recovery position, nothing like that – we don't want pooling.'

For the first time, the situation as a wave. The reality on her chest, with its own heft. A pressure builds behind Martha's eyes, and her nose stings. When she blinks, the tears come. 'Is he going to die?' she stammers. In part because she's never seen the transition up close, at least not so quickly, and the man's face seems to Martha the colour of death. Before today, she'd never seen a body – and here is the prospect of two. They'd asked Martha if she wanted to see her mum's body, the least bad outcome, given how her mum went peacefully in the end, owing to the way the cancer had breached her brain barrier. They'd said going to the chapel of rest was a useful way to say goodbye. Martha said she didn't want to say bye. She told them she wanted to think her mum had only popped to the shops, or was reading a book in the next room, or was pottering in the garden, having a secret cigarette. Sometimes the cat would take a fledgling and her mum had to run outside to stop it – better to think of her doing that than lying on a steel sheet. 'And it wasn't peaceful at all,' Martha had said. They hadn't seen what came before.

Martha hadn't gone to her mum's funeral, either.

'Is he going to die?' Martha asks the doctor.

'Maybe,' Abbas says. 'So, you must listen carefully.'

Martha nods. Martha listens. And Martha relays the instructions to Greenley. The leg injury is the big worry, especially if it does turn out to be a compound fracture. Apply a tourniquet above the man's knee. If possible, gently elevate his leg ever so slightly – will a blanket do it? Yeah, a blanket. Clean water to sip – do we have clean water? Another blanket if his skin feels cold, or clammy. A blanket. One of those foil space blankets if you've got a kit to hand. Then Dr Abbas says, 'I'm going to check something,' and shortly afterwards returns with, 'Listen, we've actually got a woman on call over your way. Brind – isn't that close to you? My mapper says so. Ask Greenley if he wants me to pull her in.'

Martha just keeps nodding. A sensation of slipping out to sea, having misjudged a fast tide. She tells them, and Greenley nods back.

'Greenley says yes,' Martha tells Abbas. 'Please.' Flinching as the injured man vomits bile down his cheek, his facial scars throbbing purple.

'I'm going to hang up, all right Martha? I'm going to hang up so I can call this woman – Agnes, she's called – and get her over to you. In the meantime, I want you to try and stabilise the man. Tourniquet, remember. No movement. And keep him warm, even if he's feverish. Agnes is coming.'

Martha nods. 'Yes,' she says. 'Yes.'

'I'm going now,' the doctor says. 'All right? Martha? I'm going now. Agnes is coming.'

And then Abbas is gone.

Martha stares at the injured man, broken on the lurid grass. The others working on him. Greenley stroking the man's cheek with a strange, unlikely tenderness. What's left of the Birmingham City shirt black with sweat and groundwater. Rolly applying pressure at the thigh. Sharon, seemingly in bits behind her scarf, clinging to the first-aid kit she was told to fetch from the lab, apparently never used before. A kit kept down there lest Greenley do something stupid with a scalpel, or a chisel, or in case one of the prostheses snaps in some dangerous way. Their false bones are honed like blades, after all – a fact Greenley always seems so proud of.

Soon through the valley comes the whine of heavy electrics. A four-by-four, dual-motored and tall on its chassis, tearing up the steep hill below the allotments.

'That better be her,' Greenley says, hand shielding his eyes. And it is her, of course: the doctor, Agnes, driving manually, face hard behind the wheel. The four-by-four slides to a stop in the mud, and Agnes emerges from the door with a captivating speed and purposefulness. She pulls out a tool bag and comes marching round her vehicle, whose engine bay hisses with coolant. A look of contempt for them, Martha thinks, imagining Agnes's internal commentary: *hemp-sniffers, hippy-bloody-dippies, half-baked dreamers*. Projection, maybe, but Agnes's disdain seems deep-set in the brow. Her red hair blows wildly about her.

'Agnes?' Greenley says.

'Naw,' she says. 'The fucking tooth fairy.' A glance across

the site, another grimace, and then she sticks her head in the damaged electric car to triage the terrible cargo inside. A cough, indifferent-sounding, before she returns. 'Good to be here,' she says. 'The auld granda's definitely gone.'

'He is,' Greenley says. 'Yes.'

Agnes motions to the injured man. 'And he's the only other?'

Greenley nods. 'He's it.'

Agnes kneels down by the injured man. 'Shite day you're having,' she says. She rummages in her coat pockets; bolts a manual stethoscope to the man's chest, counts under her breath. Sheathes his forefinger with a little white box. Finally, she taps a little capsule on her overshirt collar and speaks into herself: 'Suspect crush injury. BP and pulse elevated. Sats way down.'

'He going to be all right?' Sharon asks.

Agnes doesn't shrug, but Martha decides she was about to. It's clear the man is fading, his head lolling about on Sharon's jumper. 'Unwell, aye,' Agnes says. 'We know what happened, exactly? This all crash damage?'

None of them can answer. The unknown factors being the dead old man with the gun, whether the injured man was in some way responsible. The Birmingham City top, and the clear possibility the two men were refugees of the city, of the attack.

Agnes traces a circle in the air above the man's torso. Starts tapping his sternum. 'Blunt trauma. Dashboard or steering wheel'd do it. Wasn't driving manually, though, was he? No steering wheel in the car, right? So I'd go with the former. Hit something fast enough, you get this kind of mess. Could someone open my wee tool bag there?'

Martha, being closest and empty-handed, does as Agnes asks. Inside, a hodge-podge of elastic-banded implements, measuring instruments. A dark green cloth, wrapped with gaffer tape.

'Over here,' Agnes says. 'Quit dawdling.'

Martha pulls the bag towards the doctor. Watches, unblinking, as the doctor peels out an oxygen mask and carefully applies it to the man's mouth. Watches intently as the doctor shaves, swabs and cannulates the man's forearm with a thick needle. 'IV access,' Agnes says, apparently sensing Martha's scrutiny, or the change in her breathing. 'We push in some fluids. Analgesia.' She looks up and winks. 'I brew good junk.'

This done, Agnes begins to press her hand into the man's side, working from armpit to hip. 'Pooched his ribs,' she tells the group. 'Tenderised himself, poor fud. But it's mainly the shape of that leg that's getting to me.'

Now the doctor begins to scissor away the rest of the man's jeans, revealing twisted pulp at the knee, bone visible and bright fat ballooning like settee foam. Agnes pitches over and frowns at the tourniquet, looks along the leg. Her expression is more fascinated than appalled. 'Well, that's not the colour we wanted.' She looks up at the allotmenteers, all ranged around her. 'Derm or no derm, you're better getting him to hospital and praying for clemency. The machines won't listen, obviously – but if there's a decent goon on duty, you might be able to wangle a pass to surgery. Either way, this is gammy, and we don't have long to save it.' She tilts her head to the plots behind her. 'Unless you wanted to make a donation of your own…'

Greenley, Rolly and Sharon exchange glances, then gaze out towards the limb-trees. Agnes looks at Martha, watching the whole thing play out. All eyes fixed on the hands in their tracks, the limbs they nurse. It's there, then, right in between them: the presence of the idea, quite palpable, being made solid by consensus. Martha is stung by the realisation, a subsidence inside her. Something squirming. She wonders if this has all happened by design – if the man was already injured before the crash, knew what they grew and sold on these allotments, and aimed the car accordingly. If her shed was somehow a node on the car's pathfinder.

Agnes raises her eyebrows. 'That a yes, is it?'

'We do have some mature units ready off the shelf,' Greenley says solemnly. 'If it's really what you'd recommend.'

Martha's head is spinning. A new word on repeat: *amputation*.

Agnes licks her lips. 'I wouldn't recommend anything other than cracking on with it.'

'Then go for it,' Greenley says. 'I'd sooner that than do nothing.'

'You have indemnity? I'm not covered for foreigners, let alone non-consensual work. It's on your head.'

Greenley nods. 'For the parts, yes.'

A hush as Agnes thinks some more about it.

'I'm not a miracle worker, either,' she says. 'Just so you know.'

Sharon folds her arms. 'He's hardly in a fit state to complain, is he?'

Agnes grins. 'True. So one of you better get Abbas on the blower again. Ask him to connect me to an on-call surgeon – I'll need a guide. And Mr Greenley, come and show me where you keep your saws.'

6

The surgeon calls Agnes an hour later, when the evening is drawing in and the midges are blooming and the hooped shadows of the viaduct stretch long through the valley. With all the pieces in place – a makeshift stretcher, bucket and rags, a pallet full of cotton wool, swaddling and alcohol – things start to move around Martha at a queasy speed.

Martha doesn't want to watch the operation, if it passes as one. She keeps picturing Rolly's skinned roadkill, tendon and flesh unbonding. She helps to set up in Sharon's shed, though; stands there agog as Rolly fashions an operating table from a pair of railway sleepers and four chairs. Soon they stretcher the injured man inside, and Martha recoils as he comes round briefly to scream. Then they've got the injured man on the table, illuminated by arcs dragged up from the lab, and Agnes has arranged on Sharon's tatty sideboard her stainless instruments, a hacksaw with a fresh blade from the tool shed. The man's drip bag dangles from a coat peg, fluid lines crocodile-clipped together. Outside,

Rolly drags over one of the freshly charged solar units to serve as an auxiliary in case their stored power runs out.

Martha leaves before Agnes makes the first cut. Seized by habit, she heads for her shed – until she remembers with a lurch that it's no longer a shed at all. Then, a curiosity greater than dread. The old man's body is still in the remains of the car, and there's no one to tell her not to look.

Ten feet away from the car she can't deny a thrill, the sparkle at her fingertips. A faint high note in her ears. For some reason she expects the dead man to have shifted in his chair. Five feet, and she's taking fairy-steps around the car, whose bonnet has stopped smoking. The wind whistles across the car's open gull-wings.

Martha isn't ready to look at his body again, she realises. Instead, she goes to the car boot. Peers through the rear windscreen, webbed with hairline cracks. She runs a finger over the glass, the texture of a mosaic. Inside are two duffel bags, half-zipped. A ball pein hammer with a blackened wood handle. A large torch. A thick coil of cable, jump-lead attachments, one of which is hooked up to an array of batteries, themselves taped to a big lump of wood. A lifeless Gilper-branded navigation bug, its filigree wings singed and curled.

Martha clicks her jaw. There's a story in here, even if she can't pick up the thread. She blinks as if to simulate taking pictures with her eyes.

Martha comes back around the car. The injured man's side. At his door she's struck by the culture of the setup, the unconscious hierarchy: the dead man sits in what would be the passenger seat, were this a manual car, which meant the injured man had taken the 'driving' seat. Does that say something? Did the injured man have power over the dead old man? Or was the injured man a chauffeur?

Round the front now, with its frills and folds of metal and plastic and alloy. So much can happen in an instant. She passes the car's indicator nubbin, the A-frame on the dead man's side. And finally Martha is beside him. She stoops to be closer, at his level. She leans and cocks her head, trying to make sense of his remodelled face. Unreality expands around her; Martha inspects the old man as though he's an exhibit. It's the details, she decides, that make him less of a stranger – proof he'd lived and was not always this way. His chin has tucked into his neck like a sleeping drunk's. The string of unbroken, bloody drool stretching from his lip to his belly, somehow impossible to accept as still being wet. Cheap amalgam fillings in his teeth, visible through the hole in his cheek. The thin, white hairs of his torn scalp. She leans closer. A hint of sour peach from the car's air freshener. The man's body itself still fresh enough to conceal its own smells, even if the skin has lost its colour. In this light, the old man is a green not unlike the limbs hanging in bunches across the field. It reminds her of a glow-in-the-dark toy she had as a child.

Martha looks along the rest of him. Hairy wrists, a cheap analogue watch. Beige sweater. A weathered leather belt, whose incrementally worn holes say he's been gradually losing weight. He could be a grandfather – anyone's grandfather. But something is different to her. A change, not in the dead man's pose, his apparent indifference to death, the flap of head skin over his eyes. No – it's the wider setting. A shift in the light, maybe. The rotation of the Earth. Or the framing of his being here at all. Her understanding of him.

How do they get rid of him? Who do they report him to?

Martha imagines a rectangle of loose topsoil, patted with a shovel. A local scrapper coming up for the car, taking it to pieces in situ, leaving nothing but the wood of her flattened shed, its paint tainted by mechanical fluids. Rolly burning the car's onboard computer.

With a start, Martha realises what's different.

What's missing.

The pistol isn't on the man's knee.

Immediately she turns around, mouth open, expecting – what? Rolly to be standing there, grinning, revealing at last some clue to his past crimes, the things Sharon and Greenley chose to forgive, or had no choice but to ignore?

No. For all Rolly's brooding, the odd clumsy comment, he has never struck her as violent. His shoulders seem too narrow, for starters, and his beard only accentuates his gauntness. It's not like he's wiry and strong despite his frame – she's seen him trying to use an axe.

So who took it? Greenley? Maybe there's an argument for Greenley 'looking after it'. It's not like the crypto-paternal-figure thing never extends to his taking responsibility for things beyond his sphere of control, in part as a way to extend his sphere of control. Except the idea of Greenley even knowing how to *hold* a gun is laughable. Greenley is the man who'll scoop ants from hard standing to make sure no one treads on them.

Sharon, then? Martha can't see that, either. Sharon is

fierce to a point, certainly protective, but she wouldn't see the opportunity. Give her a hand trowel and a good motive and she'd do the same damage.

Which doesn't leave Martha many options. Except, of course, that the old man here isn't dead at all. That this is all a ruse.

'Who are you?' she asks, goose-bumped now, the forest intensely black behind her. 'Who took it?' she whispers, increasing her distance. The man doesn't tell her. The man can't answer. The dead being those who see nothing, and hardly make for good counsel.

Then a glint – a little sliver of moonlight in the car's footwell, between the dead man's boots.

Martha swears at herself. The familiar having segued into the night, and with it her rationality. There, propped against the old man's ankle, is the pistol.

She hesitates for long enough to consider the alternative. She ignores her best instincts. Martha reaches in and touches the gun. Takes it out, weighs it in her palm. Holds it to her chest as though she imagines keeping it.

She places the gun back on the dead man's knee, balancing it carefully, and does her best to ignore the creeping sense she might come to regret it.

7

The injured man's operation finishes before one in the morning. For the past few hours, Martha has been wrapped in a blanket watching the panel window of Sharon's shed from the step of Greenley's front door, and now her buttocks are part-numbed and itching from the welcome mat. The window in Sharon's shed is a warm square of light, occasionally flashing as the trio move around inside. Through the night a warped shadow-figure played on the walls, whose arms made violent motions. At one point the saw's shadow hung there like a portent.

This is the second full cup of tea to have cooled in Martha's hands. The shed step damp and freezing to the touch. She listens to the chattering forest and the mid-tone murmurings of Agnes on the phone with the surgeon. Sharon's been out twice in the last hour or so, her face sweaty. The first time to get something from the lab, stepping around Martha while tousling Martha's hair; the second to visit the limb-trees, where she switched on her hand and had it harvest a ripe prosthesis for fitment.

At five past one, Agnes comes out of the shed wearing a lubricant-smeared plastic sheet. She looks to the sky, clear and starry, and casually lights a cigarette. Martha can't get over the fact Agnes has done this here, just like that. Nor can she shake her sense that the man must've known, or at least hoped it would happen. No insurance and a catastrophic injury sustained in a crash at a limb-farm? It's all too neat.

'Why you still up?' Agnes asks, noticing Martha. She starts over and Martha doesn't stand because she doesn't want to lose the warmth.

'Hey,' Agnes says again. 'What you doing?'

Martha shrugs. 'Wanted to check he'd made it.' Then, with a frown, 'He has, hasn't he?'

Agnes exhales for a long time, nodding through the cloud. 'He's grand. Sedated for now – he'll probably wake about midday tomorrow. Be a rough hangover, that…'

Martha scowls – can't help it. The injured man is both a puzzle and a vague threat. If she's honest, she wanted him to be awake, so she could go in there and ask who he is.

'Will he be, you know – normal?'

'It's a brand new leg,' Agnes says. 'I'd call that a blessing. From the state of the scars on his face, I'm sure he's no stranger to recovering… But sure, he'll be in shock, some pain. Trauma does enough to the brain on the physical side – we've no idea what he's been through. That, and body shock. Do you know the rejection rates of your prosthetics? Abbas always says you made good stuff here – but bodies don't like things that aren't made of bodies. Being a cyborg is nice till you're honking of gangrene.'

Martha remembers the stream of people marching up the motorway. The desperation of it. She shakes her head.

'Aye,' Agnes says. 'We've done all we can.'

'And the dead guy? The old one?'

Agnes furrows her brow. She exhales. 'Good question, young team. Did anyone call him in yet?'

Martha shrugs. 'My phone's been dead since Birmingham.'

Agnes dabs out her cigarette on her boot and holds up the butt. 'I'll try and get someone on the case, eh? Here – where d'you want this putting?'

Martha throws her cold tea on the grass and tilts the mug.

'Nice one,' Agnes says, throwing the cigarette butt inside. 'I'll call someone before I get off.'

Martha sleeps in Greenley's bed for three hours tops. She dreams of finding a severed leg in her bed, and wakes before six with the taste of the car's air freshener in her mouth.

Nobody else on the allotments is up. After Agnes left, Greenley and Sharon had bunked up in his old campervan down the hill, while Rolly had gone skulking about in the forest. On past form, they'd all be lying in.

Seven comes around, and blue sky gives way to swollen, leaden cloud. Martha stands at the open shed door, breathing it in, the damp and the earth. The fresh mud. Somewhere in the forest a cuckoo is calling. Away from the allotments, the slope down to the main road is textured like the sea. A low easterly current runs through the long grass, greens and yellows moving as languidly as waves. Martha boils the kettle for the washbasin, rinses her face and armpits, and dresses in yesterday's clothes. Stands staring, for a time, at the space where her shed was. She wonders where she'll sleep tonight. She steps outside and crosses the allotments, looping round the damaged car, her flattened shed, eerie in the grey light, like the remains of a nocturnal animal. The car's been pushed off her shed. The dead man is gone. Had Greenley and Rolly moved him? She doesn't remember any noises overnight. She kneels then at the shed boundary with a knot in her throat, recognising some of her belongings; hints of brightly coloured clothing and shattered trinkets. The structure, petalling outwards, is unrecognisable as something that might have stood at all. A dog barks in the distance, and the goats emerge from their shelter. Martha goes to feed them, absently humming old pop songs as they nuzzle her arm through the fencing. When the bag of alfalfa runs out, she tugs clumps of long grass from the bank beneath the pen and lets the goats lick her palms. When her knees begin to seize from squatting, she gives in to temptation.

The injured man is half-naked on the makeshift table, still lined in to the coat-peg drip. A blanket has been pulled up over his intact leg and groin. His replacement – smooth and steely, a markedly different shade to the skin of his knee and thigh – is exposed. Getting air to it is important.

Unable to reason herself out of it, Martha taps on the shed window. The injured man stirs slightly, rolls, but stays asleep. He's facing her now – peaceable despite the sunken eyes and sallow complexion. Front on, the man's scars are most apparent across his forehead, the receding hairline, and also in front of his ears. Another rough line through the well-defined crescent of his chin, just beneath the bottom lip. It makes Martha wonder if something has bitten off his face, then roughly reassembled it.

Martha taps again. No reaction. She curses him under her breath, knowing the chance for her own interrogation has all but gone. Back in Greenley's shed, she fills the kettle, sets a fireblock going, and pulls four mugs from the cupboard. Balls to it. Greenley, Sharon and Rolly don't deserve a lie-in.

Come eleven, a police officer arrives on an armoured bike whose motor sounds like a grasshopper. A large man, leathered up, here to get things done. He unclasps his chin guard and clears his throat. The visor lifts away to reveal dimmed sun-lenses and a legacy sinus-job. The officer's jack-in ports sit on a strip running across his nose and under his eyebags, with a bundle of sensory fibre lined straight up his nostrils.

Martha has just finished wiping down her hand when the officer approaches. He turns off his sun-lenses in some attempt at humility, raises one hand against the sun. She squeezes out her chamois cloth and refits the control board.

Up close, she can tell he's studying her.

'Martha?' the officer asks, pushing out his cheek with his tongue. She looks around, but the allotments are the closest they get to abandoned: Rolly out on a drop, Greenley up the road burning the injured man's clothes, Sharon keeping vigil at the injured man's side.

'You are Martha, aren't you?'

Martha tries not to look at the officer directly, aware of his mods, the running calculus. She resents her body for giving him data. It makes her bones feel cold.

'Yeah,' she goes.

'PC Perrin,' the officer says. 'Or Geraint. Whichever.'

'Hi,' she says, rotating away.

'Chill,' the officer says, pointing to his eyes. 'I'm not on duty. These aren't even live – I messed up the last firmware update.'

Martha frowns. 'They gave you my name.'

'Proven to establish rapport,' Perrin says, grinning.

'Well, I'm not gonna throw myself off the viaduct, so you don't have to worry about that.'

Perrin halves his grin. He re-engages his sun-lenses. The effect is subtle, but unsettling. 'Is Mr Greenley on site, Martha?'

Martha hesitates, then shrugs. 'He might be back,' she says. She can smell Greenley's wood burner, now she considers it. 'If he's in, he'll be in the lab, I think. Is it about the old man's body? I don't know where they took it—'

'It's no bother.' The officer smiles delicately. 'We discussed it. If you wouldn't mind showing me the way.' He nods to Martha's robot. 'You okay leaving it?'

Martha tosses the chamois in the bucket and rolls her jacket sleeves, suddenly conscious of her heat. 'This way,' she says. And she leads the officer across the field to Greenley's shed, past Greenley's radio gear, and down the cement steps to the lab.

'Sir?' Perrin says, knocking on the main door. He goes in first.

Greenley's there to one side with two handfuls of what looks like wet seaweed. Martha remembers Sharon moaning to Rolly about Greenley developing plants and 'cultures' for a new contract; Greenley had been spending too long perfecting the mix, and wasn't going to bed.

'Constable,' Greenley says, removing his goggles and gloves. 'We so appreciate you donating your time.'

Perrin shakes Greenley's hand. The air reeks of hydroponics.

'I owed her, to be fair,' Perrin says, slightly askance. 'Been a shocker, by the sounds of it.'

Greenley smiles. 'Something like that,' he says. Then to Martha, 'Do you want to go and tell Sharon the cavalry's arrived?'

No, Martha thinks. She wants to be there, to hear this. She wants to know more – and believes she has a right to. 'Still with the other guy,' Martha tells them.

'The other guy being your injured man? The one Agnes operated on?'

'Yes,' Greenley says.

The constable smiles. 'Talk about field medicine. We'll get to him presently. For now, though, I'd like to see the dead one – if I could.'

'Certainly,' Greenley says. 'Martha?'

Martha rubs her nose. 'Yep?'

Greenley glances towards the lab door.

'I was gonna stay put,' Martha tells them. 'In case you need a witness. Or corroboration, or whatever.'

Perrin's eyes snap to her. Greenley's face hardens. His thin smile makes for a poor disguise. 'You sure?' Greenley asks. 'Don't you have stuff to be getting on with?'

Martha shakes her head. 'Cleaned my hand already. Fed the goats. I'm done for the day.'

Perrin clears his throat.

'It's fine,' Greenley says, glaring at Martha over the officer's shoulder. 'Through this way, and mind your head.' Then, almost guiltily, 'We put him on ice.'

Martha follows the men into the back. Smug, to a point, that she might have embarrassed Greenley for infantilising her. It's not like last night's strange conference with the body hasn't prepared her. Part of her wants to double-check he looks the same – that last night happened.

Greenley hovers by a chest freezer at the back of the walk-in, where much of their spring vegetable harvest is usually stored. He opens the chest. From her spot behind Perrin, Martha sees the fabric of a thick blanket, then a grey hand stuck to the wall of the freezer. Closer – all of them edging closer – the frosted tip of the old man's nose, the loose scalp folded back to where it should be. The blanket is in effect a liner for the freezer. The old man's relaxed position is oddly comforting.

Having peered at the body for a time, Perrin rubs the skin around his optics.

'Do you get many visitors here?'

Greenley glances to Martha, then back to the officer. 'The odd one, certainly,' he says. 'The odd vagrant, banished or self-exiled individual, nothing more. Normally it's local people who've had affairs and been caught out. The occasional traveller who's fallen foul of the law. We took one of those in, actually – Rolly, he's upstairs. People tend to stay, work with us a while, and drift on. I suppose people imagine allotments as a good balm for guilt. Time to reflect, atone, make peace with the earth. Which is all true. But it rains here. The hills… it does rain. You might say it takes a certain sort of person to stay.'

'Mmm,' Perrin says thoughtfully. He turns back to the old man's body. 'This is a textbook gunshot wound. Directly through the soft palate. A ricochet, out through the top. Did you look in the car? The roof liner?'

'We have the gun,' Greenley says. 'I didn't want it lying around, so I bagged it up.'

'Brilliant,' the constable continues, nodding. 'See, look here. Residue on his lips. Signed and sealed, if you ask me. Perhaps we can ask the injured friend to tell us some more.'

'If he's on speaking terms,' Greenley says.

'Mmm,' the officer says again, leaning over the body. He's taken out a foamy-looking mitt, which he places over one hand. Then he does something to the dead man's head. A flash, then another, and the officer looks away. A sound like radio chatter, very distant and minute. Martha realises it's coming from inside the officer's face.

'Results'll take a minute,' the officer says, blinking as though he's dazed. He seems amused that Greenley and Martha are staring.

'Results?' Greenley says.

'ID check. I'm prodding the database.'

'What database?' Martha asks.

'Cloud.'

'You told me you were offline.'

'No, I meant—'

Greenley shushes her.

'Bing,' the officer says. 'All right then… Here we have one Benjamin Warkin. Full taxpayer, good chunk of savings in crypto, statins for high blood pressure. Bog-standard. Wife, two grown-up kids, three grandkids, full set. Pretty spotless.'

'Then what happened to him?' Martha says.

'How do you mean?' the officer replies. 'That bomb goes off, doesn't it? Should imagine he tries to get out of there before the wolves close in.'

'I meant, why is he dead?'

'Well, he didn't fall over and bang his head on a bullet, did he?'

A pause.

'And that's it? No investigation?'

'Martha!' Greenley snaps.

The officer waves towards Greenley. 'Obviously we'll get the coroner on it – eventually. But to my mind, this isn't a crime, and given the scale of what's gone on in Birmingham – the amount of people who've rocked up in these parts – our priorities have shifted.'

Martha blinks at him. 'You don't think it's suspicious that a bloke with a family turns up at random with a gun on his knee and a hole in his face?'

Greenley can only shake his head.

'No easy answers,' Perrin says. 'Not often. Certainly not so clean-cut as this, any road. I don't see his full history without the live link. Aggravating factors. Can't have been too happy, can he? Sometimes a family isn't quite enough. Sometimes you just lose it.'

'And you don't suspect any of us? You think it's fine we bunged him in a freezer?'

'That's enough now,' Greenley says.

'No cause to suspect you,' the police officer continues. He points upwards. 'I checked the sky-eyes. Nothing amiss with the account. Everything as Mr Greenley described over the phone this morning. Plus, you've done us a favour. Every hospital round here is chock-a-block with inpatients who couldn't score beds further south. And that's before you get to the morgues, which are still filling with half-thawed bodies. Last night our commander requisitioned a wholesaler's warehouse, just for their freezer space. They're putting bodies in refrigerated trucks and setting them to run laps of the M60 until their batteries go.'

Martha shakes her head. Her eyes are hot. The casual confirmation that people really did die in Birmingham; that even the city's already-dead were displaced by the attack. As she'd watched the scene like a pervert in Manchester city centre, families were being devastated in the darkness.

'So what about the other one?' she says.

'Your man upstairs?'

Martha nods.

'He's next on the itinerary. Mr Greenley, can you cope with keeping our man Benjamin for now?'

'I... yes,' Greenley says.

'Shouldn't need more than, say, a month... Central records say we don't have notes on his file, or alerts, so it's not like anyone's looking for him just now. Unless you're running this freezer off a generator, and need the fuel.'

'Bio,' Greenley says, patting the freezer lid. The dead

man's lips are parted as though he's adrift in sleep. 'We've got plenty of waste to burn through.'

Martha clutches her belly, an old soap opera scene stuffing her throat: Benjamin's family, a life in Birmingham. The most normal night, all these years beyond the bedtime routine, telling stories with all the voices; he and his wife watching shows from the sofa, recounting the day; eating too many biscuits they promise they won't add to their next shop yet always seem to, because these small pleasures are the guts and glue of their relationship. They go to bed and hold hands until one of them gets too clammy, and the house falls silent but for the productive tinkle of preening gadgets. Then without warning the night collapses. A suffocating pall falls over the house. Awake in the dark, panicked, because nothing works – none of the torches, nothing. An ancient cigarette lighter holds out, enough to find socks and shoes and dressing gowns. And even though Benjamin and his wife get out, make good progress through the city with others from their street, they're suddenly caught in a stampede, and they're too old to run, and just as quickly as Benjamin can take his wife's hand, count her fingers in the swelling crowd, he's losing her. His grip loosens, she slips from reach. He gets lucky and free of the crowd, unaware that the softness under his feet is other people. He turns to see his lost wife screaming in the mass, too slow, then silenced and falling. And he walks and walks and walks to the city outskirts, to where the lights are still working. Here he finds the injured man, and together they requisition a vehicle, or steal it, or hack it, override it, and set course for the north via the A- and

B-roads out of the city. But his wife is back there, buried, and the pain is intolerable, and the pistol – where did this even come from? – is an instant release.

What other reason might there be for this man to be dead?

Greenley closes the freezer lid. The suck-slam makes Martha jump.

8

The injured man is sitting up when Perrin enters Sharon's shed. Martha, ordered to stay outside by a visibly irritated Greenley, loiters at the window. The shutters inside the shed are partially closed, but the timber is rotting, so she can see everything through the gaps in the joinery. The injured man's eyes are red and heavy. The drip is still attached to his arm. His legs are covered. His facial scars are a shade less raw.

Sharon stands in the far corner, picking her nails.

'Hello, sir,' the officer says. The injured man doesn't acknowledge him. His eyes are fixed dead ahead.

'I'm Geraint, a police officer. You've been in an accident. You're in a town called Dillock, and you're safe. I'd like to ask you a few questions, see how you're feeling.'

The injured man goes on staring.

Perrin comes to the edge of the man's bed. One hand close to resting on the injured man's chest. 'Sir,' Perrin says, 'I want to help you.'

This time the man moves his head fractionally. His eyes settle on the officer's face.

'Hi,' Perrin says, leaning away. 'You were lucky, you know. Is there much pain?'

The man rubs his jaw, and Sharon shakes her head angrily. 'Not a peep,' she says. 'I've had bloody nothing off him, all morning. And now you waltz in here…'

Perrin frowns at her. 'Base vitals seem okay,' he says. Then, to the injured man, 'You don't know where to start, do you? We can go from the top, or the bottom, or the middle.'

The injured man keeps his lips tight. To Martha, there's a certain poise. Like a cornered animal, calculating.

'Or how about we take a better look at you?'

Greenley's voice, then. Not protesting, just something about ethics and consent. As he speaks, Sharon looks away.

Perrin ignores Greenley. He takes the injured man by each wrist and holds up the man's fingers, moving them left and right in front of his eyes. The man doesn't resist. Next, Perrin leans directly into the man's face, and the man doesn't react to that, either. Perrin places a wire on the injured man's chest and jacks the other end into the port under his eye. Lastly, Perrin rounds the bed and carefully regards the injured man in profile, then dead on.

Perrin presses a finger to his temple, head cocked. 'Shit,' he says.

For the first time, there's a flicker of lucidity in the injured man's face. A hint of what might be a grin, gone as quickly as Martha notices it, but there regardless. She digs her nails into her arms.

'What's the matter?' Greenley asks the officer.

Perrin doesn't answer.

'Come on, what is it?' Sharon urges.

'Nothing,' Perrin says quietly, scowling at the injured man. And they watch as Perrin reruns his scans and checks. Even more deliberate this time.

'He's been scrubbed,' Perrin announces at last. 'Nothing on file. No name. No medical notes. No data. Like he doesn't exist.'

Martha swallows.

Too neat.

'Scrubbed,' Greenley repeats. 'As in, he's anonymous? How is that possible?'

'Hacks?' Perrin suggests. 'I don't know. I've never seen it before. Please excuse me one moment.'

Perrin leaves the shed. Martha crushes herself up against the shed, but the officer goes round the other way.

He's gone to look at the car, she realises.

Then Perrin is back in the shed, and his breath is shorter, his expression fierce.

'The car's not registered to you, is it?' he asks the injured man. 'Its account holder is a woman called Angelika Semolt. Do you know that name?'

Nothing. Perrin kneels by the makeshift bed and touches the man's elbow. 'Were you in Birmingham? Who was the man you travelled with? Who was Benjamin?'

This time the injured man's eyes widen. Martha bites her lip. A box of hot air surrounds her, stilling the birds and the sweep of the trees hemming the allotments. It's starting to rain again.

'I want to help you,' Perrin says.

The injured man turns his head. His mouth hangs open like he's about to say something.

'Am I there?' the man asks.

Perrin gets to his feet.

'Sorry?'

'Where is this?' the injured man says.

'A town called Dillock,' Perrin says. 'This... I suppose it's a commune.'

'Co-op,' Greenley adds.

'A co-op,' Perrin says. 'Yes.'

'Dillock,' the injured man repeats. 'Is she here?'

'Who?'

'Unggg—'

'Who?' Greenley asks.

'*Who?*' Martha whispers.

The man startles, eyes frantically searching the room. 'She can see us all,' he says. 'She will know! She will *know*.' He coughs thickly. His mouth goes slack on one side. 'The witch,' he slurs. Then, with more effort, '*Brace*.'

'Brace?' Perrin says. 'Tell us. Who can see us?'

'No.' The man says. 'Stop her now—'

'Stop her?' Perrin urges.

'Stop Brace—'

Perrin steps away as the injured man's arms lock in spasm. He arches his back, a scream cut in half as he bites down on his tongue. A ruby of blood swells in the corner of his mouth.

'Christ almighty,' Greenley says.

And with almost perfect timing, Rolly blunders through the shed door.

'Fucking hell!' he shouts, hands on his knees and heaving for breath. 'The maddest thing – the *maddest* thing. This massive fox just chased me through the forest…' he stops. 'Eh? What's up with you all? Why's it so moody in here? Someone else gone and copped it, or what?'

At the window, Martha stifles a giggle. Nerves, yes. But also relief. The tension has finally broken. The rain feels good on her face.

Later, when Perrin has left, the allotmenteers gather by the greenhouses for another of Greenley's impromptu meetings.

Martha sits behind Rolly and Sharon. 'I swear it's withdrawal,' Sharon is whispering to Rolly behind her hand, just loud enough to overhear. 'He's in withdrawal,' she continues. 'One time I did house calls for a fella who'd come off the booze, and he fitted like that. His insides were totally gone. Docs said if he wasn't careful he might end up shitting through his mouth. Telling you, Rolls: that guy is in withdrawal.'

Martha keeps her hands squeezed between her knees. Rain crinkling on the greenhouse glass. Greenley at the front, his face red and shiny.

'I realise this is twice in two days,' Greenley says softly. 'Before I start, though, I just wanted to address Martha's shed. I've seen to it that there'll be a new unit arriving this weekend. Rolly's agreed to build it, so you only need to pick a new patch.' He looks at Sharon, smiles sadly, then back to Martha. 'Tonight you can have our van.'

Martha nods.

'On top of that,' Greenley says. 'I wanted to confirm that I've been in touch with a camp near Birmingham. They'll be delighted to receive our patronage; they've seen an almost total exodus from the civic centre, and our donation will go a long way.

'Thirdly, Police Constable Perrin is arranging for the retrieval of the damaged car, in part for forensics. It's been a taxing day, and we all have questions, but I want us to try and keep things running smoothly. Which is why our unexpected guest will be staying to recuperate for another few days. Call it on-site after-care. Agnes has agreed to provide some evening respite, and will keep an eye on his dressings. And we should be proud, you know. We should take something from what we did.'

'What about the body in the freezer?' Martha asks.

Rolly and Sharon share a strange, lingering look, then turn to face her.

'A coroner will be over when the time is right,' Greenley says, reddening. 'In the meantime, we have to forge ahead as normal. We'll have to make our provisions—'

'And what about bedsores?' Martha interrupts. They had been the worst marker of her mum's deterioration. Pus-filled and clustering. Her mum would cry when the nurses washed her, and Martha never knew whether it was through pain or pride.

'As I've just told you, Agnes will relieve us as and when,' Greenley says. 'Right now, our mystery man isn't in a position to care about how comfortable he is. He had nothing before. Here he has a bed, Sharon's soup… Martha?'

'What?'

244

'Did we lose you there?'

Martha shakes her head – but he had. A flash of sheet lightning over the moors, and in the glare of it, what might have been something moving around Sharon's shed. A low, thick tail. Head and torso too large and long to belong to a cat.

'Stay with it,' Greenley says.

Martha smiles thinly, barely listening. Thinking of the injured man's scars, the colour of his new leg, and of old Benjamin's frosted body down in the freezer. Thinking so hard she's barely there at all.

9

Next morning, Martha wakes up late, sweaty in the sleeping bag, one of Greenley's army surplus cast-offs. There's a strange scorched smell in the air and a light frost on the inside of the campervan windows. She turns on the gas hobs for heat and sits on the bunk, sipping part-frozen milk from the bottle. Window blinds up, hazy light, clouds of peach and lemon. Right above the allotments, an enormous jet contrail has split the sky in two. It ends in a siege of darker clouds somewhere above the moorlands behind the allotments. The rain has passed. The trammelled mud gleams and sparkles.

Nine o'clock. Then half past. Martha absent with a brew, peering uphill through the campervan's net curtains. A normal morning: Rolly up and tending to his bike, and Sharon out on her rounds, wisps of greying hair escaping her hood as she bobs between the growing lines. For some reason, Sharon keeps hesitating near one of the hands, and soon enough she's called Rolly over from his bike. Martha watches them stand silently for a few minutes. Little puffs of smoke emerging from Rolly as he works through a joint. Something about their interaction appears odd to Martha, especially given how they usually are – bickering, or bollocking each other, or vigorously debating something daft from their old lives. Then Rolly's up close and inspecting the hand himself, and when he comes around it, Martha notices his thick brows are knitted into a frown you'd see from space. To her surprise, he points down towards the campervan.

Martha pulls one of Greenley's tweed jackets around her and slips into her boots. Rolly and Sharon watch her coming up the hill.

'Morning,' Martha says.

Rolly lets on with a nod. Sharon simply toes the base of the hand.

'What's up with it?' Martha asks. The hand is visibly out of lock mode, and some of its panels are strangely oily. The manipulator's blades are exposed and covered with a powdery black substance.

'That look right to you, Marth?' Sharon says.

Martha touches the manipulator blades, expecting soot or dust to come away on her fingers. To her surprise, the texture of the staining is smooth, and none of it rubs off. She sniffs her fingers – faint sulphur. 'Motors burn out, or something?'

'I dunno,' Sharon says. 'I didn't hear a thing. But we reckon Greenley was last to use it. I fell asleep in my chair watching you-know-who, and Greenley was in the lab – he didn't come to bed last night. Guess he could've had it running overtime in the small hours.'

Rolly looks at her, then at Sharon's shed.

'Unsupervised, though?' Martha shakes her head. 'Doubt it.'

Sharon shrugs. 'Maybe he forgot to shut it down. Got a lot on his mind. Could be that simple.'

Rolly shakes his head. 'Except it's not. Fuse board would pack in well before a fire started. Plus we'd get an alarm. This – it's like someone turned it on, opened the manipulator, then fucking blowtorched it.'

Martha frowns. It doesn't square. 'What about lightning? Weather's been grim enough.'

Sharon and Rolly glance at each other. Again that peculiar knowing look between them.

'Thing is,' Sharon says, 'the manipulator's really only half the puzzle. Go have a look at the head unit as well. Shit, man – Greenley'll go *spare* when he sees all this.'

Martha frowns and swings under the hand's main jib. Its hydraulic ram is bitterly cold on her hand. Over the other side, she places one foot in the maintenance port in case she needs to stub the emergency cut-out. She peers in at the head unit. There are three screws missing from its protective faceplate, the powder coating scratched off around the holes.

'You didn't do this either?'

Sharon nods. 'Found it exactly this way.'

'I wouldn't even know where to start,' Rolly says.

'I don't get it,' Martha says. Clearer now, though, are the facts: someone has tampered with this hand.

'Us neither,' Rolly says.

'Checked for BIOS tweaks, just in case?'

Rolly nods.

'Nothing?'

'Fuck-all. Not since the last shutdown cycle. All the code's bang-on. No loads or queries. Definitely isn't a virus, if that's what you're driving at.'

'We found it this way,' Sharon says. 'I told you.'

'Well, what about the other hands?' Martha asks. 'What about mine?'

'All good,' Sharon says. 'Faceplates are spotless, anyway. They're still asleep.'

'Okay,' Martha says. She rubs the three empty screw holes in the faceplate. 'So whoever did this was rumbled before they could get inside.' She looks towards Sharon's shed. 'Stuff like this is why we need cams up, I swear. Bad enough we've got bloody foxes roaming about.'

'Foxes?' Sharon says swiftly. 'Nah...'

Martha climbs down and crosses to the closest limb-tree. Lifts the tarp and looks underneath. Nothing out of the ordinary, except of course for the prostheses growing down there. Six rows of fresh tibia, strands of pseudo-flesh creeping up them like rhizomes from growtrays beneath. Pigment swatches sticky-taped to their nutrient lines.

Next, she goes to her own hand. She boots the terminal in maintenance mode; checks and double-checks the anti-tamper code is still firing. Noticing the others' silence, she turns back to them.

'What?'

Sharon's staring at her. 'Martha...' she starts.

'Don't even think about accusing me.'

'It's been a rough couple of days. And it's pretty obvious you're mad at Greenley. All your sloping about. The snide digs.'

Martha's chest tightens. 'Seriously? You think—'

'Don't do this, Shaz,' Rolly interrupts. The first time Martha's ever heard him call her that. 'Obviously isn't her, is it?'

Sharon spins to him, angrier still: 'Why does she get to wriggle out of it? 'Cause she's a kid?'

Rolly takes Sharon's wrist, squeezes. 'Babe.'

Martha doesn't say anything. *Shaz.* Trying not to flinch. *Babe.* Trying not to blink.

'Hang about,' Rolly says. 'Look up there.'

Rolly points up the scarp behind the allotments, where swathes of naked peat render the moorland a black lake.

'Christ,' Sharon says. 'What's he playing at?'

Martha takes a step away from the pair of them, sensing the dynamic shift. Then Rolly has two fingers in his mouth, blowing, and the peal of his whistle resounds through the valley.

'Greenley!'

A tiny figure on the hill turns towards them. It begins waving broadly with both arms, then beckoning with great paddling motions over one shoulder.

'What's the matter?' Sharon yells.

The figure points to the contrail in the sky, before holding a set of binoculars to one side.

'He's fucking lost it,' Rolly says.

'I'll go,' Martha says. Something about this is nagging at her. Everything's nagging at her.

Rolly doesn't protest. 'You better roll another spliff,' Sharon says to him. 'I can't hack this morning. And while he's fannying about up there, I'll go see if that other bastard's in a better state.' She looks at Martha. 'I'm sorry love,' she says. 'You didn't deserve me this morning.'

Martha can't tell if she means it.

Martha returns to the campervan, mud sloughing off her boots. Confusion like slow worms inside her, and her head throbbing. The air still burnt. Why hadn't she noticed a difference in Sharon and Rolly's interactions before today? She wonders if the injured man's arrival has made her look more closely at everything. She wonders what else she's missed.

At the campervan door, Martha looks up the scarp. Greenley's still there, facing the distending contrail, with what must be a mobile phone to one ear. Presumably he's found signal on higher ground. She shouts, 'What's the matter with you?' But Greenley doesn't respond.

Martha sits on the van's side-door sill and methodically unlaces her boots, cold fingers sore on the lace hooks. She slips one foot up into the van, heel freezing against her upper thigh, and drops the boot to the ground. She sniffs, starts on the other. But she doesn't stand up. There's a perfectly formed footprint in the mud next to her boots. She looks at her own feet, her baggy wool socks. Without thinking, she places one in the mud and pulls it away. The shape is indistinct, much too small to match. She slips off the sock, wipes her foot, and stands up inside the van. No question: the print was left there by a bare human foot. She can see the ball, and the arch, and even the impression of an ankle in the wet mound beside it. She leans out of the campervan, struck by the chilly sensation of being watched. There's another print, just a little further round the side of the van. Same size as the first, if less defined. And then a third, perhaps half a metre beyond the second.

She pulls on her boots and steps down, careful not to disturb the mud. A fourth, fifth and sixth print. All made by the very same foot, going by the direction of the toes, the taper of the arch. And now she's at the corner of the campervan, and she's kneeling to the ground against the rear wing, and there's a smudge of mud on the light cluster. It's a partial handprint.

She coughs. She swears. First the damaged hand, and now this. The mud is uneven and her footing less than steady. Two more footprints leading her behind the van. A second handprint, even clearer, three fingers and the heel of the palm, below the van's rear windscreen. It's obvious, now, that someone was leaning against the van. They'd leaned with their hand on the van, to try and see inside.

She says this to herself.

To try and see inside.

Martha wipes her nose, unsure what to do. It's then she notices another set of prints debossed in the slop by the footprints. She squats. They are small and vaguely hexagonal. She touches one. Two tracks, running in parallel. Pawprints. She follows them: they came from the direction of the forest.

Martha stands up. Her ears are buzzing. A taste of blood in her mouth. Now she's certain. All this really has been too neat.

• • •

'It can't have been him,' Sharon insists, holding Martha back from shaking the injured man awake. The shed is humid, the windows wet. The injured man snores loudly. 'You seen the bloody state of him? He's comatose.'

Martha pulls the blanket from the injured man's legs. She examines the soles of his feet, alternating between the woven, uniform skin of the prosthesis and the wrinkled skin of his real foot. Looking under the nails, along the gunnels of the nail beds and into the cracks of his heel. Looking for mud, grass, crumbs of soil. Evidence.

'Go look at the prints,' Martha urges. 'Go and see! He was bloody *hopping* around me while I slept!'

Sharon sighs, massaging her forehead. She lets go of Martha's arms.

'Listen,' Sharon says, 'he's that jacked up on opiates it's a wonder he's still breathing at all. I was getting up every few hours to check on him, drain his catheter bag. He's gone nowhere.'

'You aren't *listening*,' Martha says, jabbing towards the injured man with one finger. 'If it wasn't him, then who? Rolly? What's Rolly gonna do that for? You seen him after he's smoked his bedtime jay? Think he can *walk* in straight lines, let alone hop? You think it can't have been him pissing about with Greenley's hand as well?'

Sharon looks away.

'Fine,' Martha says. 'Since we're all playing the blame game today – was it you?'

'Jesus, Martha. I was in here with the guy all night.'

'So it's Greenley, then?'

Sharon frowns. She glances at the injured man. 'I doubt it. Don't you?'

'Obviously,' Martha says. 'Because if he wanted to perv on me he could come down with his spare keys and open the door.'

Sharon looks close to tears. Strung out, pallid. 'Stop now,' she says. 'I'll – we'll talk about this, okay? We'll show the boys these prints, the hand. We can suss all this out. We can take photos and call Perrin back—'

Someone trudges past the shed. Sharon rubs condensation from the window. Rolly's out there, tilting his head.

'He's here,' Sharon says to Martha. 'Greenley's come down.'

So Martha marches straight out of the shed.

'I think a plane went down,' Greenley tells Martha and Rolly, slightly manic. His lips look raw and his eyes are bloodshot. He's pointing at what's left of the contrail above. 'A small one. Definitely went down. See the dispersal? It's *smoke*. Can't you smell it? There's stuff all over my roof. It came *right* bloody over us. Something came right over and went down, I swear it. I think it landed way out on Wracklow, though the cloud's too low to be sure. Tried calling it in, but even my bloody proxy network's in and out. I went looking for blue lights, helicopter lights. I looked for flares. Something came right over and went down…'

Rolly comes forward and touches Greenley's arm. 'Chill, boss. Here.' He sits Greenley down on the frame of a manure box. Rolly gives Greenley a pill of some kind, pulled from a cargo pocket.

Martha looks up at the clouds. Heavy iron slung from one

verge to another. The smoke, if it was smoke, is all but gone.

'Shouldn't we go out there?' Rolly asks. 'Properly, I mean. Get some kit on and check it out.'

Greenley nods, excitable suddenly, as if he hadn't imagined they could do that.

Rolly looks at Martha, and then at Sharon's shed.

'What about him?' Martha says, meaning the injured man. 'We can't leave him alone. He can't be trusted. Maybe you should stay as well, Rolly. Or better yet, take him to a hospital. Get him out of here.'

'No,' Greenley says flatly. 'No.'

'Why?'

'Greenley's right,' Rolly says. 'He's still in pain. Better he sleeps it off.'

'More convenient, you mean.'

Rolly scowls, the corners of his lower lip trembling slightly. 'Jesus, kid. What's got on your tits today?'

Martha gives him the finger and turns to Greenley. 'Last night,' she tells him, trying to hold the anger back, 'someone tried to hack one of the hands. And then they came sharking me in the camper while I was sleeping.'

'You're kidding,' Greenley says.

'Obviously I'm not.'

'Who?'

Martha points to Sharon's shed. 'Him. In there. There were single footprints in the mud – go and look. He hopped down to me. I'm telling you now.'

Rolly laughs at the idea, but Greenley at least seems to weigh it. He knocks back Rolly's pill, and his Adam's apple moves up, hangs, as if it's hard to swallow it. Thinking,

thinking. Deciding. Then his mania resolves to focus – even his features seem sharper somehow. If he's surprised by Martha's allegation, he doesn't show it. He says, 'Rolly, Martha's right. You should stay on site with Sharon. Phones are still out, but there's a hard line to Abbas and Perrin in the lab. The red handset. Anything happens – anything at all – you hit eight-eight-eight. Tell them you're with me. We'll all need to talk again later. And Martha, I want you to lie low as well.'

'No chance,' Martha says, shaking her head. 'I'm coming with you.'

Greenley hesitates, then relents. 'Fine. We'll have to take the camper. You'll need your waterproofs.'

'Aren't you going to check out the footprints?' Martha asks.

Greenley avoids eye contact. 'Please go and get ready,' he says. And it isn't a request.

10

Wracklow, the given name of the moorland well beyond Dillock, is a near-featureless expanse, with gradations of purple heather between ramps of naked peat. Despite its remote feel, however, it isn't hard to get there: a fifteen-minute drive along a serpentine road, stony quiet but for Greenley's deep breathing and the camper's old turbo-diesel knocking away.

As they climb into low cloud, past sad memorials for dead bikers fixed into wet stone walls, Martha withdraws from the silence by reflecting on her links with the place. There are tales about these moors – a torso found in a suitcase in a layby, small bodies in shallow graves, unexplained light phenomena (something do with harried land and rocky outcrops, which some locals claim as ghosts). But Martha also keeps her own private stash of stories, more intimate to her than local legends or myths.

Martha's last foster home before she turned sixteen lay on the far boundary of these moors. From there, clear views over Sheffield made ideal surrounds for lazy days or late evenings spent in boys' cars on quiet lanes, or sometimes at the trig station on Lathe Head, the region's highest point. Martha never said much during these encounters, though not through shyness. She never liked the smell of spark – especially not the taste it left in boys' mouths – but by day she loved the views, which justified the trade. At night she was electrified when the headlights went off to reveal a teeming city.

One boy she used to see, a local lad with a perfectly symmetrical face, admitted to her that his older brother had once been dragged up on to Wracklow by a local hardcase and battered with a golf putter, left in the gorse. Crawling towards headlights on a distant road, the boy's brother came across the wreckage of an enormous plane, which had crashed there not long after the Second World War. It was an American B-29 Superfortress named *Blown Highlights* – so-called because it was part of the reconnaissance group that photographed the Hiroshima bombing. It'd flown out of Lincolnshire on a training flight to Burtonwood, close to Warrington. The crew, contending with heavy weather, began their descent too early, apparently without realising they hadn't cleared the uplands. All thirteen on board were killed. Their bodies were removed and, recovery being too difficult owing to the terrain, the wreckage was left in place as a memorial.

Martha found this boy's story alarming. Not because of its violence, but because she knew her then-foster parents collected war artefacts, and often said they'd moved east of Manchester to be closer to these moors, so they could visit the wreck and others like it. She told the boy this, and he stared at her, spark-droned and unable to process the link.

Now, in Greenley's camper, Martha remembers that boy's face, the long lashes and thin lips and concave chest, and tries to picture a plane wreck left up there for all this time, slowly being reclaimed by the earth. The isolation, the quiet grief of it. All those families the aircrew left behind. Are there pilgrimages, unmentioned anniversaries? Are there still tears? To Martha, it's strange to think that almost a century later, people might still go and squirrel tiny pieces of the wreck into their pockets – nuts, bolts, other fixings. How many people round here have pieces of old plane hidden somewhere in their house?

Soon the camper reaches a natural plateau in the road, where the edges have been tarmacked and gravelled. What was a grey mist from afar is now a squall that soaks their waterproofs to capacity within minutes. Zero visibility, too – no Manchester visible in the basin behind – and before them hangs a heavy shroud, underlit in places by an orange glow, which intensifies as they navigate the banks of peat, heather and hardy brown grass. When she turns, the campervan has vanished. The twisting shape of the road is described only by the cars traversing it.

'Up ahead,' Greenley comments. Martha tucks in behind him. The smell she'd noticed that morning is less ambient – and getting stronger. Another few minutes, and the cloud has fully enveloped them. They leave the path and cut into the moor proper. The rain and wind are immediately harsher without the banks shielding the path. Civilisation drops back. It's hard to hear, not that they speak. Their only markers for a while are white canvas ton-bags full of geotextiles, dropped here by drone to help re-cover the peat. At a distance, they resemble white stone blocks; up close, they are invasive, perversely out of place.

'That way,' Greenley says, motioning to a set of shelves. Martha doesn't need telling: the cloud above the feature is pulsing orange.

They ascend, sweating. At the top, Greenley turns to help her. 'My goodness,' he says, hauling her up. 'It's here.'

Martha comes over the lip. A chunk of smouldering debris directly in front of her. Next to this, a clean-looking metal rib, stitched with holes. The smell is intensely chemical.

They pick towards the wreckage. The ground is boggy, tries to claim their boots. More debris appears between moguls of peat and churned-up soil. In one bowl-shaped area they find a mostly intact solar array, perhaps twenty feet across. Its cells are cracked and charred but clearly definable. Further along, the partially slagged remains of what must be a camera, easily the size of a small car, its lens fractured. It looks like an insect's compound eye.

'No bodies,' Greenley says. 'And thank heavens it's damp. The whole moor would be burning.' Martha nods with relief. It's a struggle to see beyond twenty metres, Wracklow's harshness being a reminder, a lesson. The only thing remotely human about the place is the colour of their waterproofs, maybe the only colour in a mile radius.

'I don't think this is a plane at all,' Greenley says eventually.

Martha goes to reply, to agree, but now there's a faint rattling, steadily getting louder.

'Oh right,' Greenley says, and stops in front of her.

As they watch, a procession of soldiers in full combat gear emerge from the grey. Some are carrying powerful flashlights and stretchers. A large tracked vehicle, trailer unit on its rear, looms behind them.

When the soldiers notice the two allotmenteers across the cratered land, they take up their rifles and fan out. The point man screams, 'On your knees! On your knees! Hands out in front!'

'The bloody hell are you pair *doing* up here?' the point man says, patting them down. A SEARCH & RESCUE patch shimmers on his tactical vest. He has a bright head torch and a length of rope coiled around his shoulder.

'Saw it go over,' Greenley replies, cautiously lifting a finger from his head. 'We had no phone signal to dial it in, and we thought – well, we're close enough. We had the means.'

'Mm,' the point man says. Over his shoulder, he shouts: 'Get the dredge down there – there's more to sweep.' The soldiers trudge past Martha and Greenley, young men mostly, and the tracked vehicle lumbers after them.

'Can I get up?' Martha asks. 'My knees are freezing.'

The point man nods backwards.

Martha stands up. Greenley is more tentative. Martha grabs his hood and tugs. Over by the solar array, an enormous grid of green laser light springs into the cloud, expanding outwards. It phases in and out of view as it adjusts itself, sharpens and finally settles, shivering, above the territory.

'Mapping,' the point man says through one corner of his mouth. 'They're big on their mapping.'

'It's a satellite,' Greenley says. 'That thing.'

The point man glares at him. 'Says who?'

'I just think it might be a satellite,' Greenley offers. 'A spy satellite. I saw a camera. It smells funny, doesn't it? Smells foreign.'

The point man looks at his gloved hands, shifting weight from foot to foot. He spits into the peat bank. 'No,' he says. 'It's not a satellite.' The lasermesh clicks off. He's eyeing them both suspiciously. 'It's a spy drone. You really haven't heard, have you?'

'Heard what?' Martha says.

Greenley shoots her a sideways look.

'The reports,' the point man says.

Greenley shakes his head. 'Reports,' he repeats.

The point man squats over his boots. Rubs at the grime on his face. 'Your network's patchy because all the networks are going down. After Birmingham... how do you not know?'

'We're only peasants,' Martha says sharply.

Greenley adds nothing.

The point man takes a breath. 'They're pulling reports from all over the shop. Top to bottom. Cornwall, right up to the Scots border. Facility after power station after network hub after local substation. Electrics. Factories. Server farms. Defence systems. Power infrastructure. Like a fucking tsunami. We're going offline, see? We're being turned off.'

'Turned off,' Martha says.

Without a word, Greenley doubles over and vomits a thin stream of bile into the heather.

Martha recoils. The point man takes Greenley's shoulder. 'Sir? Sir?'

'It's fine,' Greenley replies weakly, leaning on his knees. 'It's just a shock.'

The point man passes Greenley the camelback tube from his vest. 'Try supping that,' he says.

But Greenley has to straighten up first. His skin – hands, neck, face – the picture of frailty. He touches Martha's shoulder and it doesn't calm her at all.

'Birmingham was the distraction,' the point man goes on. 'I shouldn't be telling you, but we're dealing with wave attacks from small cells all over the country. Going in for machines and electronics, automated stuff. A bloody surveillance drone like this bad boy comes down for no one, I'll tell you. Those things are built to last the end of days.' He gestures to the burning debris. 'So, what don't they want us to see round here? What was this keeping an eye on? It's not the first, either. Downed units all over the region. And I ask myself: why are we out here in this dismal fucking sog? Why are me and these lot having to clean up, unless we're trying to keep the sheen on? Pretending the seals haven't come off?'

Greenley doesn't reply. It strikes Martha he might already know. That really he vomited because this wreck wasn't a shock, but actually confirmation of something.

Martha's insides harden. It's all so alien. Even if their cities vanish, wink out, the allotments will surely survive.

Sharon had told her. Sharon promised her.

And yet. The gear in the back of the injured man's car. The fact his identity was wiped. The dead man – a hostage? Guilt-ridden? Was he a decoy?

She sees it now in high contrast. The allotments are part of this. And so is the injured man lying in Sharon's shed. When Martha looks at Greenley, she knows that Greenley knows this, too. Nothing else would explain his physical reaction. His mania, his coming steadily unstitched.

'We missed it,' Martha says. 'Didn't we? We had the pieces, and we put them together all wrong.'

Because the wolf is among them, and the crashed drone can no longer monitor what the wolf is doing.

'We need to go back,' she tells Greenley. 'We need to go home.'

Greenley nods without blinking.

'Good plan,' the point man says. 'Good plan.'

In the camper, Greenley is hysterical to the point of driving dangerously. Martha is shivering and gripping the roof handle, holding her seat belt across her. She's not sure she's ever seen anyone more alone or frightened, more lost in themselves. He wrenches in breaths between his sobs, his back and shoulders shuddering like he's trying to get out of his own body. This isn't the man who took her in. 'Oh God,' he keeps saying, face puffy. 'I'm so sorry. I should have listened.' The headlights of other cars diffuse in the rain on the glass. The glare is all Martha can hold on to.

When they're back on the narrow track down into the

allotments, Greenley stops the van and cuts the engine. They sit in a corridor of silver birch, bramble and nettle, brilliant pink foxgloves emerging on lengthy stems from the mid-foliage.

There's a click. Martha looks at Greenley. He has the pistol in the campervan with them. He has the dead man's pistol between his legs.

'I couldn't believe it,' he tells her softly, voice catching. 'I think some things you have to see before you can.'

'What are you doing?' Martha asks.

'The thing is,' Greenley says, wiping his nose up his sleeve, 'I didn't want to believe any of it. It was Perrin. Perrin called me on the hard line – oh *God*. He told me, "Contain that man until I can get back there." He had finally found the car's registrar – that woman named Semolt, you remember? – through the sky-eyes network. They have footage of her – of them – in that car. She was one of the bombers. She was right there. Which means our man was *involved* in the Birmingham attack – not fleeing it. And I didn't, I *wouldn't* believe it was true. I wouldn't. He was a victim, surely!'

Martha kneads her legs. Martha can't speak. Greenley knew this before she challenged him to look at the footmarks around the campervan.

'Snippets were coming over the ham, on my scanner,' Greenley continues. 'I sat up late, trying to follow the movement of the refugees, telling myself it was the best way to direct our donation. But as the night wore on, the stories started to reveal something to me. Call it pattern recognition, cognitive bias or not. People were talking about railway signals failing. A chain of autonomous factories was firebombed almost simultaneously in three different regions. One woman was wailing about a whole estate of smart-homes going haywire and trying to suffocate their residents... And then Perrin contacted me again, well into the early hours, and it was there in his voice – he was *icy*, Martha. He was afraid. He said, "Tell me the man is contained." And I said he was, even though the word "contained" froze my blood. I knew I had endangered Sharon, and you, and Rolly. And now I was certain. It's just like that soldier told us: Birmingham was the start of something, even as Perrin insisted it was nothing to dwell on. I could tell he was lying. An insurrection has arrived. And we are one of their targets. The allotments. Our work. The lab... We are on the wrong end of it.'

Martha tries to get out of the van. The door's locked. Her feet are like concrete. She wants to piss, and she needs to run, and she can't.

'As soon as I came off the phone,' Greenley goes on, 'I went outside to wake Sharon and Rolly to explain. To seek their counsel. We needed a plan to keep this man captive without him knowing. I felt I had a responsibility, that together we could work out how to deal with him. How to respond. It was so late, so first I came by Sharon's shed, because I knew she'd be in there asleep with him. Except she wasn't. The man's drip had been refreshed and his pain relief was set to a timer, but she wasn't there – she had left him alone. So I left, too. The allotments were more silent than I have known them. There was nothing out there. No birds, no cloud. The starfield was astonishing. The Milky Way...'

Martha's skin is livid. She wants to peel herself. She gets

the idea she should try and moult, like a snake; slip away through the corrosion in the campervan's chassis.

'I wasn't alone,' Greenley says. 'There was a fox on the allotments. The most extraordinary creature I have seen there, for all its mundaneness. It came to my legs and rubbed itself on me. I had the sense to try and photograph the thing with my phone, but each time I did, the camera – the pictures – were corrupted. It had eyes unlike any I have seen in a fox. I was almost inclined to believe it was a holotype, a wholly new species, though of course I grasped that this could not be the case.

'I stroked the fox, Martha. It had such exquisitely furred ears, these impossibly long whiskers. It nuzzled me with an affection I cannot explain. I stood in shock and the creature closed its jaws around my knee, gently, and tugged at me. "You want me to move, do you?" I laughed! Talking to this fox in the middle of the blasted night while the country is starting to collapse around us. It worked, though, whatever it was I did: the fox released me, trotted a yard or two ahead, and turned its head to me. I followed it. I followed the fox around the greenhouses, across the vegetable patches. When it came to the tool shed, the fox stopped and stood still as a rock outside it.

'I looked inside the tool shed. They were together inside. Sharon and Rolly were in the tool shed, fast asleep. He was wrapped in one of her blankets.' Greenley turns to Martha, eyes hollow. 'Please. You have to forgive me.'

'I'll walk,' she manages, unable to meet his gaze for the dread, the shared humiliation, the sheer velocity of her world being upended. 'It's not too far.'

'Don't you see?' Greenley says, weeping again. 'That man, on the allotments. Whose leg we replaced. Oh, Martha. Please forgive me. Oh God, oh *Christ*, please. He was sent to us, for the work we do. He came because of what we're doing here. Our contracts. The hands. He came to take our little future.'

'Please,' Martha says firmly. 'Let me get out.'

'I haven't *finished*,' Greenley hisses. 'I forced Perrin to tell me. To explain the urgency.'

'I don't want to hear it,' Martha says. 'I just want to go—'

'You *must*. You must know. Perrin told me there was a siege in London. Another man involved in Birmingham was captured and flipped, and the Met were led to a woman in a converted warehouse, an old MI5 safe house. An old writer called Brace who was apparently squatting there. When they finally broke in, they found she had hanged herself from the roof bars of what Perrin called a Faraday cage. She was surrounded by pages and pages of a typewritten manuscript; dozens of folders containing the intimate details and portraits of various people. She was dead, but Perrin told me his call to me was technically a threat-to-life notice – and still I *wouldn't believe him*. I couldn't believe it. Perrin had got word of the contents, and asked for some photos to be uploaded. He cross-checked the pictures he took of the old man's body in the freezer, and several of the man Agnes saved. Two of the pictures matched. One of these folders down there contained the details of a man called Remi.'

The answers are there. Martha holds her face.

Remi.

Greenley produces something from his pockets – a square

of glossy paper. He passes it to her without a word. A baby scan picture.

'The man called Remi was carrying this,' Greenley says. 'It was in their car when I was clearing it. It had fallen under the seat. I suppose he was holding it when they arrived.'

Martha stares at the scan. The full date in the top left corner has been partially obscured by dried blood and abrasion. The month, year and presenting hospital, however, are visible: May 2015, Manchester Royal Infirmary. Next to these details is a surname. A maiden name.

Martha doesn't say anything. The memory of mourning – but not for him; for her mum. She watches the square tremble between her fingers and can't steady it; she focuses directly on the foetus, its outsized head and soft features, the otherworldly whiteness, the grain and hollow patches bounded by its skull. The early makings of a life, swelling in darkness. Her life.

'Why didn't you tell me sooner?'

'I didn't know how to,' Greenley says. 'Perrin explained that the dead writer had amassed all these names, locations and targets. And leverage. Each of her recruits had some sort of emotional attachment to their respective targets. Remi was blackmailed, or seeing you was a reward. I couldn't begin to guess.'

Martha stares out of the window. How? How is this true? He doesn't even look like her father.

'Look,' Greenley says. 'I made a bag up for you. It's in the back. Those jeans you always wear, that were soaked the other night. One of Sharon's jumpers. I didn't dare touch your underwear.' Greenley smiles to himself and removes the keys from the ignition barrel and puts them in her lap. 'I can't tell you where to go, but I can give you this, at least. The rest of it is done. I just had to be sure. I won't go back there. I can't see Sharon and Rolly. And I won't let myself see what your father has done.'

Then the pistol has slipped into Greenley's mouth, barrel squeaking over his teeth. Saliva and snot stretch down his chin, down the barrel, on to his chest. Martha looks at him, then past him, into the thicket, the thorned edgelands. She's down a dark tunnel, her limbs in recession. There's a flash and a pop, very dull but excruciating, felt in the roots of Martha's hair and in her teeth, and her ears seem to fill up with liquid. She pitches over, instantly back in the childhood she thought she'd had; a single picture of the father she thought she knew, just one, with the face she remembers. She was on her father's shoulders with her fists in his thinning hair, his bright smile, possibly a fake smile. Boxes long closed are breaking open: the day he left them, the day he died to her. The house was on fire and her father had gone, and Martha didn't understand. Her mum was sitting on a kerb wrapped in a child's garish duvet, her face like one of those miners' faces Martha had seen in history lessons at one of those schools she went to. Eyes wide and wet. Sirens and lights and neighbours with hot drinks, and someone with cigarettes, a cigarette being pushed into her mum's mouth, between those parched lips, smoke shaking from it. The taste of ash when she kissed Martha's face.

'That isn't my dad,' Martha tells Greenley. 'He can't be.' Her voice like the distant intrusions you hear while deep underwater, when the pressure mounts around your head.

Greenley doesn't reply. His neck muscles have gone taut. His lower lip is downturned. His hair is a mess. His mouth is leaking badly. Behind him, the headrest has been remade as a terrible pink flower. The rain is a slow roll on a loose snare.

11

Part-deafened and disorientated, Martha staggers on to the allotments. The grass is desaturated under cloud, not much lighter in colour than Wracklow. The wind is muffled, a hard static, how she imagines her blood would sound in the vacuum of space. Mizzle on the air, vibrating rather than falling. Something new is burning.

Martha closes on the sheds. The radio antenna on Greenley's shed has been pulled down. Half-grown and ripe prostheses are scattered on the wet ground. The goats are watching her, crammed into one corner of their pen, and her presence does nothing to reassure them. She comes across a long, deep stripe in the mud. It starts under the empty tarpaulin outside Rolly's shed. Rolly's motorbike is gone. Martha holds her belly on approach; not the worst thing, all this considered, but a wrench. A note has been nailed to the shed door. Even before she reads it, she knows Rolly and Sharon have taken their chance, too.

TRIED TO WAIT
COULDN'T
WE LOVE YOU KID X

The *WE* sets Martha going. Picturing Sharon and Rolly together, a couple. All this time, right under Greenley's nose. All those little clues she'd missed, or noticed too late. Turning away reveals the source of the burning, anyway. Smoke pumping from the chimney pot above the Greenley's lab. She wipes her eyes and approaches Greenley's shed, convinced her heart might stop soon. The shed's windows are all that seem to contain the heaving bulk of black and grey inside. A plastic stench, caustic and dense, somehow concentrated because she can't hear properly.

The lab is on fire. Greenley's work is gone.

Martha runs into Sharon's shed. Ready now for what must happen, the confrontation. Except, of course, the injured man's makeshift bed is empty, and his drip bag is on the sheets, leaking.

Outside once more, pulse at full tempo. Desperate to find something she might be able to salvage. Beyond the sheds stretch the growing slopes, upon which three of the hands are pointing skywards, their manipulators splayed and grasping. Martha's hand, conversely, is stationary, its jib pointing away from her and down into the valley. The limb-trees around it are missing their protection, tarpaulins snapping in the wind. Whole branches have been torn out, wires and pipes trailing in the grass. The cables that link the solar arrays and growing lamps have been turned from the soil and severed. Most of the solar arrays have been tipped over and had their cells smashed in.

Their guest, she accepts, has chosen his moment to strike.

Martha rounds the nearest set of limb-trees. The next set, and the third, until she's approaching her hand unit from behind. It's still pointing away from her, down into the valley, as if to blame Dillock itself.

Just as she reaches the back of her hand, Martha trips on a prosthesis. A complete lower leg. In anger she kicks at it, this wet and lumpen thing, and baulks to see its skin flex. The leg has been unwrapped, which means the leg has been used. Which means it belongs to someone.

Martha kneels to the leg, bile rising. Its connecting face is scored and bitten. Chunks of ersatz flesh are flapping off the ankle and sole, as though it's been tugged at; impressive damage, given the leg's compactly layered construction. The leg's core, its 'bone', is also protruding from the connecting face, as though rammed upwards from the heel. There are pocks and serrations across its blade. She adds it all up. She has to steady herself. The injured man must have found a way to get his new leg off, then used it as a cutting instrument. To sever things. She squints, noticing irregularities in the calf's smoothness. Martha touches it, the leg's clammy skin. She runs her finger along the calf towards a tiny object, dark and thorn-like, embedded in the ankle. She picks at it until it's out in her palm. An amber tooth – a long, curving canine. Too thin, too sharp, to be a human's. She squeezes the tooth and clears her throat. Standing there in the breeze, beneath the smoke suspended on damp air, she sets her eyes on the hand, on the valley beyond. How many times has she walked over to her hand like this? Martha holds out the

274

tooth in front of her and presses her finger into the point until it's close to breaking the skin. 'Where are you?' she asks. But that question is already answered. When Martha focuses beyond the amber tooth, its used edge, she can see for herself. Someone is standing behind the upright beam of her hand.

Instinctively, Martha drops to all fours and into the shadow of the nearest limb-tree. A stench of leaking disinfectant and latex as she tries to control her breathing. Slowly, carefully, her knees and hands sodden with mud and growing fluid, she follows the row uphill, then edges round it. From here she can see what's waiting on the other side of her hand. She covers her mouth with a muddy palm, a soundless scream. It's the injured man, held fast by the hand's manipulator. His whole forearm is caught in the clenched metal, mangled and bloody. His hand hangs limp, and his head is low, eyes shut. A sticky bubble of blood expands and retracts from his nostrils. Evidently he can't squat owing to the hand being out at full extension. In fact, he can barely stand at all: his half-leg is crossed behind the thigh of his complete leg for support, and his toes are just about grazing the mud.

The fox is curled up in the grass at the man's feet. Martha squeezes the tooth, understanding. She darts forward, closing the gap quickly, and takes the man beneath his jaw. She tightens her grip, feels his glands slip beneath her thumb and forefinger. His eyelids flutter. If she balls up her fist she could crush his windpipe, throttle him, finish him—

The man comes to. His left pupil is slower to react. He blinks at her. Her heart is raging.

Then a stillness as he searches her face. 'Martha?' he

mouths, and it's clear he's straining against more than the metal around his arm. His eyes swell, shimmer, then brim over. Spittle pops between his lips. 'You came back,' he manages. And he smiles a sad smile.

Martha squeezes. The man's face contorts. His trapped hand twitching madly above her head. She squeezes again as she studies him, his shocked face, seeking herself in him. She follows the ragged scar tissue into the crags of his cheeks, the lines around his mouth. Down his body at the weft of his clothing, the shuddering of his leg. Back to her warped reflection in his pupils. He's soaking from the rain, his blood and sweat, and he can't be her father, he can't be, and not only because this isn't her father's face – not as she remembers it. Her father died when she was seven. She has already mourned him once – that rift has long since closed and hardened. She turns away to swallow her desperation, to try and deny she feels it. She reminds herself he deserves cruelty for what he's done to them, to the allotments. She sets her jaw and turns back to him, glaring.

Confronted with this expression, the man's back arches. He tries to wipe the mucus from his top lip, some attempt at dignity. The gesture is so pathetic it shocks her. Above the anger, she finds herself pitying him. She releases his throat.

'Like a flytrap,' he says loudly, coughing. 'Your robot.'

Martha steps back, unsettled by his sudden change in tone. It's like he's remembered something; remembered to be a certain way. Martha crosses her arms to stop her hands from shaking, then nods curtly. Her anti-tamper patch worked. She responds in kind: 'We'd have caught you last night if the others had bothered listening to me.'

Her voice sounds distant, cold, but the mid-tones are starting to filter through.

'Teach me for being hasty,' he says. 'But I think I've done things properly today.'

'Like killing him?'

'Killing? Who?'

'Greenley.'

The man scowls. 'Greenley?'

Martha goes on glaring at him. 'That pistol you brought.'

'That's… unfortunate,' the man says, shaking his head. 'But try to understand—'

'Look at the state of it!' Martha snaps. 'You've ruined us. What's to understand?'

'It's not personal,' he says. 'That's all I meant.'

'How isn't it?'

'It's just bigger. It's a movement. A revolt.'

'Against *what*, though? Electricity?'

Now the man's face goes very blank, so that he appears to be hypnotised. 'Automatic England!' he shouts.

Martha sighs. She could almost laugh. 'We're not even halfway there,' she hisses. 'You know these hands cover the town's healthcare, don't you? Everyone round here gets their chip. And we give people more time – to do things. They can paint, or rebuild old motorbikes, or, I dunno, parent their *kids*. Now what?'

The man takes a deep breath. 'Don't be an appeaser,' he says. Still with the overloud voice, like he's performing for someone. 'Don't be so *naïve*. You're young. You think you've escaped real life, don't you? But the state still knows you. Every little thing – they know you all right. They'll have had that drone keeping an eye on this place since day one. And they let you carry on so they could swoop in and suck it all up when you're done.'

'Fuck off,' Martha says.

'It's true. The stuff you make here – where do you think it'll all end up? It goes overseas, that's where. It goes on war medicine. On killing machines. You think you're doing good, but all they see this technology as good for is to maim and kill, and control. You can chase utopias all you like, but one day they'll invert it. Your robots generate cash. That's what matters.'

'Well, they won't do anything now, will they?'

'And that's *right*,' the man urges. 'Try to see it. We have to do this. It's one encroachment after another. Machines rob honest work from honest people.'

'Bollocks,' Martha says. 'You're embarrassing. Everyone your age voted down basic income, which would have freed us full stop. You weren't protecting us – you went out and protected what you all found comfy.'

'No,' the man says. 'People voted against robots doing charity work. People voted to earn their own way.'

Martha narrows her eyes. 'Then you're fighting the wrong thing. There are still other ways, better ways. We were proving it.'

The man shakes his head. 'It's too far gone. You can only do this – your co-ops – for so long. It needs zeroing; the whole country does. A hard reset.'

'And what does that look like?'

Another long silence between them. The man gazes at the fox, apparently studying it, and closes his eyes. When he opens them again, Martha gasps: his face has returned to its vulnerable state. The lines are softer, and more recognisable to her. Certainly he's more frightened. And now it's somehow easier to find herself in the shape of his ears, the underlying structure of his brow and forehead. These are shapes she knows of herself, indivisible. Martha swallows, and her throat is dry. The man takes her wrist in his hand, a roughness closes around her veins. She swallows again, and the lump won't go. Suddenly there's a smell of decaying leaves at the turn of autumn; she's a little girl in dungarees and too-big wellies and her father is picking rotten conkers from a pile in the elbow of a dry-stone wall; the pair of them scrubbing then soaking mouldy conkers in jars of vinegar, her mum tutting at the shell fragments and soil on the table. Martha does know these hands, these shoulders, these eyes.

It's him. He's her father.

And he's gazing down at the fox, and he's trembling.

'Martha,' he whispers.

'Don't,' she says, shaking off his hand.

'Please.' Still whispering. 'I had to make sure she was sleeping. I can't string it out much longer. The fox – she's idling. It's her recharge state. You need to finish her now, before—'

'What?'

'*Kill it*. I mean destroy her. It'll buy you a few minutes. I let the other two go, your friends, but it'll be obvious if I slack off again.'

The fox is curled around itself. Its chest rising and falling.

'You let them go? Sharon and Rolly?'

'Martha…'

'Stop *calling* me that—'

'The fox is my monitor. They know I'm done here. If Greenley's really gone, then it's over. You can leave.'

'But this is my home,' she tells him.

Her father shakes his head. 'You won't be hurt. That's the deal. I had to see you again, even if it was just once. To have a chance. They knew it. They showed me. To do this was to free myself.'

'Stop lying. Stop talking.'

'I'm telling you the truth, now. Forget what I said before.' He bows his head. '*Please*. The fox has been recording us. I had to say that stuff.' The whisper is insistent. 'She's idle now, but she's been relaying it. She's electric. She follows me. All you have to do is cave her head in.'

Martha kneels by the fox. Its fur is filthy. There are shreds of wool and prosthetic skin at the corners of its mouth.

'If you do it,' her father says, 'I can help you. It's the deal. I finish the job, I do the fox in, I close the loop. And I'm free. We both are.' He touches his trapped arm, which has turned a livid blue. 'Look at me, love. I can't do it myself.'

'I'm not touching the fox,' Martha says, and turns away. She follows the pointing hand down into the valley. Late sun lancing cloud, distant Manchester veneered in copper. For the first time, she notices plumes of dark smoke rising from the city centre. Emergency lights flashing in the distance. The silhouette of a lone raptor tracking over the valley. No, Martha isn't ready to leave. She isn't ready to move on from here.

Her father spits on the ground. It's thick and white, like glue. 'He showed you, didn't he? Greenley – the scan picture. I knew he'd found it. I felt him take it.'

Martha keeps her head still. Her face still. She doesn't turn back. The fox purrs.

'You don't look like him,' she tells her father.

'They used machines on me,' he says. 'To make me hate them even more. The programme resets you. I see it so clearly in hindsight. I knew it even as the car drove us here. They had me, and they still have me. She – the fox – she makes sure.'

'And now you want me to forgive you?'

'It's not that.'

'I don't even know you.'

'Then at least know I never wanted to harm you, or your mother.'

Martha snorts. The grief and the rage. All these years in the rain. She swivels and slaps him, and it feels good. She slaps him again. She spits on his chest. 'I don't know what you think happened,' she shouts. 'You left, and the house burned down. I was seven. I was *seven*.'

'I know. Please—'

'You *don't* know. And you don't deserve me standing here.'

'I'm sorry,' he says. 'But the fox—'

'No – you're getting it out. To feel better about yourself.'

'That's not what this is. But you'll wake her—'

'And the other one. In the car – Benjamin. He had a family as well.'

'Ben was never quite over the line.'

'So you shot him?'

Her father's eyes widen with alarm. 'No! Jesus, no. He did… He did it. When the first news broke from Birmingham, we were nearly here. Ben started questioning what Laurel had done – what we'd done. Close to the allotments, he lost his mind, tried to get out of the car. Screaming that he couldn't go through with it. So Laurel took control and locked us in. We were meant to be a team... Ben had broken his contract. She didn't even need to say anything. She crashed us into that shed to make sure, and we sat there in the wreckage and he just did it. Just shot himself, like it was nothing.'

'Laurel is your handler? Is that her name?'

Her father nods. 'Birmingham was her op – we were the second wave. She's an illusionist, Martha. Her trick was convincing each of us that we would be heroes.'

'So you were meant to, what, come here and wreck Greenley's lab? Kill us?'

Her father looks down, defeated. 'There was a charge, a device, in the car. It wouldn't go off. Not after the crash.'

'I saw it. And there was the woman called Semolt.'

Her father nods again. 'Angelika. There were three of us. Me, Ben and Ange. It was her car.'

'You murdered people.'

'No!'

Martha gets in his face. 'This Laurel woman you follow has murdered people.'

'It doesn't matter. Only you matter. If you don't kill the fox, you'll suffer. Laurel keeps her promises.'

'Well, she can't keep this one. The police found her swinging – Greenley told me. She's dead. So I'm not doing this, and you don't get to tell me. You don't.'

Now the fox responds, stirs at Martha's feet. It stretches

over its hind legs with a casual elegance, licks around its mouth. Watching them. Assessing them.

'Oh Christ,' her father says. 'She heard you.' But instead of bracing himself, he leans forward and draws back his lips. There's a glint between his teeth. In one rapid movement he drags his mouth across his free wrist. He squawks and convulses, then repeats the action. When he pulls his arm away, his chin is stippled with fresh blood. He reveals a wound in his wrist, which he immediately begins to suck at, thick red saliva swinging into the grass. He cups his hand and opens his mouth, and a tiny red square slides out and drops into the mud at Martha's feet.

The fox darts for it. Martha's father drives his foot into the fox's abdomen, then stamps down on the fox's neck. 'Rupal!' he screams, and shifts to put more of his weight over the animal. His stump waves hopelessly.

Martha is horrified. The fox is yelping.

'Take it!' her father screams. 'It's Greenley's lab work, the research! Take it!'

But Martha, shaking her head, is backing away.

'Take it!' he screams. 'Take the bloody memory chip!'

This time she hesitates. Staring down at it. Her name like a refrain – repeated and amplified and head-splitting. The fox writhes under her father's weight. It snarls and snaps at her, tongue thrashing.

'Now!' he says.

So Martha moves to snatch up the chip. As she does, the fox bites into her sleeve, a spike of pain. Martha slams a fist into the fox's neck and staggers backwards. Her father, clenching his teeth, bears down. The fox strains at her, raw and frenzied. Martha retreats again. Her father doesn't say anything, or can't. His eyes have glazed; his face looks serene. Martha's fist tightens around the chip. The fox is rabid, hyperextending, tearing strips from her father's foot.

Martha moves away, slipping in the mud, accepting that she's about to leave her father with the fox trapped beneath him; man and beast conjoined and shrieking, some terrible new creature, held captive by Martha's machine. Soon she's on past Greenley's shed, by now well alight. Past what remains of her own shed, the wet slats and personal rags. Past the growing patches, the greenhouses and groundwater pumps, where the shrieking finally stops.

At the forest, right on the edge of it, a pigeon comes to rest on the powerlines that once connected the allotments to the main grid. It coos once at Martha, jerks its head, and flies away. She pushes through the bushes on the boundary. The trees welcome her in.

She runs.

12

Greenley is heavier than he looks. It vexes Martha, his body's weight, as she tries to unfasten the seat belt – she'd always figured if you tapped one of his limbs it would ring like a length of scaffold tube. She keeps looking through the windscreen, waiting for the fox. Smoke from the lab fire is filtering down through the trees, settling above the road as a dark gauze, stationary in the light. The air is bitter with it. At last she gets Greenley's belt off, and his head lolls forward. His crown is like a mouth of broken teeth, chewing raw mince. She retches, though not at the sight of his wound, but rather the slackness and absence of him; at the way his skin is the same temperature as the seat belt, the dashboard, the air moving on her neck. She pushes his head back against the rest. She wants to respect him. She remembers the nurses with her mum, and how they would speak to her as if she were still conscious. 'Okay, Joan,' they'd say, 'we're just going to clean your top half now,' and they would gently sponge the topside and underside of her arms and around her ribs. 'Okay, Joan, I'm just going to dab your neck now,' and they would, because the sweat had left a salty crust there, and it was hard to go near her when she was more alive, still fighting.

Greenley falls to the road, shoulder first. Martha rolls his body into the long grass beneath a bough of ripening berries. This way, she tells herself, the falling ash can't settle on him.

Martha drives the campervan through the burning allotments, and directly down the steep hill towards the main road out of Dillock, using Agnes's recent tyre tracks as a guide. Too late does she notice the fox track its passage and move to intersect her; too late does she notice it skitter and roll down the hill behind the van, teeth bared and unnaturally bright in her mirror. The van nose hits the flat of the tarmac. The chassis meets the verge. A bomb-crack, then the protest squeal of springs. It feels for a second like the van's chassis has split in two.

The camper bounces, skitters across the road. Wrong side, veering back, where it slows, judders and stalls. Passing cars with automatic braking slow off in sequence. The camper's radiator is steaming. She looks right as the fox clears the hill with uncanny speed. It's coming directly for the driver's door. It's going to hit her.

She turns the key but the old van chokes, won't start. Her hands fumble at the ignition barrel. The fox is metres away, full tilt. Jaws closed and eyes perfectly set. Turn the key again. Into gear, just as the clutch pedal slides out from under her foot. Mud and gravel spraying, then a lurching movement, and momentum. Despite herself, Martha finds second, dumps it. The campervan roars and weaves under its own torque, tractionless on its wet, grassy wheels. At last it digs in properly, rocking back, and Martha fights to keep the wheel steady. Just off target, the fox hits the van's sliding door behind Martha; the weight of the impact splits the old panel windows and fully bursts one of the kitchen units. Then the fox rallies – from nowhere it has come under the van and climbed the passenger door, using the left wing mirror to scramble over to the bonnet. Here the fox starts rending back the wipers, gnashing at the glass. Martha accelerates hard, screaming, as the fox gets right down into the wiper motors, narrow eyes fixed on her. She can smell the fox through the ventilation system – stagnant water and heated copper. It has its forepaws on the window, its torn mouth slobbering on the glass. The engine's howling, so Martha slams into third gear, and the fox begins to beat its face and head against the windscreen with a terrible ferocity. Some of its teeth shatter and its snout seems to break, starts foaming from splits above the lips and gumline. Its neck slackens. And then the windscreen cracks enough to allow the fox's lower jaw inside, where it bites futilely at glass, paws scrabbling desperately, its tongue dripping a foul oily liquid into the van. Martha seizes the opportunity: she pushes the fox's mandible right up into the glass, stands on the brake pedal, and gives the steering wheel a sudden wrench. The fox's lower jaw detaches with a bright *pop*; the rest of the animal shears away. Martha glimpses what might be steel plate beneath the matted fur of its chest and belly. The lower jaw falls into the cabin with a metallic ring. Framed in her rear-view mirror, the fox rolls over on itself, limp and wet. It doesn't stand up.

Martha reaches down for the fox's mandible, a greasy thing lodged behind the gear stick, and weighs it in her hand. She recognises alloy and composite beneath the distressed skin. Her father's electric fox. She winds down the window and throws the mandible outside. The co-op's work is on the chip in her top pocket, and that's enough to keep. The rain is easing. The fox is already well behind her. Martha changes into fifth, cruising gear, and the campervan, ancient and untrackable, continues along the cold electric road. Into the unknowable future, freed from the certain past.

PART V

2041

ENGLISH COMBINED TASK FORCE INTELLIGENCE
CASE REPORT: BLACK COUNTRY/309921
STATUS: FROZEN
RATING: HIGHLY CONFIDENTIAL

Introduction

On 10 October 2041, combined task force intelligence THEMIS detected a breach of Scotland Yard's encrypted case archive. An anonymous user spent eighty-nine seconds scraping internal records pertaining to the recently declassified COLD VEIL case of 2032 [see supporting material *1a*], with searches focused on author LAUREL M. BRACE and one named follower, ANGELIKA SEMOLT.

Based on case sensitivity [incl. ongoing investigation – see notes under *1b*], THEMIS responded to the violation within 0.3ms. THEMIS routine FENCER logged a defunct browser and modified mobile operating system in breachspace, and probed for locale. While sophisticated countermeasures [chaff, Garblr] concealed the user's activity, THEMIS successfully commandeered ~1,300 nearby devices to produce detailed magnetic imaging of approx. 70m³ of local environment, inside which were found fourteen people. Of these, only one person was seen to be using a handheld device during the infraction window. This suspect was profiled as female, approx. 160cm in height, 26–36 years old, with comprehensive dazzle-tattoo coverage.

THEMIS bugs determined the infraction space as an outbuilding beside a small town named BILMSTEAD, less than 10km south of BIRMINGHAM. In 2038, Bilmstead was designated one of Birmingham's suburban 'no-go zones'. Given the case material scraped, and Bilmstead's proximity to the 2032 'zero bomb' attack site [see supporting material *1c*], the case was assigned priority status.

Owing to restricted jurisdiction in the area, and with limited operational signal available, a budget for human investigation was approved by THEMIS committee.

OFFICER QE of Black Country sector was sent by dropship to Bilmstead.

Officer QE's statement

I arrived on the outskirts of Bilmstead at 1600 on Saturday, 12 October 2041. The town's border was protected by a concrete wall, around 10m in height and crenelated with anti-drone turrets. On the ground, militia guards conducted patrol cycles around a well-fortified checkpoint. The footing was good, the weather was clear.

I began my search of the target building, a derelict warehouse overlooking the wall. It proved empty across three levels except for a single mattress on a mezzanine and some discarded ration packs and sanitary items. There were no obvious subfloors, nor signs of disturbed earth/ excavation works on the ground floor. I judged it unlikely that tunnels ran from the warehouse into Bilmstead, so I left and approached the checkpoint. As expected, militia guards sought my documentation. Ingress was achieved by means of **[REDACTED]**.

Inside Bilmstead's walls, I found the remnants of what I would describe as a traditional town square. Hanging baskets of flowers hung from crude breeze-block shelters, whose doors were brightly painted. A bandstand was being constructed in the square's centre. I gathered that locals filtered rainwater from the multiple bowsers positioned around the site. Solar generators appeared to supply power, with abandoned shopfronts housing batteries and ancillary plant. Despite these simple amenities, the town's roads appeared swept and well maintained. Rumours of open sewers, malnourishment and 'cholera pits' were clearly false. Almost all of the locals were dressed in workers' overalls or denim. None appeared downtrodden or oppressed.

Within forty minutes, I was stopped four times by locals seeking donations towards 'the cause'. I took the opportunity to offer money in exchange for information on recent movements in and out of the town, particularly around the time of the recorded infraction. All four locals were somewhat offended by the idea, refusing payment. I was told my donation required 'only time and expertise', as money was not necessary or even circulating within the town. I took from further responses that people could enter and leave Bilmstead freely. One woman, perhaps fifty years old, suggested that Bilmstead having its reputation for violence and destitution provided ample cover. Then she told me that a growing number of people were arriving at the community every month, and made it clear I would be welcome to join them.

Elsewhere in the settlement I found evidence of rudimentary schooling. While mapping the square for THEMIS analysis, I came across a thin rope lashed to a wooden telegraph pole that had been implanted with several plant species. As I got closer, I noticed the rope was teeming with leafcutter ants, which were harvesting the plants. I followed this rope for approximately 30m towards a large terrarium in the corner of the square. Observing the ant colony were several children, overseen by a single male adult. EyeDent logged him as MOSRI ROTRA, M, 28, a lapsed dissident reported missing from London five years previously. The children with him were unregistered. Rotra told me they were learning about 'teamplay', and we struck up a conversation. During this exchange, I asked what it was like to live in Bilmstead; Rotra told me he was contented, 'even if it doesn't last', and that, 'It means something to feel looked after in these times.' I tried to press Rotra on these points, but he became distracted by two of the children squabbling. I took images of the terrarium and returned to the square.

With my mapping completed, I continued to **[REDACTED]**, an approved observation point inside the wall. Here I established a weak THEMIS link and uploaded my collected data. It was then agreed that I should pick up my inquiries the next morning. Based on committee analysis of my uploaded map, I was to make use of a communal shelter in the square, presenting myself as **[REDACTED]** to evade suspicion.

THEMIS analysis of my images revealed the presence of a synthetic queen ant inside the terrarium. This was of secondary concern to the operation, but if possible, I was to take a soil sample at the first opportunity.

By promising to volunteer my time, I was able negotiate the use of a private room in the town square's communal shelter. The room was sparse but comfortable, with a window facing the wall and checkpoint. A sweep for monitoring devices found nothing.

At approx. 0120 on Sunday, 15 October, I was woken by the sound of machinery moving outside. Through the window I watched a crane being wheeled into position near the wall. The crane then elevated a narrow section of the wall and held it in place. This, it transpired, was to allow the safe passage of five despatch cycles with human riders. Each rider wore a bubble-carrier of the kind associated with blood transfer. Presently the wall section was returned to its original position, and the crane was taken away. I could see no other locals outside, and because this felt significant, I dressed and prepared to go and inspect the wall section at close quarters. When I tried to leave the room, however, I found that the deadlock had been engaged from the outside. Despite repeated attempts, I was unable to open the door, and had no means to call or communicate with the front desk. I decided my time would be better spent observing the wall. I recorded no further incidents. None of the hydrocycles returned. I was told that THEMIS was unable to detect any of the hydrocycles on the local road network.

At around 0700, I found my room's deadlock had been disengaged. A notice was fixed to the door's exterior that read: SLEEP BETTER, MEATSWEEP. I saw no other guests or workers in the shelter. No receptionist was present on the front desk. Outside, I knocked on the doors of other shelters in the row: no less than six residents denied hearing anything during the night; a seventh laughed at me and closed their door without speaking.

With my cover essentially blown, I consulted THEMIS on the best mode of extraction. While I did not feel unsafe, nobody approached me, and the square seemed much quieter than it had the day before.

Instead, THEMIS endorsed a deeper incursion. I was ordered to travel three miles north from the village into open countryside, where I would collect various samples for analysis. I undertook to walk, using a route planned for me with recent satellite imagery. I saw no ground vehicles. Curiously, there were no birds. The wind was brisk and carried the smell of latex. Beyond wildflower headlands, healthy-looking oilseed rape and wheat fields lined the road towards a large industrial unit at Bilmstead's north wall. In places, the road surface bore marks of heavy transporters. Autonomous crop harvesters lay dormant in the fields; much of this equipment appeared to be in good working order.

On reaching my target location, I took various samples of local soil. My field analyser reported contaminant levels were nominal, with lower than expected traces of lead and mercury. Air samples were also normal. I then spent around half an hour imaging local insects in several locations, including a large ants' nest on the verge of the road, and a zone of adult wheat where ladybirds were being used to control aphids. While imaging the ladybirds, I was surprised to see that large clusters of ladybirds were actually repairing damaged wheat stems with what I would describe as a bile-yellow secretion. In just five minutes, I watched approximately 300mm of one stem being 'reconstituted' in this way. This secretion set quickly, leaving a metallic finish, and then the ladybirds moved on. I decided to catch three ladybirds to test their origin; though my kit could not materially confirm their exact composition, all three ladybirds were synthetic.

At approx. 0930, I became aware of a faint hum on the air. I used my optics to identify a small drone circulating a flightbox above a distant section of the wheat field. The drone became immediately twitchy, as if it had caught me looking. Seconds later, the drone began a rapid approach, making a series of low passes clearly intended to intimidate me. In line with rules of engagement, I pulsed the drone with my PDW, causing its motors to stall. On reignition the drone rose to face me, hovered for around ten seconds, then immediately set course for its original area of operation. I followed it through the field.

I lost visual contact with the drone as I ran into a tall, opaque fence, disguised with photorealistic images of wheat. On the presumption that the drone was monitoring (or protecting) whatever lay on the other side of the fence, I climbed it. At the top I found a large sheet-like structure covering approx. 50m^2. Like the fence, the surface of this sheet was also rendered to appear from above like the fields surrounding it.

I made a small slit in the sheet and descended from the fence. Beneath the sheet, which let in only a small amount of natural light, I was met by a grid of tightly plotted hedges, divided into squares. Each of these squares was being tended by its own highly advanced-looking machine. These machines were equipped with agricultural manipulators, and bore no corporate logos. Their operation was silent. I went between the hedgerows and found growing what appeared to be synthetic body parts, including limbs, organs and large swathes of what I can only describe as bioluminescent skin. Owing to the darkness, or possibly to jamming systems in use beneath the sheet, I was unable to capture any useable images.

At this point I sensed a disturbance in the air, followed by a light pressure exerted around my trunk. A numbness spread through my arms and legs, and I was struck by the sensation of vertigo. Something whistled behind me, and with some difficulty I turned around to find myself opposite a woman in a khaki-coloured vest top and shorts, her hair tied up in a bandana. Despite the dimness, I noticed that she had intricate dazzle-pattern tattoos on all visible skin up to the chin, with obvious implants in both eyes. There was also a distinctive fox tattoo on her left bicep.

The woman approached me with a hand raised above her head, but said nothing and did not appear armed. Noting the woman's likeness to the primary suspect – her age range, height and tattoos were certain matches – I challenged her and used a verbal command to engage EyeDent. Apparently the suspect recognised this, and had darted into a space between two hedges before a full scan was complete. Moments later my sense of paralysis gave way, and I was able to pursue the suspect for approximately twenty seconds, constantly attempting a lock with EyeDent. The woman remained silent as she moved, and scaled the fence with unnatural speed. I followed her, but caught my foot near the top of the fence and fell down heavily on the other side. There was a brief, searing pain in my wrist and neck. I heard boots in the soil near my head, and somebody sighing. Then I lost consciousness.

Additional notes

At 1100 on the morning of Monday, 16 October, ~23 hours after her last contact with THEMIS, Officer QE was delivered to an EPIONE health intelligence clinic in Birmingham city centre by persons unknown. She was treated for the mild side effects of an undetermined sedative.

Key witnesses at the clinic report seeing at least two people arrive with Officer QE in a Mk. II GILPER FLECHETTE, later found alight on a charging forecourt less than 1km away. Both people wore what witnesses describe as 'partially invisible clothing'. Neither of their heights or builds matched that of the primary suspect. Combined surveillance footage of the care facility and its surrounds has proved inconclusive. THEMIS returned no positive ID of the persons responsible.

Forensics confirm that Officer QE's comms had been deliberately blacked out, and a vitals monitor tampered with. Officer QE had made no attempts to communicate with THEMIS or operational control. Tissue scans suggested a corrective operation had been performed on Officer QE's scaphoid bone, with bruising indicative of shoulder and neck massage. Organ and blood scans yielded otherwise normal results.

Officer QE has no memory of being recovered, operated on or transported out of Bilmstead. She was released for THEMIS debriefing at 1615, and later demobilised for a period of two weeks. Therapy was offered, but declined. Officer QE has complained of some intense nightmares and hallucinations of insects, but no other effects.

Current status

Three subsequent expeditions into Bilmstead have yielded no comparable data, nor any confirmation of synthetic growing operations, including the machinery seen by Officer QE. This is despite positive identification of the 'field' in which Officer QE encountered the primary suspect.

While it is strongly suspected that Bilmstead is running with hyperlocalised, unregulated civic services in place, alongside an advanced programme of robotics engineering and medical research, Bilmstead community members are reluctant to testify to this, and to date there is no other admissible evidence (samples of synthetic insects collected from Bilmstead have disintegrated under lab conditions).

For these reasons, ongoing operational and budgetary challenges preclude the continued use of THEMIS assets in this investigation. Resources have been diverted to more pressing affairs [see notes on anti-militia operations in Sutton Coldfield, Wolverhampton], and case 309921 will be frozen. As a precautionary measure, however, all database entries related to the Cold Veil case are scheduled for deletion. As a priority, all available copies of proscribed novel *The Cold Veil* by author Laurel M. Brace are to be located and destroyed.

ACKNOWLEDGEMENTS

Endless thanks to those who read drafts, answered weird questions and kept me at it: Alex, James, Nina, Penny, Matthew, Steph, Holly, my agent Sam Copeland, and the much-missed Ed.

I'm massively grateful to my editor Gary Budden, not least for his incisiveness and patience. Thank you also to PR queen Lydia Gittins and the rest of the Titan Books crew, with special thanks to Julia Lloyd for her stunning cover art.

Lastly, my love and gratitude to close friends and family, especially Suze and Albie.

ABOUT THE AUTHOR

M.T. Hill was born in 1984 and grew up in Tameside, Greater Manchester. He is the author of two novels set in a collapsing future Britain: Dundee International Book Prize 2012 finalist *The Folded Man*, and 2016 Philip K. Dick Award nominee *Graft*. He lives on the edge of the Peak District with his wife and son.

For more fantastic fiction, author events, competitions,
limited editions and more

VISIT OUR WEBSITE
titanbooks.com

LIKE US ON FACEBOOK
facebook.com/titanbooks

FOLLOW US ON TWITTER
@TitanBooks

EMAIL US
readerfeedback@@titanemail.com